On the run . . .
It's been four months since the head of the Institute of Supernatural Research was murdered. But that doesn't mean June Coffin is out of hiding yet. In a world where being different can get you killed, it's best to keep a low profile. Especially for a Siren who can control other people with the call of her voice. That goes double if your powers might be inexplicably growing...

On the hunt . . .
But June isn't the only one trying to clear her name. There's Sam, the charismatic paranormal rights leader, and Micha, the first human on record to go paranormal. All of them must bargain with a mysterious vampire named Occam Reed if they want to stay alive.

Out of time . . .
As tensions increase between humans and paranormals, June must decide who to trust. If only she could hear the song inside her heart...

Visit us at www.kensingtonbooks.com

Books by Megan Morgan

The Siren Song Series
The Wicked City
The Bloody City

Published by Kensington Publishing Corporation

The Bloody City

A Siren Song Novel

Megan Morgan

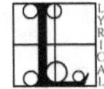

LYRICAL PRESS
Kensington Publishing Corp.
www.kensingtonbooks.com

Lyrical Press books are published by
Kensington Publishing Corp. 119 West 40th Street New York, NY 10018

All Kensington titles, imprints, and distributed lines are available at special
quantity discounts for bulk purchases for sales promotion, premiums, fund-
raising, and educational or institutional use.

To the extent that the image or images on the cover of this book depict a
person or persons, such person or persons are merely models, and are not
intended to portray any character or characters featured in the book.

Special book excerpts or customized printings can also be created to fit
specific needs. For details, write or phone the office of the Kensington
Special Sales Manager:
Kensington Publishing Corp.
119 West 40th Street
New York, NY 10018
Attn. Special Sales Department. Phone: 1-800-221-2647.

Kensington and the K logo Reg. U.S. Pat. & TM Off.
Lyrical Press and the L logo are trademarks of Kensington Publishing Corp.

First Electronic Edition: November 2015
eISBN-13: 978-1-61650-685-8
eISBN-10: 1-61650-685-7

First Print Edition: November 2015
ISBN-13: 978-1-61650-686-5
ISBN-10: 1-61650-686-5

Printed in the United States of America

For Jamie Edford, who had my back at the beginning and kept my head up.

Author's Foreword

This book didn't take as many years to write nor go through as many revisions as the first in the series. If you read the forward in the first book, you know that story went through many mutations before it reached its final form. This book, mostly, came to me as it is, with only some slight alterations along the way.

In this book, I introduce the vampires hinted at in the first novel. Though I try to give the paranormal world in this series a 'scientific' slant, I hope readers will forgive me for taking some liberties. A little bit of magic must be left after all, and a little bit of disbelief suspended. I do hope you'll enjoy my version of vampires. The main vampire in this book was a delight to write and I had a great time putting him on the page. I'm a big fan of anti-heroes, which I tried to create him as. Maybe you'll love him; maybe you'll hate him. Either reaction is acceptable.

June, as always, remains beleaguered and suffering, though she's finally starting to come into her own. I hope you'll stick with me through the rest of her journey.

Thank you for reading.

Acknowledgements

To my family and friends who have supported me in every effort over the years. Thank you for listening to me, encouraging me, and believing in me. Also to my wonderful son Cain, who is by far my greatest piece of work.

Chapter 1

Vampires made a badass gluten free blackened chicken dish; however, their interior decorating skills were woefully lacking. June Coffin didn't need to be an artist to realize this. A colorblind hillbilly would attest the diner was the tackiest thing on the planet, and June had seen drag shows in San Francisco.

The diner, on Chicago's North Cleveland Avenue, was called Zing's and had a campy fifties feel crossed with Steampunk, which went together about as well as the concept sounded. The fixtures were bulbous and metal and the walls decorated to look like the interior of some retro spaceship that also served hamburgers and Coke. She sat in a black leather booth with a brass frame, the seat cracked and dingy from previous occupants. The scuffed black Formica table held her empty plate.

A sketchpad lay open in front of her. She drew in it with one of the few luxuries she'd been afforded in the past four months: a set of colored pencils. They weren't quite a tattoo gun, but her fingers itched to make art. All the other things she'd lost she'd been able to get used to—a cell phone was useless when she couldn't contact anybody, she'd forgotten how to put makeup on, and entertainment felt hollow and pointless. The outside world in general remained easy to access, though. They had laptops and cable at the house. Unfortunately, the news was always bad.

"How was everything?" a lilting female voice asked. A tall, curvy blond waitress stood over her. The woman had fangs.

"Great." June slid the empty plate toward her. "Can I get a refill?" She tapped her pencil against her coffee cup.

If she had to sit around, she might as well work up a good caffeine buzz. The restaurant didn't serve alcohol, though they should have, if they were going to torture patrons with the décor.

"Certainly." The waitress smiled unnecessarily wide.

Yes, I've seen your friggin' fangs. She wore a fifties style waitress outfit, but black—the only thing in the place not completely ridiculous.

June had learned a great deal about vampires. Sam Haain, erstwhile—if currently sequestered—leader of the Paranormal Alliance, had insisted she get a thorough education, and June didn't argue. She needed to know what she was up against, after all.

Vampires didn't naturally grow fangs. Those who had them either had veneers or had their natural teeth filed down. As Sam had explained, normal human teeth could bite through flesh. It was no more difficult than biting through an orange skin. He demonstrated this with an orange, which squirted her, prompting her to swear and throw a cup at him.

Biting proved much easier with fangs, though. Fangs were a sure sign of a militant vampire. The pussy ones went to the transfusion clinics to cleanse their blood.

She paused drawing and nibbled on the end of her pencil. She hadn't smoked since a certain incident in which a bullet went into her lung, but the compulsion to stick something in her mouth remained. She'd already endured the jokes.

The diner wasn't crowded—a few people sat at tables and several at the long curving black lunch counter. No one paid attention to her, though she was probably one of the few non-vampires in the place. Most of the other patrons were young and hip, with stylish haircuts and way too many vintage accessories. She didn't understand why more vampires weren't punks.

A girl sat a few booths away, alone, facing June. She had long dark hair and wore a halter top and a short jean skirt, her legs crossed beneath the table. She sipped from a coffee cup while reading a magazine, but occasionally, she glanced up at June.

The waitress returned with a silver carafe and refilled June's coffee cup.

"Thanks."

"Nice drawing. You an artist?"

June only had an outline at the moment, a skull with a cat winding luxuriously around it, the cat's eyes narrowed viciously at the viewer.

"Yep," June said.

"That's a badass little kitty."

"She certainly is."

"Looks like a tattoo or something." The waitress tilted her head to the side, exposing her neck. A faint pink scar traversed the tendon there.

"I'm a tattoo artist," June said.

"Oh, yeah? Where do you work?"

Steam rolled off the black surface of June's coffee cup. "Nowhere close."

The waitress smirked. "Didn't think you were from around here."

June took a sip of the coffee as the waitress sauntered off. The liquid burned her tongue. Hot coffee was one of the best things on earth, right up there with a clean shot of whiskey, a smooth red wine, and getting finger-banged in a stolen Porsche.

As June set her cup down, someone at the counter turned on his stool: a young sinewy black man. A mass of red-tinted dreadlocks peeked out from under the slanted baseball cap he wore.

She pulled the menu over and eyed the dessert page. This was her first night outside the safety of the house in weeks. Vampires were alive and physiologically human and so had all the old human needs, including the need to consume food. The myths were wrong. They didn't drink blood for sustenance, but to battle the bacteria that infected them.

While June pondered if there was anything on the dessert menu that wouldn't give her hives or death, a shadow fell across the table. She looked up. The young black man stood over her. He had starter gauges in his ears and snakebite piercings in his lower lip. He was cute.

"This seat taken?" He gestured to the booth across from her.

"You've been sitting at that counter as long as I've been here," she replied. "Do you think it's taken?"

The guy grinned, showing brilliant white, slightly crooked teeth and fangs bigger than the waitress's fangs, narrow and curving. How could he even eat with those things? He slid into the seat, dark eyes glittering. June closed the menu.

"I'm Zack." He leaned on the table, arms folded. He had tattoos winding down both arms, black on his shiny brown skin. His nails were pale and manicured. A scent like patchouli wafted across the table.

"Hi, Zack." June picked up her pencil. She started sketching again, adding detail to the cat's fur. She would have a hell of a time tattooing an image of a Tortie, with all the different shades and patterns.

"You ain't a vampire, are you?" Zack said.

"How'd you guess?"

"The clinic dogs don't come around here much." He leaned closer. "And you don't have fangs. But it's pretty obvious even without that."

"Are you looking to bite me or pick me up? Just so I'm clear."

He sat up, his fang-baring grin coming back. "Which are you hoping for?"

She put her pencil down. "Well, I'm not letting your mouth anywhere near my sensitive parts, that's for sure."

Zack laughed, a nice masculine soothing sound. June tilted her head. Vampires didn't have any sort of glamour, but Zack seemed to glow with attractiveness. Maybe he was just naturally hot. He leaned forward again.

"You're June, aren't you?"

She reared back and arched her eyebrows. "Finally! Jesus."

"Sorry to keep you waiting. You seemed to be enjoying your food. Didn't want to interrupt."

She slapped the sketchbook shut. "I haven't been enjoying sitting around here while the waitress tries to figure out which part of me is the most tender." She paused. "You said your name is Zack...."

"I'm not Occam. But I can take you to him."

"Good." June stuffed her pencils back in their pouch. "I'd like to get this over with."

"It's not that simple." Zack placed a dark hand on hers, stilling her.

A tingle shot up her arm.

He patted her hand. "I need to make sure you are who you say you are. Who we've been told you are."

"And how are you going to do that? I don't exactly have an ID. They took that at the Institute along with everything else."

"You do have a special power." He slid his hand off her. "Siren."

"Which I can't use on you," she pointed out. "Vampire." Vampires were immune to supernatural influences. No one knew why.

Zack sat back. "That girl over there." He nodded at the girl absorbed in her magazine. "She's not a vampire, either. Tell her to show you her panties."

The girl had her head ducked, her hair swooped forward.

"Are you serious?"

"Quite. She's been checking you out."

"Maybe. But that's not exactly my...thing."

Her savior-turned-friend, Cindy, had mistaken her for a lesbian once too. Why was that a thing with her? Was it her gruff exterior? Her lack of makeup? Her thick fingers?

"You want to meet Occam or not?" Zack said.

June finished jamming her pencils in the pouch. "I already hate vampires."

Zack smiled widely, showing his fangs.

June tossed some money on the table for the bill, gathered up her sketchbook and pencils, stuffed them angrily into her bag, and slid out of the booth. After a moment's hesitation, she strode toward the girl. Zack remained in the booth.

June stopped next to the girl's table. She looked up at June, her brown eyes questioning.

June cleared her throat and said softly, "Show me your panties."

June held her breath. A moment passed. Then slowly, the girl turned in her seat and unfolded her legs. June backed up but tried to shield her from view of the other patrons.

The girl gripped the edge of her jean skirt and slid it up. Her thighs were unusually thick for a woman. She hiked the skirt up until she exposed the triangle of her white silk panties.

A low laugh drifted over from June's former booth.

"Thank you," June said. "Go back to your magazine and forget about me." She turned and marched back to Zack, who was still laughing.

"Can we go now?" she said. "Take me to your freakin' leader."

"Occam is no leader." Zack slid out of the seat and rose to his feet. He stood a few inches taller than she, but then, everyone did. "Occam is a visionary."

"Yes, he's certainly got some clever disciples." The girl had slid back into the booth and returned to her magazine. "That's the first time I've used a junior high parlor trick since I made my brother's friend show me his dick."

"Now that's enchantment." He led the way out.

Despite the late hour, the streets were crowded. They were in the Nocturnal District, the main hangout for vampires in Chicago. Every vampire that passed eyed her, their leers more unnerving than the usual ones she got out on the streets, as if they wanted to eat her.

"Slow the hell down," she eventually huffed, a few paces behind Zack.

Zack slowed. The night was warm and humid, typical mid-May weather in Chicago, unlike Sacramento where it was dry and cool at night in the summer. June had discovered humidity was not her friend.

"I got shot in the lung." She struggled for breath as she fell in step beside him. "I smoked like a chimney every day until it happened, so it's taken a long time to heal. I don't have any lung capacity anymore." She also had limited use of her right arm, the muscles connecting it to her torso having hardened with scar tissue.

"You were shot at the Institute?"

"Escaping the Institute." June cringed as a tall Latino man looked her up and down with slow deliberateness.

"I don't know much about you." Zack slowed his pace more. "They don't talk about you anymore. Every once in a while someone will say, 'I wonder what happened to the Coffin twins?' but the papers and the news have bigger fish to fry these days."

"Yeah, Chicago seems to have forgotten we were ever here." Had they forgotten about them in California, where they were from, too?

"Most people believe you're dead," Zack said. "Normals think you were killed by the SNC or the Paranormal Alliance, and paranormals think you were killed by the Institute. It's convenient. A dead woman no one cares about. Best subterfuge you could ask for."

They stopped at a street corner, vampires sliding past them. Music thumped, muffled and distant, from nearby clubs. Neon seared the darkness. The smell of smoke, booze, perfume, and car exhaust hung thick in the air, making it even harder to breathe.

"Yeah, being dead is great."

Did their mother think they were dead too? Had she accepted the idea? When June closed her eyes at night, it wasn't thoughts of the Institute that plagued her, or the war that was slowly building, or what they'd do if the police—or worse, Eric Greerson's supporters—finally found them. Her mother's face loomed in the darkness. Her friends back home in Sacramento, uninformed and uncertain, haunted her thoughts. She was a spectator at her own funeral and she couldn't get her balance.

They crossed the street. On the other side, Zack slowed again.

"Not far now," he said.

Fewer people walked this side of the street. Shadows crawled across the pavement and cloistered them. She raked a hand through her hair— her right one, because Aaron's doctor told her the more she used her arm the better it would get, which so far had proved to be bullshit. Her arm fell limply to her side again when she lowered it. Her long hair was badly in need of a cut and shaping, not to mention her roots were showing like a bitch. Haircuts and shopping trips were infrequent while in hiding.

"Don't feel bad about being forgotten." They turned a corner onto a darker, quieter street with low-rise buildings and a few houses. "This whole city is about to collapse. It won't matter soon." He chuckled, an oddly tantalizing and companionable sound in the darkness.

"Sounds ominous."

"At the end of the coming clash, the vampires will be the only ones left standing. That's the beauty of neutrality. We'll be sifting through the ashes when the fight is over."

"Like scavengers. Picking the bones for treasure."

The media heralded the "coming clash" every day on TV and in the papers. The Paranormal Alliance grew more and more radical by the day. Members of the SNC—Aaron's secular non-paranormal group—had either joined forces with Sam's group or splintered into rogue factions. All of them wanted the Institute closed down. Unrest swelled: violence, riots, even bomb threats and arson attempts on the Institute.

"The scavengers will inherit the earth," Zack said. "When the rest of you get done killing each other, we'll gather up what's left and rebuild this city in our image."

They stopped outside a brick building four stories tall, a small porch attached to the front. Lights were on in many of the windows. Music drifted out.

"How's your lung feel about climbing stairs?" Zack asked. "Because we're going to the top floor, and the elevator's been out of service for months."

June groaned.

Chapter 2

June stood in the dimly lit dingy foyer of the building, a wooden staircase rising in front of her. Music thumped from the floors above. The scent of pot hung on the stuffy air. Stairs were not her friend these days, along with humidity and walking and...everything.

At least she'd get a good bout of physical therapy.

By the second floor, she had to stop. She slumped against a wall, panting, her bag drooping off her shoulder. Zack waited a few steps above her.

"Is the bullet still in you?" he asked.

June nodded. Every breath burned on the right side, her chest tight. She had turned into a weak, bedraggled old woman.

Zack seemed to think differently. "It's kind of sexy and dangerous." He flashed his fangs in a grin. "So's that ink." He slid his gaze over June's bare, heavily-tattooed arms. "Nice work."

"Thanks. I did most of it myself." Her breaths evened out. "It's a good thing I'm ambidextrous. I doubt I'll be tattooing again with my right hand." She lifted her arm and flexed her fingers. *I doubt I'll be tattooing again at all. Especially if I'm dead.*

"Want me to carry you the rest of the way up?"

"In your dreams."

She was winded again by the fourth floor, but she didn't take another break. People crammed the fourth floor hallway, doors open, music and voices issuing from doorways. Smoke filled the air with an opaque haze. Though mostly pot, the underlying cigarette smell caused her to salivate.

The vampires here were not trendy young hipsters like at the diner. Most of them were older and much more grizzled. June hung in some rough circles in Sacramento. Leather, ink, and shaved heads were not foreign to her, but these vampires were blatantly malicious. Their dark, brooding presence and their defensive stances oozed danger and warning.

No one spoke to her, but they watched her pass with keen, glittering eyes. This was the wrong party house to stumble into unaware.

Zack led her through an open door near the end of the hallway. They stepped into an apartment, noisy with voices and music. The place was a shit hole—sparsely furnished, trash and clutter everywhere, stained carpet, cracked paint. The walls were white, but the corners and ceiling were yellow with cigarette smoke, like nicotine wallpaper. June's tiny apartment above her tattoo shop seemed homey in comparison, though her place was admittedly cluttered and not in the best condition either. People sat around on the few pieces of furniture and on the floor, drinking from bottles and cans, smoking and talking.

Eyes followed her as Zack led her into the apartment, down a hallway, and into another room. This one held a couch, a couple of chairs, and a widescreen TV that several people were playing a video game on. Some sort of military-type shooter. Two people sat on the couch, lazy-eyed, bottles in hand, passing a joint back and forth.

"Occam," Zack said. "Your appointment is here."

The man he addressed sat slumped in one of the chairs, in front of a set of windows that were open, making the room less hazy than the outer one. He had his legs draped over the arm of the chair and a video game controller in his hands, a cigarette dangling from the corner of his mouth. Someone immediately paused the game.

If this was Occam Reed, June was a little flabbergasted and a lot disappointed.

He was middle-aged, paunchy, and wide-shouldered, with a square jaw and short, messy, spiky blond hair. Behind him on the windowsill, an array of liquor bottles sat, most of them empty. He lifted his arm and looked at a clunky black watch on his wrist.

"Is it three already?" He had a deep, low-pitched voice, smooth and vaguely creepy, like the kind serial killers used to lure people into bushes.

"Yes." Zack stood in the middle of the room. "June Coffin." He jerked his head at her. "June, Occam Reed."

A guy and girl sat on the floor, video game controllers in their hands as well. A tiny, curvy black girl sprawled in the chair next to Occam.

"I guess it is." Occam slung his legs over the side of the chair.

He tossed his controller on the floor. The girl there grabbed it up. A vast presence emanated from Occam, making it clear he was the head honcho in this room, maybe the whole building. His piercing stare reminded her of Sam's—as if he wanted to drill into her aorta with his eyeballs. He plucked the cigarette from the corner of his mouth.

"So you're the messenger?" he said. "The poor child Sam and Aaron sent into the woods?" He jerked his chin at Zack.

Zack turned and left the room.

"I wouldn't call myself Little Red Riding Hood." She tried to maintain a cool façade. "Though you do look like a bunch of big bad wolves."

Titters and snorts went up. Occam took a pull off his cigarette, bouncing one of his legs. He narrowed his eyes and blew the smoke out.

"Clear out, guys." He glanced at the TV. "Leave it paused, I'm winning."

Everyone got up and filed out, except the black girl, who remained in her chair, gazing at June.

Occam gestured to the couch. "Sit, June Coffin."

Her chest hurt and she needed to rest, despite her reluctance to relax. She walked to the couch and sat down on the end closest to Occam. The thing nearly sagged to the floor and reeked of cigarette smoke. Occam smoked down the last of his cigarette, knee still bouncing, the corner of his mouth pulling and jerking. His tic reminded her of Sam's bodyguard, Muse, whom June had grown so accustomed to she barely noticed her little tremors now. However, Occam's tics were more familiar to June. They were chemically induced, not neurological.

He slid his tongue over his cracked lips. He took one more puff and then swiveled and ground out the cigarette on the arm of his chair. A wide black burnt spot showed it was his favorite ashtray. He flicked the butt into the space between the couch and his chair.

"So." He rubbed his hands together. He thankfully quit bouncing his fucking knee. "They sent you into the belly of the beast to ask for our help fighting the mean old Institute." He had little stubs of fangs, brighter than the rest of his dull, yellowed teeth. "This is dangerous territory, Little Red. You think you'll get out alive?"

June reached down and slid the bottom of her T-shirt up, revealing the butt of the gun tucked into the holster on her hip. "Yep."

Occam chuckled and flopped back in his chair, legs splayed in front of him. June dropped her shirt back down over the gun.

"Belle," Occam addressed the black girl. "Make me a drink. You want one?" he asked June.

"More than you know. But I think I better keep my wits about me. I'd rather you didn't get me vulnerable and make me into a blood milkshake."

Occam laughed, loud and jarring.

Belle stood up. Her features reminded June of Zack. Were they related? Her hair was dark blond and she wore all white, like a vampire angel. She turned to a set of shelves on the wall cluttered with bottles and glasses and grabbed a rocks glass.

"You know how to use that thing?" Occam gestured to June's hip.

"Yes." She'd been practicing. Not easy with only one good arm.

"I heard about your plight." Occam lifted his leg and rested his ankle on the opposite knee. He started bouncing his foot. "What they did to you and your brother at the Institute. Your daring escape. Your terrible wound." His voice dripped with sarcasm. "Sam and Aaron filled me in when they were lobbying to get you here."

"They wanted to gain your sympathy. But don't feel sorry for me. I'm doing just fine."

Belle turned the glass over and pushed the rim into a shallow white bowl on the windowsill. She twisted it back and forth, as if rimming a margarita glass with salt.

"Just fine?" Occam said. "Hiding in the shadows like a rat, while everyone thinks you're dead? Sucked into their war?"

"Maybe it's a war worth fighting. I was under the impression you didn't like the Institute, either."

"I don't." He quit bouncing his foot. "But I don't like the SNC or the Paranormal Alliance, either."

"I can understand why."

Belle opened a bottle and poured clear liquid into the glass.

"But?" Occam said.

"But I'm neck-deep in shit right now, and I've got to swim or I'm never getting out."

Belle sauntered over to Occam's chair and held the glass out to him. He took it. The top was rimmed with something white, too fine to be sugar or salt.

"Thank you," he said. "Sure you don't want one?" he asked June. "It's my own creation. A Russian Donut."

"Russian Donut?"

Belle went back to her chair and sat down.

"A shot of vodka." Occam sat forward, holding the glass aloft. "Powdered." He lowered the glass, pressed a finger to one nostril, and snorted the rim by rotating the glass. He then downed the shot and flopped back in his chair, sniffing and rubbing his nose, eyelids fluttering.

"I think I'll pass," June said. He got points for style, though. Like they were at the druggie Olympics.

Occam thrust the glass out. Belle took it from him. She set it aside on the windowsill.

Occam sat bolt upright and focused his glassy eyes on June.

"The great thing about being a vampire," he said, "is I can fuck myself up as much as I want, and there's no lasting damage."

"At least you're not using your powers for evil." June shifted, trying to get comfortable on the lumpy couch. "Now, can we get down to business by any chance? I came here to negotiate."

Occam dug into his jeans pocket and pulled out a crumpled pack of cigarettes.

"The only way you're going to get what you want right off the bat is if you've brought me Micha Bellevue's head." He nodded at June's bag. "Is it in there?"

"Not quite."

"Well, then." He pulled out a silver-plated Zippo. "Guess this'll take a while."

June presented the terms she'd been instructed to give by Sam and Aaron. She didn't need them written down, as they'd been drilling them into her head for a week. They would give Occam their information on the serum—a nasty potion distilled from the stolen abilities of numerous research subjects, meant to give a "normal" their powers—if...

"We turn the information over to our scientists?" Occam's cigarette burned away between his fingers. "And then what?"

The vampire's "scientists" were collectively known as the FPS—the Freelance Paranormal Scientists—a group of researchers who didn't involve themselves with the Institute, and to hear tell, were in the vampire's pocket.

"And then they tell everyone what the Institute has done," June said. "And the Institute goes down."

"You think it's that easy?" Occam took a drag.

"Honestly? No. But I'm just the messenger."

Occam blew the smoke out in a slow stream. June longed for a cigarette. Her chest hurt from the smoke in the air, though.

"So what's in it for us?" Occam asked.

"Blowing the lid on the Institute isn't enough for you?"

"Is it enough for you?" Occam focused on her. His eyes were deep and intense beneath the drug-induced haze on the surface. He might be sharp behind that shabby exterior.

"Why wouldn't it be?"

"You just want them called out on the carpet and shut down, so you can declare a default victory? You don't want more than that? You don't want revenge?"

"This isn't my war. I'm a soldier in it because it's the only thing I can do right now. The things I want are a lot more complicated than revenge."

Occam ground his cigarette out on the arm of the chair. "So I ask you again, what's in it for us?"

June took a deep breath.

"Micha Bellevue is willing to tell you everything he knows about his wife's research."

The late, not-so-dearly departed Rose Bellevue had been the top vampire researcher at the Institute, the person the militant vampires despised for revealing them as little more than perpetual bags of bacteria. She was also, questionably, the reason Micha became the first victim of the serum. They still had no definite proof Rose had trussed her husband up for experimentation, and her ghost seemed to be trying to refute it, but for Micha it was another torment in his currently long list of tortures. He had agreed to give up her research so the vampires could hand it over to their scientists for shooting down.

Occam sat silent. He bounced his foot. Sniffed.

"Now you have my interest," he said. "Beating up the Institute is fun and all, but beating up the Bellevue legacy is even better."

Just don't beat up Micha Bellevue, please.

"So those are the terms," June said. "Help us expose the serum, and you can have—whatever it is Micha can give you."

"Why should I trust you'll keep your part of the bargain?"

June sat forward and slid her bag off her shoulder. She placed it in her lap and unzipped it. "I was told to give this to you. You can have your scientists look at it." She pulled out a glass tube with a stopper in the top. The tube was full of blood. She held it out to him.

He sat forward and took it.

"It's not quite his head," she said, "but will it do?"

"Is this a party favor?" He brought the tube to his nose and waved it under his nostrils. He then laid it aside on the arm of the chair, as if it didn't contain the most valuable and damning ounce of liquid in the entire city.

"Do you understand why they sent you to present me this deal, June Coffin?"

"Because I'm a victim and you'll take pity on me?"

Occam snorted. "Do you believe that? Do you believe I have tremendous amounts of pity for all the Institute's lab rats?" He rested his elbows on his knees. "Do you trust Aaron Jenkins and Sam Haain that much?"

Megan Morgan

"I don't trust anyone in this city, but they've helped me a lot. They got my ass out of a sling more than once."

He chuckled. "They didn't send you because I'd take pity on you, and you don't really believe you're a victim. Oh, you're a victim. But you're not victimized."

She narrowed her eyes.

"They sent you because you'd make a wonderful vampire."

She blinked at him.

"You're an insurance policy, Little Red. They're taking a shot in the dark. If I was offended, I'd at least have a nice peace offering, because God knows they have enough problems right now without me on their backs."

A chill rushed through her. Her brain protested "that's not true!" but her instinct, her gut, doubted.

Before she could answer, or contemplate betrayal or her fate, a commotion rose in the outer room.

Zack reappeared. He wasn't alone, but was dragging someone by the arm, someone who was fighting him.

The girl from the diner.

"What the hell?" June gasped.

The girl looked around wildly, eyes bulging. Zack held her firmly, despite her struggle.

"Good work, Zack." A smile quirked Occam's cracked lips.

"What are you doing?" June demanded. "Why did you bring her here? Let her go. She has nothing to do with this."

The girl shrieked and tried to yank out of Zack's grasp again, her hair flying around her face.

"Oh, stop it," Occam said. "I'm not as stupid as you think I am, Sam."

The girl stopped struggling. Suddenly, she wasn't there. No fade or a shimmer, the transformation didn't seem to happen in time, more like an imperceptible blink. One moment she stood there, and the next she was Sam Haain, seething and glowering, his dark, straight hair brushing his shoulders.

"Occam," Sam said. "You're such a fuck."

June slumped and rubbed her forehead.

"We're not idiots." Zack released Sam's arm. "I was watching you two from the second you came into the District. You weren't disguising June."

"Of course I wasn't," Sam said. "She needed to find Occam. He needed to know it was her."

"Sam Haain." Occam hauled himself to his feet. "What are you doing in my territory, exactly?"

Sam huffed. "Your territory? This is an open area. Anyone is allowed here, even normals."

"I thought we had some unspoken rules." Occam strolled over to him. "You wouldn't react too kindly if my entourage went traipsing about on your turf."

"I wasn't going to let June wander into your 'turf' without backup. I'm just watching over her in case any of you try to open a vein."

"As if you could stop us if we wanted to do that. If you tried, you'd have two wars on your hands."

Sam gritted his teeth. "Your threats hold no weight with me." He sneered at Zack. "Hilarious joke with the panties, by the way."

"You're not as strong as you used to be, Sam," Occam said. "I'd watch your tongue. You're out of favor. Your group is becoming more fractured by the day, without you there to herd them into place."

"I'm not out of any favor. My true followers are still keeping my edicts."

"And Robbie Beecher's followers?"

"Were never my people to begin with."

June scooted to the edge of the couch. "What are you going to do with us? Now that you've found out Sam is here. Kill us?"

Occam swiveled toward her. "If I were going to do that, I would have done it the instant the two of you showed up in the Nocturnal District." He walked back to his chair and flopped down. He folded his hands on his stomach. "I'll help you. Your offer intrigues me."

Sam stared at him. "Just like that?"

Occam picked up the tube. "Just like that." He rolled it between his fingers.

"And we can walk out of here?" Sam asked.

"Of course. But I expect you to enjoy my hospitality first."

Sam huffed. "I'm not sure I would enjoy your hospitality, Occam."

"You can't seal an agreement without a celebratory drink. Fix us some drinks, Belle."

Belle got to her feet.

"You want to seal the agreement, don't you?" Occam arched an eyebrow at Sam.

They'd probably need to seal some wounds before they left.

June took a shot of vodka but refused the powdered rim. Sam sat beside her on the couch. Zack sat on the arm of Belle's chair. Side by side, they were clearly related. Occam did two shots and a line of coke to seal the deal. He oh-so-politely offered his mirror, but June and Sam refused.

"You're a mess, Occam," Sam informed him after he threw back his own shot. "How you seized any respect around here is beyond me. And how the hell did you know it was me?"

Occam snorted and set his mirror aside. "I've learned the tells over my many long years."

Suddenly, it wasn't Occam sitting in the chair, but Sam.

"I can see through the glamour," Occam-Sam said.

June's head was already spinning from the one shot. She thought she might be having a nightmare.

"Great," the real Sam said. "So that's what you are. I'm so pleased to call you my brother."

Occam blinked back to himself.

"Thank you for sending June," Occam said. "She's an absolute delight."

"I take it you didn't actually have a conversation with her?"

"You know what?" June shot at him. "Eat me."

Occam gestured at Belle. "Why don't you make June another drink?"

Belle got up and poured another shot. June flexed her fingers. They were tingling, but it was only an alcohol buzz. Occam hadn't poisoned her. Yet.

"We can't hang out here all night," Sam said. "We're not safe out in the open, not even here."

Belle sauntered over to June, glass in hand. June lifted her hand to take it, but instead of handing it over, Belle fell into her lap, all warm, soft flesh, and perfume. June froze, arms raised, frowning.

"Um…"

Belle smiled a tiny smile and lifted the glass to June's lips. June jerked her head back, staring at her.

"What the hell?" Sam said.

"Occam." Zack shook his head.

Occam arched an eyebrow. "Oh, my bad. I'm not very good at this, am I? I thought she might like your sister, Zack. Belle." He waved at her.

Belle crawled out of June's lap, taking the drink with her.

June gritted her teeth, getting it now.

"I'm not gay!" June shrieked. "Oh my God. Really?"

Zack stood up, and in passing his sister, took the drink from her hand. He walked toward June. The movement of his hips, the swagger in his stride instantly, inexplicably distracted her. He plopped in her lap, as his sister had. June relaxed, warmth spreading through her limbs. When Zack lifted the glass to her lips, she drank without hesitation. Belle crawled into Sam's lap, straddling him.

"You can stay for a while," Occam said. "The night is young. Dawn is far away."

June gazed at Zack, enraptured. So gorgeous, perhaps the most gorgeous man she'd ever laid eyes on. A heat spread through her that had nothing to do with the vodka. His body was solid and firm, and he smelled heady and mysterious. She gripped his thigh and massaged it, the muscle taut beneath his tight jeans. He stroked his fingers through her hair, smiling beatifically, his dark eyes gleaming. The heat inside her expanded and flashed across her skin. Her entire body went molten. She grew painfully horny.

A heavy thud sounded, followed by an angry feminine yelp. Sam leaped to his feet.

"Occam, you bastard, how dare you!" He snarled at Belle, "Stay right there, or I swear I'll jam my boot straight up your ass."

June tried to ignore the distraction. She locked an arm around Zack's waist and pulled him closer. Zack placed his hand on her breast and plucked her hardened nipple through her shirt. She had never been so glad she didn't wear a bra.

"I want you," she whispered, close to Zack's lips.

Sam loomed over them, and he grabbed a handful of Zack's dreads, jerking his head back. Zack snarled, baring his fangs.

"You call this sex witch off," Sam demanded. "Get him out of her lap, or I will!"

Occam watched placidly.

"Is this our punishment for interloping?" Sam asked.

"Did you think you'd get out of here without so much as a slap on the wrist?"

Sam yanked Zack, snarling and struggling, off June. Belle lay sprawled on the floor, but she sprang swiftly to her knees. June's skin seemed to have turned to goo, and Zack pulled strands of it away as he went. She clutched at the air. Her insides burned.

Sam flung Zack against the opposite wall, between the TV and the chair Belle had been sitting in. As he slumped to the floor, he locked eyes with June, and she jerked forward, her heart jumping into her throat. Zack leaped up and sprang toward her, but Sam checked him with an elbow to the chin. Zack hit the floor beside his sister.

"Call them off, Occam!" Sam swiped Belle with his leg as she tried to get up, sending her crashing back to the floor.

"They're hungry, Sam. Not for blood, though."

Zack had gotten back to his feet. June tried to get up and go to him. However, Sam flung himself at the couch and landed in a heavy heap on top of her. June squirmed beneath him, her senses filled with Zack, everything in her body churning, wanting. She would burst into flame if she didn't get to him. Sam reached down to June's side, whipped around, and jerked his arm straight out. He had taken June's gun and he trained it on the two vampires charging at the couch. They immediately stopped.

"Stay back," Sam warned. "Stay the fuck back. I know how to hit a vital organ."

They remained in place, though Zack's eyes were hard and glittering and fixed on June. He flexed his fingers at his sides. June balled her fists against Sam's chest and tried to push him off, but her right arm was too weak.

"Get off me!"

Sam kept her pinned with his weight across her hips. He kept the gun pointed at the two. "You're gonna hate me for this later," he said to her. "But I'm saving your life right now."

Sam jammed his thigh up between her legs. June convulsively locked her legs around it and began humping, wet and trembling with arousal, eager for anything to give her stimulation. Sparks shot into her stomach, raced up and down her back. She blanked out everyone else in the room apart from Zack, whom she focused on with desperation.

Sam leaned over, his hair brushing her cheek. "I hope this is enough. I don't want to violate you." He whispered, "I'm sorry."

Zack seethed. His sister retreated a few steps. Sam still had the gun pointed at them. Occam hadn't moved from his chair.

June remained locked in the intense grip of need. Her insides ached as she slid against the firm, hard length of Sam's thigh. She wished her jeans would disappear. She was too hot, too aroused, tense and filled up with an energy like her skin would burst at any moment, paralyzed apart from the rhythm of her hips. Her orgasm built sharp and hard, and she wailed—in anguish, in pleasure, she wasn't sure—when the tension finally broke and she came, thrashing beneath Sam's body. She had soaked through her jeans. She had probably soaked his.

As the tremors subsided, her head cleared. The heat trapped in her skin seemed to radiate off. The tension gripping her muscles subsided. Zack stepped back, his chest heaving.

Coming back to reality sucked. Her entire body shook, her crotch was soaked, and she lay prone underneath Sam, who studied her with actual concern in his eyes, making the situation even worse. His hair brushed her neck and jaw, and it smelled like the shampoo they'd all been using for months. A small comfort, somehow.

"Oh God," she said, her voice small and quiet. The vodka churned in her stomach.

Sam lifted off her and stood. He walked over to Zack and jammed the barrel of the gun against his temple.

"I should paint this room with your brains," he said, low and fierce. "See if you survive that, vampire."

Occam cleared his throat. "You won't leave here alive. Just an FYI, Sam."

Sam still held the gun to Zack's head.

June struggled into a sitting position. "Sam, it's not worth it. Let's just go."

Zack leered at Sam. "You smell like her pussy."

Sam dropped the gun to his side; then he brought it up in a swift arc and across Zack's face. A sickening crunch sounded, and blood sprayed and splattered across the floor. Zack collapsed to his knees, hands to his face, yowling.

Sam's eyes burned with rage. "We're walking out of here now," he said to Occam. "And if you try to stop us, I might die, but I'll take your sorry bullet-riddled ass with me."

Chapter 3

June and Sam sat in an empty car on the night owl red line L train. June had learned all about public transportation in Chicago, especially at night, since that was the only safe time for needed excursions or clandestine meetings. The car was empty so they didn't have to disguise themselves. She'd held hands with girl Sam on the way there—for his power extended to others via touch—while he disguised her as a young man. He released her once they were safely inside the District, allowing her to be herself so she could meet with Occam.

They sat silent, June awkward in the aftermath of their vampire rendezvous. She still buzzed with the energy Zack had ignited in her.

The car wobbled along. The click of the rails and the city lights sliding by in the darkness calmed her.

"You all right?" Sam finally asked.

She nodded.

"I'm sorry," he said. "Sex witches can be vile creatures. They get you hot and bothered and suck the sexual energy out of you. It makes you weak and vulnerable. Over time, it can really damage you, make you horribly sick. Even kill you."

Cindy was a sex witch. June had never feared her, not for her supernatural abilities, anyway—she was kind of crazy on her own—but maybe she should.

"Do you think they would've—could've—killed us?" June asked.

"I think they would've weakened us so Occam could keep us as his playthings. And then, yes, perhaps eventually killed us."

She stared out the window across from them.

"I'm sorry," he said again, "that I had to do that to you."

"You didn't do anything. I did…all the doing." She cringed. Too much embarrassment, too soon.

"I won't tell anyone. I won't tell Micha."

"Thanks. And thanks for saving me from getting my life sucked out through my vagina. I'm glad Belle didn't get the better of you." She paused. "She couldn't bewitch you? You don't like black chicks or something?"

"I knew what was happening, from the second he got in your lap. I don't like evil murderesses. And I don't like vampires."

June could get behind that.

"I hate vampires." He slipped down on the plastic seat, legs splayed. "I'd cut off a vampire's head before I'd allow one in the Paranormal Alliance."

"I might have called you an extremist before, but I can totally see why you feel that way now."

"I can't believe Occam is a goddamn shapeshifter. There's not a whole lot of us."

"There's not a whole lot of Sirens, either. I'm pretty glad he's not one of us."

"This is what we explained to you, though. They don't turn normals. And the ones with the rarest abilities float to the top, not to mention the ones with the strongest abilities. It's a pissing contest." He fell silent a moment. "Are you impressed by them?"

"Impressed? With what?" She shifted and crossed her legs. "The drugs? The drinking? The utter filth? Their penchant for trying to rape and kill people?"

"They live like pigs, don't they? It's a result of their physiology, actually. They're not susceptible to germs and illnesses, or overdoses. They don't have to be clean or careful. When you can't really die, you tend to get careless."

"It sounds like an existence that would get really old, really fast."

"I guess it's better than our existence right now."

"Doesn't mean I'm impressed by them."

"Unfortunately, they're very strong and very well-connected. We need them for this."

She took in his profile. He was handsome, his jaw strong, his nose big, but it fit his face. His features were chiseled and blatantly masculine. Maybe the remnant of Zack's power made her fixate.

He narrowed his dark eyes at her. "What?"

"Why did you send me to talk to the vampires?"

"We went over that."

"You really thought they'd take pity on someone, even someone who's been victimized by the Institute? They don't seem to give a damn about non-vampires."

"Well they certainly wouldn't have taken pity on me or Aaron. You were holding a better hand." He sat up on the seat. "Don't let what happened haunt you. Vampires love to mess with people. It could have been much worse. They actually did take pity on us. They let us walk out of there."

June resisted the urge to press. The people she trusted most couldn't have possibly used her as fodder.

They had to get off the train and take a bus to Hyde Park, where they were hiding out. They'd left Aaron's downtown penthouse before the end of winter, since downtown wasn't the ideal place for slipping in and out. Aaron owned a house in the quiet, residential, and university-focused area of Hyde Park where people were unlikely to be looking for the city's two biggest villains—or heroes, depending on whom the media asked.

The house wasn't in his real name, and Aaron wasn't there. Sam and Aaron had agreed not to hide out in the same place, so if one of them was captured, the other remained free. They actually didn't know where Aaron was—another safety measure. Most news outlets believed Aaron and Sam weren't in the city. The favorite bit of speculation at the moment was they had fled to Canada.

The bus wasn't empty so they had to disguise themselves, but the streets were quiet and deserted in the pre-dawn darkness, and the walk from the bus stop to the house proved uneventful. The house where they were hiding was simple, middle class, and non-descript, though canvassed with a sophisticated security system. Robbie would have been proud of their paranoia.

Despite being around five AM, all the lights were on in the house. As soon as they started up the narrow cement walkway—having tripped the beams at the gate—the front door opened. June hadn't reached the porch steps yet when someone swept her up in big, strong arms.

"You're safe," Micha whispered against her hair. "Thank God."

She squeezed him. Sam climbed the steps.

"This has been a long night." Micha drew back, his arms still around her. His eyes glistened in the light from the door.

Another person walked down the steps, and Micha released her.

"I'm so glad to see you in once piece." Her brother Jason hugged her tightly. "How were the vampires?"

June huffed against his shoulder. "Complete assholes. Not a surprise."

"I'm glad everyone is happy I'm safe!" Sam called out.

Despite his griping, inside the house, Muse, Sam's ironic little bodyguard, gripped him by the arms, relief evident on her face. She wore a white terrycloth robe. She had to tilt her head back to look at him. June considered her a sister in shortness.

"I'm glad you're back," Muse said. "I hate when you get out of my hearing range." Muse was a powerful telepath. So powerful, it was killing her.

The living room where they stood was spacious, sconces on the walls filling the space with a soft yellow glow. A wall of TV and stereo equipment dominated one side of the room.

"So what's the news?" Jason asked. They had all waited what seemed like ages for the results of tonight.

Sam pushed a hand through his hair. "Occam accepted our offer. I'm sure we'll be hearing from him soon."

"Good," Micha said, but his voice was grim.

Micha had become the epitome of their seclusion. His hair had grown out shaggy, and dark roots dominated his faded blond highlights. They shared a communal pile of genderless shirts and jeans. Everything Micha wore hung from his frame and his bones stuck out at odd angles. His cheeks were hollow.

"I guess my fate is sealed," he said. "I wanted to make a difference. Now I will."

June clenched her jaw, forcing herself not to say anything. Sam and Aaron were using him as a pawn, and they couldn't do anything but use him. Micha had lost his power to choose long before they'd turned him into a bargaining chip. He'd lost it when Eric Greerson injected him with the serum. He'd lost it before that, when his wife prepared him for it.

The serum worked, to an extent. Micha had experienced every paranormal ability one could name, aside from aural captivation, though they all came and went, and he could never control them. Thankfully, he didn't seem to be infected with the vampire virus.

"God must be getting some kind of sick pleasure out of kicking us around," June said.

"I don't believe in God anymore." Micha walked out of the room, toward the kitchen.

June went upstairs, to the bedroom she shared with Jason. A TV sat on the dresser, rarely turned on, because June was forced to watch the news too much downstairs.

She took off her jeans—the crotch still damp—and changed into a pair of pajama pants. She sat down on her bed, facing the window. They were usually awake at night and asleep during the day, ironically like vampires. When dawn arrived, they pulled curtains against the world, against its taunting memory and the blossom of approaching summer. They were prisoners of their own fate, and the outside world was too painful a reminder of what they'd lost. Would her life ever be normal again, or would she spend the rest of her days a fugitive, in seclusion, hiding from the sun, cursing God?

Jason entered the bedroom and crawled into his bed across the room. "Good night," he said softly.

His voice remained raspy from the torture he'd endured at the Institute. He couldn't speak loudly, or it would crack. It sounded ragged and guttural when he woke up, crying out from nightmares.

"I'm glad you're safe," he whispered. "I was worried all night."

Safe. Was she?

She waited until Jason's breath grew soft and even, and quietly left the room. She went downstairs. Her insides still burned, an energy that wasn't wholly her own churning low in her gut.

She envisioned Sam on top of her, felt the pressure of his thigh between her legs. She saw the consternation on his face as he ascended the porch steps, when Micha hugged her.

The kitchen light was on. Micha stood at the sink counter, sipping from a coffee cup. His blue eyes—they hadn't dulled, at least—were questioning as June walked over to him.

Maybe it was guilt, or need, or some leftover thing from Zack that made her grip Micha's T-shirt, made her yank him forward and against her. Her head had cleared, and what was left, raw and disfigured in that clarity, terrified her. She wanted someone to suffer, like she had suffered. Maybe she was more of a monster than she gave herself credit for.

Micha seemed to get it. He set his cup aside, grabbed her, and pushed her against the counter, close to the hulking steel refrigerator, so one of her shoulder blades bumped into it. *He doesn't mean to hurt me.*

Maybe she wanted to be hurt, and she deserved it—especially to be hurt by him.

Micha crushed his lips against hers, stealing her breath and forcing her mouth open, the kiss wet and harsh. His tongue pushed against hers, and she pushed back, bringing her hands up to grip his shoulders, digging her nails in.

A million thoughts raced into her mind and right back out, but the one that stuck was that Micha was not as fragile as he seemed.

He broke the kiss, leaving her lips tingling, and she would have been able to breathe if not for her heart pounding in her throat and the hitch in her right side. Micha kept her trapped between him and the refrigerator, looming over her, his body heat and trembling muscles all she could focus on. He wanted her. She wanted him to want her.

"June." His voice, next to her ear, came out intensely intimate.

She yanked his shirt up. Maybe those sharp points of bone beneath his skin would cut her, so she could bleed and feel again.

Things needed to be said. She had to tell him things, ask him things, be reassured of things, but silence dominated. Her body wanted something, some kind of contact, some satisfaction. Zack's power left a mark on her that was still raw.

Micha gripped her around the waist and lifted her onto the counter, so she was face-to-face with him. She shoved a hand down the front of his pants. He did the same to her. She moved her hips on instinct, rubbing, grinding, rolling against his hand, her own hand full of him, thick and hot. Their mouths met, and they sucked in each other's breath.

Sex had become a weird thing between them—weird, and emotionally jarring. They hadn't done it, not properly, for a while. But this, they could do. This they could walk away from without too much internal bleeding.

Maybe.

June planted her foot against the drawers beneath her, her heel catching on the lip of the bottom one. She drew Micha tight against her. He had a foot braced on the cupboard door for leverage, so he could slam his fingers up into her. She stroked him hard and fast, like a piston.

The air between them thickened, sticking to the inside of her laboring lungs. The world wobbled as her head grew woozy from the lack of oxygen. Micha had his head turned to the side, face tilted down. His hair filled June's static-dotted vision. She licked her lips and stared aside as well, at the red-and-white checkered floor.

She stifled the ribald moaning that wanted to rip out of her. Micha's breath came quick and shallow. Occasionally he moved his head, a slow rolling of his neck, but they kept their faces turned firmly away from each other. With a twist of his wrist he pushed her closer to the edge. The slickness, the scent, but mostly the soft, moist sound of flesh slapping intensified the burn in her stomach.

Micha came first. Wet heat splashed over June's hand and trickled down her wrist. He breathed sharply through his nose, but emitted one small sound at the end, a faint, whiny grunt, and June clenched hard inside and succumbed, finally finding release from the torment. The musky scent hanging on the air changed, getting stronger and thicker. June stroked, slow and firm, until Micha gripped her forearm, indicating enough.

They remained in silence, June's sticky hand still wrapped around him. Micha still had his fingers inside her. She struggled to get her breath. Her chest ached.

Finally, Micha drew back.

"Jesus Christ, June."

Jesus Christ, indeed.

Chapter 4

"You should dye your hair," Micha said.

He and June were lying in Micha's bed, the late afternoon sun blocked out by thick curtains. The cursed light still crept in around the edges, though, and fell in a sharp line across the sheets. The house was quiet. Micha's body rested warm and clammy against her bare side.

"Why?" Instinct in edgy moments drove her to reach for her cigarettes on the bedside stand, but they weren't there anymore.

"Because." His head rested in the crook of her shoulder and chest, his hand on her sternum. "You'd be surprised how much changing your hair makes you look different. Every picture people have seen of you, your hair is black. Maybe you should go blond."

June reached up and slid her fingers through her hair.

"The roots are already like five feet long." Her natural hair color was light brown, like Jason's hair. She could have dyed her roots, she supposed. Cindy could have brought her dye and done it for her, but June didn't have the heart. She almost fancied herself one of those warriors who didn't cut her hair until the battle was won. She couldn't look good until they got out of this.

Micha shrugged. "You'd look good as a blonde, I think. And you wouldn't have to worry so much about being recognized."

June focused on the light fixture above the bed dangling from a dusty chain. The air from a fan in the corner caused it to swing in a slow circle.

"No one remembers me," she said. "And I think I have slightly more distinctive features than my hair." She plucked at one of the gauges in her ears. By now, she should have been at a two gauge or maybe a zero.

"I can't keep doing this." His voice fell an octave, infused with desperation. "I can't handle it. I worry all the time. About our situation. About them finding us. About you."

She rolled her head toward him and gazed into his eyes, those clear blue depths, troubled, strange, but more familiar to her than anyone else's eyes, including her own.

"Why?" she asked softly.

"I have this nightmare they'll break in and kill you. Or kidnap you."

"It's not me they want to kill or kidnap. I don't exist anymore. I can't change the situation we're in. I wish I could."

"I wish you'd leave Chicago. Get the hell out of here, go back to California. You've had plenty of opportunities to do so."

"When Sam tells me to go, I'll go. I trust he knows what he's doing."

Micha sat up, his lip curled. "Why do you trust Sam? He's done nothing for months. He's waiting instead of acting. We can't just hide here for the rest of our lives."

"When did you stop trusting Sam?"

"When did you start?"

He scooted away, toward the edge of the bed. His typical behavior of late. He was coming unhinged, distrusting everyone in the house, even her sometimes.

"Micha—"

"If it wasn't for him, we wouldn't be in this situation." He got to his feet, naked. The faint light outlined the tight muscles of his buttocks.

"Yes," she said. "It has abso-fucking-lutely nothing to do with the Institute, now does it?"

"You were a victim. Do you want to be a victim again? Because that's what you'll be if you keep sitting around here, taking orders from him. Letting him send you into the Nocturnal District at a time like this. That could have been a death sentence!"

Occam's words rang in her head. You'd make a wonderful vampire.

Micha bent and snatched up a shirt from the floor. As he tugged it on, a knock sounded at the door.

Micha pulled the shirt down. Before either of them could answer, the door opened and Sam poked his head in.

"There you are," he said to June. Then he jerked his head back, apparently having gotten a glimpse of Micha. "For God's sake."

"I don't believe anyone said come the fuck in," June shot at him.

"Come downstairs," he said from the other side of the door, his voice grim. "There's breaking news on TV."

June's stomach lurched. She hated the news, breaking news even more. She sat up.

When Sam left, she looked at Micha. "If I leave, you'll probably never see me again."

Micha wiggled his pants on. "If you leave, maybe I can leave too."

Downstairs, everyone gathered around the TV in the living room. A blond woman spoke in a serious voice.

"There have been many acts of violence and civil unrest since the murder of Eric Greerson earlier this year. Most of them perpetrated by the two groups believed to be responsible for his death—the Secular Normalists of Chicago and the Paranormal Alliance, the two most prolific extremist paranormal groups in the city."

Sam stood with his arms folded in front of the TV. He grumbled.

"However, this is a grisly and unfortunate reminder of how far this unrest may go if left unchecked."

The scene cut away to somewhere outside—a parking lot cordoned off with yellow police tape. The lake stretched out in the background. Police gathered around a four-door white car. At the bottom of the screen it said: BODY FOUND: POSSIBLE INSTITUTE RESEARCHER.

"What's going on?" June asked.

"Robbie sent us a message," Sam said. "Someone found a car down by the lake with a message written on it, in blood. The police found a body in the trunk, with the throat slashed. All they're saying is they think it's an Institute researcher."

The woman spoke again. "Police say they will not reveal the identity of the victim until the family has been contacted. However, the message written on the trunk of the car, in what is believed to be blood, says"—she spoke succinctly—"Sam Haain is dead. We act now."

Sam glared at the TV, shifting his jaw.

"Sam Haain, of course, is the former leader of the Paranormal Alliance, having disappeared earlier this year after his alleged involvement in the death of Eric Greerson."

"It has to be Robbie," Sam said.

"I don't doubt it," June said. "Throat slashed? Messages in blood? Taunting you? Definitely him. I wonder how his face is these days?"

The last time they had seen Robbie, Muse slashed his face up good. Or bad, depending on the viewpoint.

Sam turned away from the TV. "Muse has gone to see Aaron. Maybe she'll find out more about this."

Muse often sneaked out on information-gathering missions. June didn't ask where she went or how she got the information she did, but she usually returned with something helpful.

Megan Morgan

"I wonder if it's really a researcher?" Jason said, his tone hopeful. He disliked Institute researchers more than June did.

"Are you going to do something about this?" Micha addressed Sam. "How far will you let this go before you take action?"

"There is no action I can take right now." Sam glowered at him. "Not one that won't put us in greater danger. We need the means to prove our innocence before we can crawl out of this hole."

"I'm tired of being a prisoner." Micha's voice rose. "I'm tired of hiding. You still have power, but you sit here and do nothing. If this is a war, we need to fight it."

"Don't bark at me, puppy." Sam advanced on him. "I'll kick you."

"Hey." June held a hand out to Sam. "The last thing we need to do is start chewing each other's legs off."

"Puppy?" Micha stepped toward him. "You wanna see how hard I can bite?"

"Enough!" June positioned herself between them. "If I have to use my voice on you two, I will."

She wouldn't.

She might.

"How dare you say I've done nothing," Sam growled. "If I hadn't done something, you'd be dissected by the Institute. June and Jason would be rotting in their basement with their throats ripped out."

"You're doing nothing to get us out of this situation."

"I'm trying! What do you think last night was about? What do you think this deal with the Devil is for?"

Micha huffed. "You think throwing us into the lion's den is going to save us? You keep claiming you're so smart, but every day you sit here and do nothing, and all you can come up with is to throw us to the vampires. You're as dumb as Robbie thinks you are."

Micha stalked across the room, toward the stairs.

"What the hell else can I do?" Sam yelled after him. "If you can come up with something better, why don't you tell me what it is!"

Micha thundered up the stairs and disappeared. Sam snarled and stormed off to the kitchen.

June spread her arms at Jason, begging him for some sort of answer. He shrugged.

"Men," she muttered.

She weighed her options: soothe Micha or talk Sam down. Or let them both stew.

She followed Sam, because Micha's issues were complicated and not likely to be resolved in one conversation. Sam took affront to the lack of appreciation for his efforts, and that was at least understandable. She could have left them both alone, but she was bored.

A stone patio jutted from the back of the house, and Sam sat at the umbrella-shaded table on it. A tall wood plank fence ringed the backyard, impossible to see over or through. The grass had grown tall since no one had been mowing it.

She flopped in a chair across from Sam.

"Your boyfriend is pissing me off," he said. "That little cocksucker."

June squinted against the sunlight. "I like how I'm the only one who doesn't use that word."

"Cocksucker?"

"Boyfriend."

Sam eyes were particularly dark under the shade of the umbrella, black and bottomless.

"Sorry." He flicked a leaf off the table. "The guy you've been screwing for the past four months. I thought it was a commitment."

"Shows how much you know." She pulled one leg up and propped her bare foot on the edge of the chair seat. She smoothed a hand down her calf, trying to come up with something comforting to say. She was not a motivational speaker.

"To hell with Robbie," she said. "You knew he would do this. He wants to show you how wrong you are for not being crazy like him."

"I never killed anyone—well, except for Eric Greerson. But I argue that was in the utmost self-defense."

"I agree. Also, he had it coming. Big time."

"I never killed anyone to make a point. I never thought violence was the answer. I never tried to give my followers that impression. We raise a lot of hell, yes, but that's only because no one in this city listens to the paranormal unless we're yelling. We never hurt anyone, even the bastards at the Institute who deserved it. But that monster was right there in my ranks, turning my followers, killing our own kind and letting the SNC be the scapegoat for it."

"Being a leader means setting an example, which it sounds like you did. But some people can't be directed or convinced." How she'd managed to crap out that gem of wisdom, she didn't know. "Some people are just crazy. They don't have morals."

"If I don't resurface soon, they're all going to turn to him."

"No, they won't. Losing the good guy doesn't mean people automatically go to the dark side."

"Times are tough. People want action. Like your boy—" He paused. "Like that self-righteous asshole in there."

"Don't call him that, either." She put her leg down. "And yeah, people want action. Desperate times and all that. But being desperate doesn't mean you don't think for yourself. Most people won't give up their morals for a quick and violent fix. Your followers are still loyal to you. You know that. You hear about it. They'll do the right thing."

Before Sam could respond, the patio door slid open. Jason stood inside. "Code red." His voice came out strained.

She and Sam jumped to their feet. "Code red" meant the silent alarm around the perimeter of the property had been tripped.

"Muse?" June asked Sam.

"She's not due back for another hour."

Jason left the doorway and they hurried inside.

"Maybe it's an animal again," June said.

"Hopefully the four-legged kind." Sam rushed across the kitchen.

They grabbed their guns from the kitchen cupboard where they kept a small arsenal of weapons and ammunition.

"Go upstairs," June told her brother. "And make sure Micha stays up there."

"Don't treat him like a child," Jason said. "He knows what to do."

She wasn't sure when Jason decided to be Micha's champion, but this wasn't the moment to argue. "When he stops forgetting his blood is more coveted than a porn star's dick, we'll stop making him hide every time the alarm gets tripped. Go upstairs and lock yourselves in one of the bedrooms."

Jason left the room, scowling. If she babied anyone more than Micha, it was Jason. She had to protect Micha's blood for their cause, but she had to protect her brother for their mother.

"It's like a nursery school around here," June said. "I'm going to start putting people in time-out for their sass."

"Now do you feel my pain?" Sam tossed her a Glock.

June turned off the TV so she could hear and moved stealthily around the house, peeking out windows.

The street was quiet, no unfamiliar cars parked outside.

Sam called from the kitchen in a loud whisper, "June!"

She rushed to the kitchen. Sam stood in front of the sink, hunched over and peeking out the window above it. June joined him, hunkered down as well.

"Someone's outside," he said. "A man. He was looking in windows at the side of the house, and then he walked around back."

Sam had his shotgun. June learned quickly why Sam chose such an unwieldy, un-concealable weapon: he hardly ever had to use it when the sight of it alone subdued most people.

"Awesome," June said. "Someone knows we're here."

"Let's not panic. If it was someone from the Institute, they would have sent a squadron to oust us."

"How do you know they haven't and they're not just lying in wait?"

"Good point."

Maybe Micha would get his longed-for action.

Staying below the windows, they slunk over to the glass doors of the patio. They positioned themselves on either side of them and waited.

When no one appeared on the patio, Sam whispered, "I'm going outside."

"Are you nuts?"

"If I have to shoot someone, I can't do it through the glass."

Sam reached out and slowly slid one of the doors open. June held her breath. Sam crept out onto the patio. Tall shrubs grew around the patio, boxing it in on both sides. Sam moved behind them, peeking through the branches.

June waited for a signal, her Glock clutched in both hands. She'd shot only one person ever, a vampire, and though her aim was a lot better these days, she still wasn't ready to take a human life. She wasn't sure she'd even killed the vampire she shot.

Sam yelped, and June leaped up.

Sam didn't bother going down the patio steps to chase the interloper. Instead, he sprung up on the railing and jumped right through the shrubs, sending leaves and twigs flying. While this was certainly a more direct approach, it left June confused for a moment. She ran across the patio and jumped down into the yard.

Around the side of the house, Sam had someone on the ground. The person lay flat on his back, hands raised in supplication. Sam had his shotgun pointed in his face.

"Sam!" June ran over. "Who—" She stopped dead in her tracks.

Shock nearly dropped her to her knees. The man on the ground wasn't a stranger to her.

The man widened his eyes, mirroring her surprise. "June!"

"Diego!" She gaped at him, her eyes about to shoot from their sockets. "What the hell?"

He dropped his hands. "Holy shit, it's really you, June."

"You know this sneaky bastard?" Sam asked.

She pushed the barrel of Sam's gun away. "This is Diego, my best friend. We own the tattoo shop together."

She offered Diego a hand up. He clambered to his feet, all six-foot-three lanky inches of him. His dark, straight collar-length hair had streaks of bright red shot through it, complimenting his olive skin tone and brown eyes. Though most of it wasn't visible at the moment, Diego had as much ink as she did. Some of it peeked from under his T-shirt, crawling up his throat and down his biceps.

They embraced so hard June's chest hurt. Seeing a familiar face made her heart soar so high she could kiss him. With tongue.

She couldn't form words through her surprise, though she had a million questions. Sam stood with his gun at his side, lowered, but body still poised for action.

"That's nice," Diego said, gesturing at Sam's gun. Sam—or someone—had customized the barrel, the black metal decorated with silver antique filigree. "That a Winchester?"

"You better stop worrying about my gun and start talking," Sam said. "How the hell did you find us?"

This was the foremost question in June's mind.

"I've been searching for you for months." Diego looked at June. "Your mother sent me."

She sucked in a breath.

"I've been asking everyone about you. Trying to find someone who had seen you or knew what happened to you. I haven't had much luck. Then I ran into these people who said they were part of a group called the Paranormal Alliance."

Sam narrowed his eyes. "Are you a normal?"

"Yes."

"This is going to be funny, then. Continue."

"They sent me to Old Town," Diego said. "They told me the vampires could help."

Sam shrugged. "It's what I would have done. Test his mettle."

"Yeah, well—" Diego yanked the collar of his T-shirt down to reveal his neck and shoulder. Even through the copious colorful ink, dark puncture marks were visible. "I did a lot of bargaining for information, but they didn't actually have any."

"Goddamn it, Sam!" June turned on him.

"I didn't do it!"

"I was about to give up." Diego righted his shirt. "Then I saw you, June. Last night."

"You did?" She widened her eyes.

"Yes. You were walking with a guy, a black guy with dreads. I wasn't sure what was going on, so I didn't approach you. You looked fine. You look fine now." He sounded cautious, even a bit accusing.

"Looks can be deceiving. I have a bullet in my chest, and we're hiding here because some scientists want to cut my vocal cords out."

"I don't think they'd actually cut them out," Sam said.

"Would you shut up?" June glared at him. "So you followed me here?" she asked Diego.

"I've been lurking around, watching the house. What's going on?"

June heaved a sigh. "It's a long story. You can't imagine how long."

"Is Jason all right?" he asked. "Is he with you?"

"Yes, and he's fine."

"There's no one else with you?" Sam peered toward the front of the house.

"No." Diego shook his head. "It's just me. I've been doing all this searching on my own."

"Good," Sam said. "Let's get inside before someone sees us."

Sam ushered them into the house. Once inside, she clutched Diego in another huge desperate embrace and held on.

"I'm so fucking glad to see you," she whispered against his shoulder. "Oh my God, I can't believe you're here."

"The feeling is mutual," he whispered back, and trembled as she held him.

"I wish Muse were here," Sam said. "So she could make sure you are who you say you are."

"He is who he says he is." She pulled back. "Trust me, Sam. I know my best friend when I see him."

"And how do you know he's not a shapeshifter, pretending to be your best friend?"

"What?" Diego flinched. "I'm not... I'm not a shapeshifter."

"Can't you tell?" she asked Sam. "Like Occam could tell?"

"No." Sam shook his head. "That's an Occam thing. He's been at it a lot longer than I have."

She pondered. "I have an idea. If it's someone pretending to be Diego, they wouldn't have Diego's thoughts, would they?"

"No."

She breezed past Sam to the stairs. "Jason!" she hollered up. "All clear! Come down here."

A door opened, and a moment later Jason appeared at the top of the stairs.

"Was it an animal again?" he asked.

"No. Come here."

Jason walked down the stairs. She led him into the kitchen.

"Look who found us," she said.

Jason gasped. "How did he—Diego! What are you doing here?" He yanked Diego into a hug.

"Jason." A blush crept across Diego's cheekbones, visible beneath his dusky complexion. "I'm so glad you're both all right."

"It's him." June smiled at Sam. "He's been nursing a crush on Jason for as long as I've known him."

"I have not!" Diego yelped over Jason's shoulder.

Sam rolled his eyes and laid his gun on the counter. "Great, we need some more soap opera around here."

Chapter 5

"Mom doesn't think we're dead?" June asked.

They were all sitting around the dining room table. June had made coffee, but Micha, sitting next to her, had a glass of water. He had a phobia of coffee now, since he suspected his late wife had used it to sneak him the receptors that turned him into a guinea pig for the Institute.

"She never even entertained the idea." Diego sat across from June. "She's been contacting everyone: the Institute, the police here, even the papers. No one could tell her anything, though. That Institute place kept telling her you guys went home, but no airline has a record of you guys having flown out of Chicago. I think she's even been in touch with the FBI."

"I wish she hadn't," June said. "I know it's unrealistic she'd do nothing, but all this questioning, she's put herself in danger. She's on their radar now."

June had told Diego the entire story, from their arrival at the Institute, to their botched escape attempt and Jason's imprisonment, and June's rescue with the help of Sam and Aaron, to the situation that led to them being viewed as assassins and having to go into hiding.

"They're not gonna mess with her." Jason shook his head. He sat next to Diego. "Mom's a normal. What would they want with her?"

"She's asking a bunch of questions about some really sensitive stuff," June said.

"That's why she sent me here," Diego said. "She thought I might have better luck if I came to Chicago. She wanted to come with me, but I convinced her to stay. I told her she needed to be there in case you guys showed up."

"Thank you," June said softly.

Micha spoke up. "We can't keep hiding here. If you were able to find us, someone else will too."

June wasn't in the mood to listen to him rant again.

"We have a plan," Sam cut in. He sat at the head of the table. "We're going to get the truth out to the public."

"Because the public is interested in the truth," Micha said.

The door to the patio opened. Everyone fell silent. Muse walked into the room a moment later.

"Come join us for coffee and gossip," Sam said to her, patting the table. He jerked his head in Diego's direction. "We have a new friend. Do you mind?"

Muse stood next to Sam and stared at Diego. The corner of her mouth jerked. Diego regarded her warily. She was obviously scanning him with her telepathic…head scanner.

"June's best friend," Muse said. "He saw her last night, followed her here."

"Sam!" June smacked the table. "I told you he is who he says he is!"

"Forgive me if his hard-on for your brother isn't reliable enough for me."

"What's going on?" Diego asked.

"She just read your mind," June told him. "Try not to think about that time we met those drag queens in Lavender Heights."

"I admire his perseverance," Muse said.

Diego sank down in his chair. "This is kind of new to me. Really, June and Jason are the only paranormal people I know. So I'm not—up-to-date on this stuff."

"I can see what makes you two friends," Sam said.

"Yes." June glowered at Sam. "I'm sure he'll find you smug and annoying in no time at all as well."

"It's not like I don't want to know about this stuff," Diego said. "I just—I guess I never thought about it. And June never cared if I knew. She never talked about her power and stuff."

"There's plenty of education out there for normals," Micha said, sounding like he did when June first met him, pithy and eager to teach. "Plenty of ways to educate yourself on their conditions and struggles."

"This isn't the time for activism." June rubbed her forehead.

Sam glared across the table at Micha. "How dare you use the word 'condition.'"

"Hey," Muse spoke up. "I have something important to tell you." She stretched her lips over her teeth in a grimace. "I have a message for Sam."

Sam turned his full attention on her, seeming to forget his usual "condition" of being offended.

"Occam wants to meet with you," Muse said. "He wants to negotiate."

"Does he now?"

"Negotiate?" June frowned. "I thought we already 'negotiated' with him. I gave him a tube of Micha's blood. What the hell else does he want?"

"I don't know," Muse said. "He sent a message through our information network. He says he wants to meet with Sam." She cleared her throat harshly. "And he wants Sam to bring Micha with him."

"What?" June gasped.

"Right." Sam snorted. "Does he think I'm actually stupid enough to bring Micha to one of his vampire tea parties?"

"I take offense to this," Micha said. "I wasn't the one who revealed their infection to the world. It's Rose they have an issue with."

"Yes, but they can't kill her, now can they?" Sam rolled his eyes. "Occam is out of his skull."

"I'm also supposed to tell you," Muse said, "if you don't do as he requests, he's going to drink the tube of blood and pretend he never spoke to you."

June sat back and rubbed her face. She was completely done with this city and all the hardheaded, manipulative people knocking her fate back and forth like a ping-pong ball.

Sam sighed. "Where does he want me to meet him? I find it hard to believe he doesn't know where I am. Vampires are notoriously good at tracking people. I don't think it's a supernatural quality. They just cultivate being sneaky bastards."

June pondered. Was that why Kevin hired them to find Sam's brother's murderers?

Muse widened her eyes. June wasn't supposed to know that information. Muse had revealed it to her in a moment of strife. June bit her tongue and stared at the wallpaper over Jason's head.

"At a hotel downtown," Muse said. "Tomorrow night. He wants neutral territory, in public, he says so you won't try anything." She snorted. June wasn't sure if it was a sound of derision or one of her ticks.

"Yes." Sam lifted his hands. "Why don't I take Micha Bellevue out in public and parade him up and down the streets for everyone to see?"

"You're a shapeshifter who can shift other people," June reminded him. "That's how we got into Old Town, remember?"

"I don't suppose I have any say in this?" Micha asked. "Of course not. My power to choose was taken from me months ago."

June squeezed his shoulder. "If you're taking Micha to meet with him, I'm going with you."

"Because that's practical," Sam said.

"You'll need some backup. You don't honestly think Occam will be on his own? You'll need help protecting Micha from them if they start to act up. We're all in this together."

"I don't like having more heads on the chopping block than necessary." Sam stood up and started pacing, head down, hands on his hips.

"I held my own when you sent me into a den of bloodsuckers," June said.

Sam stopped. "Yes. Except for the part where they immobilized you and would have killed you if I wasn't there."

Everyone at the table looked at June. Micha furrowed his brow. They hadn't discussed what happened at Occam's place.

"I'm going." She pushed her chair back sharply. "And that's the end of the discussion." She stood up and stalked out of the room.

She walked outside and sat on the patio. Afternoon had faded to evening. A cigarette seemed like the answer just then, but the hitch in her side reminded her she had to find new ways of coping. She still had a pack hidden upstairs, in case things got really bad. The cigarettes would be stale as hell, but they'd give her a buzz.

Diego emerged from the house a few minutes later and sat down in the chair next to her. They had so much to catch up on, not just current events.

"Is the shop still running?" she asked.

"Oh, yeah. Or it was. I closed it to come to Chicago and everything. But your mom is still paying the rent while I'm gone so we don't lose it."

"Ah, Christ." June sighed. "She doesn't have the money to be doing that."

"She's holding out hope you'll come back. It's all she's got."

She sat forward, elbows on her knees, rubbing her hands together. "Does everyone else back home think I'm still alive too?"

"I don't know what's going on back home. I've been here almost as long as you have, looking for you. But before I left Steve and Cody, they said there was no way something happened to you. Steve joked you probably found a guy and ran off with him, but after we read the stories about the press conference where you disappeared, he wasn't joking anymore."

She didn't live all this drama in a bubble, and this point was suddenly driven home. Steve and Cody both worked in the shop. Steve was an artistic prodigy. Cody was learning. They were usually both founts of optimism.

"So"—Diego stretched his legs out—"what's going on with you and the tall cute blond guy?"

"Are we that obvious?"

"Well, when you told me it was his wife that got killed, I assumed he was still dealing with some crap. But the way you reacted back there says something else. So is it unrequited?"

"Not exactly."

"You and tragic guys June, what the hell is it?" He was referring to a single isolated incident with another "tragic" man, a year before, who, in her defense, was actually more dramatic than tragic.

"I don't know." June sat back. "Trust me, I feel guilty about it every day. It's not black and white, though. He's been through a lot. We all have."

"You know, there's this whole thing about how people who fall in love during times of hardship don't last once the hardship is over."

"We're not in love. It's just—I don't know what it is. We need each other. It's comforting."

"Jason hasn't met anyone to comfort him, has he?"

She side-eyed him. "You doth not protest too much now, do you, good sir?"

They both laughed. God, when was the last time she'd actually laughed, from her gut?

Diego squeezed her hand on the chair arm. "Damn, I've missed you."

"I've missed you too," she said softly, her momentary mirth fading. "What did you plan to do when you found me?"

"Take you the hell home. But it doesn't seem like you want to leave."

"Oh, I want to, trust me. But it's a lot more complicated than that."

"At least I can tell your mom I've found you."

June swallowed. "Don't. At least not yet."

Diego frowned.

"If she knows we're alive, they might use her to get to us. Don't tell anyone back home you've found us, not yet. They're watching people. They want to find Sam and Aaron, but I doubt they'd pass up a chance to snag me and Jason, too."

"You think they're watching your mom?"

"They might be. I can't risk it."

"What if they're watching me? What if I've led them right to you?" He looked around.

"Nothing lasts forever. This will end, sooner or later. Doesn't matter if it happens now or months from now."

They sat in silence for a few minutes, still holding hands.

Finally, she squeezed his hand, released it, and got up.

"You're not allowed to date my brother," she said. "Even if you do charm him to the other side. It would just be too weird for me."

"Killjoy."

The usual nightly routine followed: dinner thrown together from the groceries Cindy regularly brought, watching the news, and waiting for Aaron to call with any updates he had. He did have some—his information gatherers had confirmed, indeed, the murdered researcher stuffed in the trunk was a gift from Robbie's faction.

Sam seemed agitated by this, more than usual, a bit emotional even. He went upstairs, and Muse followed him up a few minutes later.

June wouldn't let Diego go back to the hotel where he'd been staying. She made him a bed on the couch, telling him they'd get his things the next day, when they went out to meet with Occam.

Micha remained in a stormy mood all night, and June finally sent him up to his room with the promise she'd be up soon. When Diego fell asleep, she went to join him.

However, she didn't go directly to Micha's room, but to Sam's. The door was open a crack. She knocked lightly and nudged it open, peeking in.

"Sam?" she said cautiously.

The room was dark, but light from the hallway shone in. Sam lay on his side, his back to the door. He wasn't asleep, though, as he immediately lifted his head and looked over his shoulder.

"Sorry," June said. "I just wanted to—" She stopped, eyes widening.

Sam wasn't alone. Muse lay curled up next to him, and she peeked over his shoulder.

"Oh, sorry." June averted her eyes, though they were both fully clothed. "I just needed to talk to you, but it can wait."

"I'll be out in a minute," Sam said.

June went and sat on the steps, awkward. A few minutes later Sam came out and sat down on the step next to her. He was barefoot. He pushed his hair back.

"What?" he said.

"I just thought we should talk about this meeting with Occam tomorrow. How we're going to protect Micha from the vampires."

"Maybe we won't have to." He folded his arms on his knees.

"I don't think Occam just wants to chat. Doesn't seem his style."

"I'll think of something." He curled his toes in the carpet on the stair beneath him.

June frowned and ducked her chin, trying to meet his eyes. "Something wrong? It seems like something's bothering you."

"Oh, no, what could possibly be bothering me? Everything's just peachy in my perfect, blissful life."

She rolled her eyes. "I mean, besides the obvious. Is this about Robbie?"

Sam gazed down the stairs. "Muse isn't feeling well, that's all."

"Oh. Is it, um"—she touched her face, indicating the ticks—"the nerve damage? Or something else?"

"She's dying," he said flatly. "We've both known that for a long time. It's no surprise she's going to feel under the weather now and then."

"There's nothing that can be done for her?"

"What's to be done?" He shrugged. "You can't lessen her powers or take them away. Even the Institute hasn't figured that one out yet."

June hesitated; then she spoke carefully. "So are you and her…?" She gestured, a little wave, though she had no idea what it was supposed to indicate.

Sam frowned at her.

"Never mind." She unfolded her legs. "But I think we should figure out a way to protect Micha, if there is one." She stood up.

Sam grabbed her wrist. "Why do you care?"

She arched an eyebrow. "Because I don't want him to die?"

"No, I mean about…" He paused and shook his head. "I'll figure out something. I still don't think you should go. I don't want a repeat of what happened before. I truly don't." He sounded like he truly didn't.

"It won't. We'll be careful." She pulled at his grip. "Can I have my arm back?"

He let go.

He remained sitting, as June stepped up into the hallway. Should she sit back down and console him? Her consoling always ended up hurting more than helping.

"I trust you'll figure something out," she said. He probably needed to hear that, at least.

"Still the smartest man in the city," he said.

"Given how many times you've saved my ass, I can't argue."

Chapter 6

Sam's voice came from the kitchen when she walked downstairs the next evening. He was talking to someone.

"You have to be extremely careful. No one can see you. Those are our allies watching the place, but it'll blow our cover. They can't know where I'm at right now."

June stepped into the kitchen. Sam stood, lecturing Muse and Cindy, who were sitting at the table—Muse with her bleached-out white hair and Cindy with her unnaturally bright red hair. They looked like a pair of superheroes.

"Morning." June went straight for the coffee pot.

"We'll be careful." Muse's voice sounded rougher than usual. "I know that building and area like the back of my hand."

"Our people will be guarding it," Sam said. "At least I hope so."

"I know your guards like the back of my hand, too."

"Pour me a cup." Cindy swiveled around to June. "I'm about to play lookout and I need to be alert."

"We don't have any whiskey," June said.

"It's all right. I've already had some." Cindy controlled her "psychic sexual" powers with alcohol, as she was a sex witch. Not a healthy option, but June was far from one to give advice.

June paused in pouring Cindy a cup. Something struck her. Despite Occam's drug and booze buffet, Zack and Belle hadn't partaken.

They didn't want to dull their powers, since they were about to use them.

June resumed pouring, trying to ignore the crawling sensation on her skin. "What are you guys up to?"

"Stuff," Sam said. "If you two aren't back here in two hours, I'm coming after you myself."

"I would caution you not to be completely impractical," Muse said.

"Noted."

After a few sips of coffee, June grew a little more clear-headed. Micha was still asleep upstairs, and she had been worried the past few hours, as he'd been running a low fever. Random flu-like symptoms were the norm ever since his injection. Fussing over him increased his agitation, though.

Cindy came over to the counter and grabbed her cup of coffee. Sam and Muse left the room.

"You seem to be getting healthier every time I see you," Cindy said to June. "Chest feeling better?"

"Better than it did when I was first shot."

"I met your friend. Brave guy, hunting you down like that."

"Yeah, I can't believe he's really here. I had to peek in the living room to make sure it wasn't a dream."

"So, is he like…your ex-boyfriend?"

June reared her head back. "No."

Cindy shrugged. "Thought it might be love. That's a lot to go through, following a woman across the country, searching for months, braving untold dangers to find her. Kinda romantic."

"He's gay."

Cindy blinked.

"God, you really have no gaydar, do you? Of course, we found that out a long time ago." Cindy had thought June was a lesbian when she first met her. Just like the stupid vampires.

"Too bad. He's cute." Cindy took a drink.

"How's Dipity?"

Cindy lowered her cup. "She misses you." She pouted. "I've been thinking about bringing her over, but Sam says the last thing you need right now is a pet."

"We had her in the penthouse, though!"

"I know, right? He says this is different. It's more dangerous here. You might have to run, or they might throw tear gas through a window, or shoot through the walls with high-powered rifles. I don't want Dipity to get shot."

"Yeah, me neither."

"I can't imagine what tear gas would do to a cat."

Jason walked into the kitchen, bleary-eyed and ruffling his hair. He noticed Cindy and smiled.

"Hey," he said. "Didn't know you were here."

She flashed him a quick, tight smile. "Hey." She set her cup on the counter. "Well, I better get out of here. Gotta get ready for this. Good to see everyone again."

She exited the kitchen. Jason watched her go with a frown.

"Why does she keep running away from me?" he asked. "We were getting along so well for a while. Really well, if you know what I mean."

June leaned against the counter. "She's trying not to possess your cock, would be my guess. It's...probably not a pleasant experience."

Jason turned to the refrigerator and opened the door. "Everyone wants me."

"Welcome to my world." Something caught her eye. "You're wearing the watch."

Several weeks ago, bored, June went rooting around in the attic. All kinds of crap had been stored up there—maybe it was Aaron's old stuff, or the people who had lived there before. She discovered a box of old jewelry, most of it junk, but she found a silver wristwatch that still worked. Since it was obviously a man's watch, she'd given it to Jason— not because he needed a watch, though.

Jason had a scar on his right wrist, from the restraints they'd held him in at the Institute. He rubbed and picked at it a lot. He told June he hated it, that the sight of it always took him back to that place.

The watchband covered it completely.

"Yeah." He held his arm up. "It's cool. Thanks."

She smiled. "No problem."

She went upstairs to check on Micha. He was awake, sprawled on his bed, shirtless. She sat down on the edge.

"How are you feeling?" She rested a hand on his stomach, surreptitiously checking his temperature. Still too warm.

"As well as I ever do."

"Are you worried about tonight?"

"No. I'll be glad to get out of here for a while. I feel like a prisoner. I'm going crazy."

"Out there, you're a target."

He turned his head toward her. His eyes were dark in the shadowy room.

"In here," he said, "I'm ineffective. Idleness has always been something I feared. Lack of motivation. It's an advocate's worst enemy. You have to get out there and make a difference."

"This isn't like getting equal rights for mind readers, Micha. The Institute wants to finish turning you into an abomination and then dissect you. That's a good reason to lie low."

"I'm not an abomination. I'm just becoming that which I wanted to protect."

"Except that which you wanted to protect isn't what you are. Who knows what it's doing to you on a cellular level, or how it's messing up your organs. You can march for gay rights too, or if we were in the fifties you could be fighting for civil rights, but you can't take an injection to make you gay or black."

Micha was silent.

"We're doing all we can do, to keep them from doing what they want to do. To you."

Again, no reply.

June curled up next to him. She rested her head on his chest. His heart thumped against her ear, fast and hard.

"How did we end up like this?" she whispered.

"Which do you mean, like this?" He waved a hand in the air. "Or like this?" He lowered it and stroked her hair.

"Take your pick."

"I don't know what I would have done without you these past few months," he murmured.

"Likewise."

She could stay there forever, listening to his heart, cuddled up to him, making believe all the drama was outside and not right here, sitting on their chests.

"Have you seen Rose lately?" he asked.

"No, thankfully."

"Thankfully," he repeated, the word tinged with bitterness.

She lifted her head and moved up until her face rested next to his. Despite never having seen a ghost prior, she was haunted by Micha's wife, who was apparently trying to give June a message. Rose always appeared confused, but seemed to be proclaiming her innocence.

Micha didn't buy it, though.

He draped an arm over her. She kissed him, because she didn't like the tone of his voice, and she didn't like what it implied—the anger, the betrayal. If she could make him stop talking, stop thinking about it, she would.

A knock sounded at the door. Sam stepped in without being invited, his usual method of entering a room. She broke the kiss and scowled at him.

"I think you have another supernatural power," she said. "The power to sense when you're least welcome."

"I need to talk to you." He stared directly at her, ignoring Micha.

"I doubt I can stop you," she said.

"What can I do to convince you not to come to this meeting?"

She shrugged. "Kill me."

"I can disguise myself and Micha. But it's going to be a good deal harder to disguise all three of us."

"You don't have to disguise me. I walked around Old Town and no one messed with me. I'm a missing person that no one misses."

"It's still a risk."

"This whole thing is a risk. You need help protecting Micha, plain and simple." She squeezed Micha's hip.

"Hopefully what Cindy and Muse bring back will do just that," Sam said.

"Unless it's a bomb, I'm going."

"I think you ought to go home instead."

She frowned, blinking.

"I'm serious," Sam said. "I think you ought to take Jason and go back to California."

"Yes." She sat up. "Why didn't I think of that? Because I haven't wanted to go home before now."

Sam sat down on the edge of the bed. She jerked her feet out of the way.

"Leaving hasn't been practical until now. If you took a plane or a train, or a bus, someone out there might have recognized you. But your friend is here now. He can take you back in his car."

The idea was marvelous, tempting, yet...

"You don't want me fighting the good fight with you anymore?"

Sam looked away, his jaw tight. So much emotion had come from him lately the Institute must have sneaked in during the night, snatched him, and left behind another shapeshifter, one who was a conscience-riddled human being.

"Things should be different," Sam said. "This isn't how I meant for this situation to turn out."

"Oh, please. This isn't gonna work." She untangled herself from Micha.

"What do you mean?" Sam looked back at her.

"You, pretending to be all sorrowful to manipulate me into being safe. I think we're past that bullshit, aren't we?"

"I'm not manipulating you. If you have a chance to go home, you should take it."

"Don't tell me what I should do."

"Maybe he's right," Micha said behind her.

"Don't you tell me what to do either." She pointed at him. "I'm the one with the voice around here, remember?"

"This could be your only chance," Sam said.

"And do you think they'll leave me alone in California, if they decide they're interested in me again? We go back there, we're sitting ducks. So is our mother."

"You could get your mother and take her somewhere safe." Sam knew exactly where to strike. He didn't even have to strike that hard.

"Now you are manipulating me," she informed him. "You're trying to play me."

"I'm trying to help you. Getting you away from me is probably the best help I could give you right now."

"I would have to talk to Jason about it first. It wouldn't be safe."

Sam frowned. "Your whole argument for going tonight is that no one knows who you are or cares about you. Now you're arguing you can't go home because people are going to know who you are?"

She waved a dismissive hand at him. "I'll think about it. Now get the hell out."

Sam stood up. "Please think about what I'm saying very carefully. You know it's the best option for you. For Jason."

"Get out of here!"

He left.

"Do you think I should go?" she asked Micha.

Micha had sprawled on his back again, gazing at the ceiling. "I think you should do whatever you can to help yourself."

"I knew you would say that."

Sam was right. However, part of her was completely tangled up in this mess, and it wasn't that easy to cut her way out. She couldn't just take off and leave everything, everyone behind.

Could she?

* * * *

Cindy and Muse returned in their allotted timeframe, so Sam didn't have to go on a reconnaissance mission, thankfully.

Cindy had a wooden box, about the size of a milk carton. She set it carefully on the kitchen table as they all gathered around. Sam had summoned the household to a meeting.

"It wasn't hard to get in," Muse told Sam. "No one is patrolling."

"Things are falling apart without me." Sam sighed. "They're not being vigilant. My wandering sheep, lost without their shepherd."

June rolled her eyes. "Maybe they don't listen so good since you call them 'sheep.'"

"What were you breaking into?" Micha asked.

"A building where we keep special things, a storehouse," Muse said. "We weren't really breaking in. I have a key." She turned to Sam. "And to be fair, only you and I know the extent of what's in there. You've never over-stressed the need for security."

"I don't know what this is." Cindy eyed the box. "Nothing alive, I hope?"

Sam pulled it toward him. "It's something dangerous. But not to us."

Sam popped a latch on the box and carefully opened the lid. The way he behaved, June expected a dazzling light to issue forth and the answer to all their problems to spring out. Instead, he took out a narrow tube. June flinched. The tube reminded her of the Oracle of the Dead, a seemingly innocuous tube of blood that, once magically activated, could literally wake the dead. This tube wasn't a vial, though, more like a fluorescent light bulb, with metal fittings on each end. The tube was the length of Sam's hand, fingertips to wrist.

Sam held the tube out to Micha. "Recognize this?"

Micha narrowed his eyes.

"No? It really was top secret, then."

"What is it?" Micha asked.

"Something your dearly departed wife was working on." He held it up by one end. "This was the prototype, anyway. My spies at the Institute stole it."

"What does it do?" June asked.

"It was the beginning of the cure," Sam said.

"The cure?"

"The cure to vampirism." Sam lowered the tube. "Of course, this version does more harm than good, but we can certainly use that to our advantage. It emits UV light."

June tilted her head, brow furrowing. "Fake sunlight?"

"Yes," Sam said. "That's not the point of it, though. Obviously, since they want to help vampires, not kill them, altruistic scientists that they are. UV light is also used for germicidal irradiation. It kills bacteria."

Micha gasped. "Like what the vampires have inside them."

"Yes." Sam nodded. "Only problem is, this early model is dangerous. They hadn't yet perfected how to kill the germs without burning through vampire flesh as well. With Mrs. Bellevue in the dirt, I'm sure the project got tanked. Sad."

"So…" June said. "You want Micha to take that with him when you meet Occam?"

"Now she gets it." Sam snapped his fingers.

"You think that'll keep them off me?" Micha asked.

"You'll have to be careful." Sam placed the tube back in the box. "UV light can harm humans, as well. Too much exposure will burn your skin and fry your corneas. You'll have to be careful whom you flash it at. But it'll work much faster on them than it will you."

Sam closed the box. June squeezed Micha's hand. His fingers were cold.

"Told you I'd figure something out." Sam looked at June.

"Are you coming with us?" June asked Muse. "For extra protection?"

"I can't read vampires' minds," she said. "But I'll be close. With my knives."

"I like your knives," June said.

After they dispersed from the kitchen, Diego pulled June aside in the living room.

"Sam said he wants me to take you and Jason home." He gripped June's upper arm. "There's nothing I'd rather do. We can leave tonight if you want, when you get back. I have a rental at the hotel."

Worry shone in his eyes, the same worry her mother must have had in hers every single day since her children went missing. She hated Sam even more for his manipulation.

"I don't know yet," she said. "I'll give you an answer when I get back tonight. Don't fill Jason's head with false hopes while we're gone, though."

"June…"

"I'll think about it, Diego." She squeezed his hand on her arm. "It's not that easy."

Chapter 7

Occam arranged their meeting at the Hotel Burnham on West Washington Street, or rather, the restaurant adjacent to the hotel. The place was ridiculously fancy. Red pillars held aloft a high ceiling hung with chandeliers, the walls painted smooth black, the tables draped in white tablecloths. Tall windows provided a panoramic view of the nighttime streets around them.

Patrons filled the restaurant. The chatter of voices and clink of silverware and glasses created a nerve-wracking cacophony of humanity June hadn't realized she'd gotten so unfamiliar with. All the people put her on edge.

Occam had reservations under a false name, and despite being for one less, since he hadn't expected June, they were shown to a table. June trailed behind Sam, who was disguised again as the woman from the Nocturnal District, and Micha, disguised as a dark-haired swarthy man, arm-in-arm with Sam.

June wore a red slinky dress Cindy had provided. The dress was undoubtedly short on Cindy but fell to June's knees, and Cindy had to pin it in the back, since June was nowhere near as busty as Cindy. A black jacket accompanied the dress, hiding this embarrassment, as well as most of June's tattoos, which might spark a memory more than her face would. Muse had provided a pair of black heels in June's size, to match the outfit.

June had been stunned Muse actually owned some non-white clothing.

Occam lounged in a curving gray booth, waiting for them. He wore a black jacket and a white dress shirt, the top three buttons undone, his hair a wild blond tangle.

June had no choice but to sit next to him, as Sam and Micha had to sit across the table together to maintain contact. June looked around, seeking out the sommelier, before she had to do this completely sober.

"Hello, Little Red." Occam draped his arm across the seat behind her. "What a nice surprise. I didn't expect you to tag along. You smell nice."

"You don't," June informed him.

He reeked of cigarettes. In the light, she could tell he was middle-aged, bony, and grizzled. His eyes were pale gray.

"You look good too," he said. "Good enough to eat."

She scowled. "I'll get up and piss on you, Occam. Right here. I'll do it."

"Reminds me of an ex-girlfriend."

"You're an asshole, Occam," Sam said. His voice, disturbingly his own, came out of his pink lipstick-painted mouth. "You could have picked a more discreet location."

"Discreet." Occam held his wineglass aloft as a waiter sped by. "Why, so your band of yahoos can attack me?"

"Why would I want to harm you?" Sam's voice was sardonic. "You're my only hope right now, unfortunately."

June tried to slink farther away from Occam and glanced at Micha, silently willing them both to have strength. Micha looked handsome in his current form, like a negative of himself, though she still preferred him the other way. He remained the same size and height.

June had learned a few things about Sam's power: he could change appearances, but not dimensions. His power worked on the same principle as ghosts, in that it used energy to project an image to the observer. He could stretch it over the available canvas, no farther, and he couldn't make things invisible. This left him a rather burly woman, though somehow, it worked. She was pretty.

"I'm not stupid enough to think you don't have people watching me," Occam said. He held his glass up again and a harried waiter stopped to fill it.

"I'd like something red when you get a moment," June said to the waiter. "Do you have a wine list?"

"Of course, madam." He slid off.

"Yes, I have people watching you," Sam said. "Like you don't have people watching us."

The only "people" Sam had was Muse, and as usual, June had no idea where she was.

Occam shifted in the booth, surreptitiously closer to June. "Well, now that we've established our mutual paranoia, let's get down to business."

Their waiter appeared. He introduced himself and delivered a spiel about specials, and they all listened with mock-attentiveness, except

Occam, who downed his fresh glass of wine. He didn't make an effort to hide his fangs, and the waiter seemed unnerved.

June ordered a glass of high-end Cabernet, since Occam was paying, and Occam ordered an entire bottle of rosé. Amazingly, he didn't drink straight out of it, but actually poured the wine into a glass.

"What exactly do you want to negotiate about?" Sam asked once they were alone again. "We gave you Micha's blood."

"A stick full of blood isn't enough to do proper research. We want the source." He flicked a finger at Micha.

"What do you want with him?" June demanded.

"We need him. We need him to help us help you."

"What are you talking about?" Sam asked.

"Our scientists need to examine him."

Sam narrowed his eyes. Her eyes. Pale green, ringed in silver eye shadow. "The blood is enough to prove the experiments the Institute has been doing."

"It depends on who you want it proven to." Occam stroked the stem of his wineglass. His nails were dirty. "You have your stolen files, but don't you want the evidence as well? Is it the easily swayed citizens of Chicago you want to prove this to? The biased and sensationalized media? Or do you want so much damning evidence the federal government will have to get involved and close the place down?"

They were all silent. This was a much bigger proposition than they'd expected. June could practically sense Sam's boner, which was weird since he currently had breasts.

"How do we know you won't do something to him?" June asked. "Like tear him to pieces?"

Occam focused on her and smiled widely. In the light, his natural teeth were markedly more yellow than his fangs. "Now why would we want to do that?"

"Yes, why would you?" Micha asked. "I had nothing to do with my dead wife's research. I don't understand your vendetta against me."

"Call it guilt by legacy."

"She screwed us both over." Micha raised his voice. "That's why I'm a bargaining chip right now."

"So tragic," Occam mocked.

"What do you get out of this, Occam?" Sam asked. "If we let you take him, do the research, and get the Feds involved, what will you gain from it? I know you're not doing this out of the kindness of your black heart."

The waiter returned with their salads. They all fell silent again. He asked if they were ready to order. Occam obnoxiously ordered for the entire table, but no one intervened. At least in Sam's case, it was necessary. June would pick at what she could digest, whatever he ordered for her.

When the waiter left, Occam picked up the conversation thread.

"There's about to be a shift in vampire society. New things on the horizon, changes that have been long coming. Most of them are none of your business. Micha is to be part of that. We'll need him. So we can't cut him to pieces, unfortunately."

"Need him?" June said. "For what?"

Occam leaned forward and lowered his voice, as if imparting a secret. "We're going to correct the mistakes of the past. When the Institute goes down, he'll step up." He jerked his head at Micha. "He's going to tell the public his wife's research was false."

Sam huffed. "Except...it's not?"

Occam sneered, baring his teeth. "Truth is subjective. He'll say she made it up, falsified her research. It'll be easy to believe after the other things they find out."

"And what about the transfusion clinics?" Micha asked. "They're making stuff up as well?"

"As I said, there's going to be a shift. You let us worry about the rest."

"How am I supposed to convince people her research was false?" Micha asked. "I never had access to it."

"You'll think of something." Occam sat back. "You better, or we'll call this whole thing off. We take you, get you checked out, let you go. Simple as that, not a hair on your head will be harmed. In return, you call bullshit on your wife when this whole thing implodes."

"What if I don't hold up my end of the bargain?" Micha asked.

"We'll know where to find you. And all your friends." He slid his hand over and tried to touch June's shoulder.

She jerked away.

Sam grabbed up his wineglass. "I had a feeling this 'negotiation' would be nothing but us bowing to your stupid demands."

"You're an astute man, Sam Haain."

Sam drank his wine, glowering over the rim of the glass.

"Your options right now are slim," Occam said.

"Obviously"—Sam lowered the glass—"or I wouldn't be here talking to you."

June pushed everything off her salad that would make her break out in hives, or worse: croutons, cheese, nuts, the cup of dressing—she was okay with oil and vinegar, which were on the table, at least. She wanted to just ask for a pile of washed vegetables and make things easier.

Occam drowned his salad in dressing and gorged disgustingly, making June lose what appetite she had.

"Let's hash out the details," Sam said. "We're not sitting around here waiting for someone to figure out who we are. This isn't a fun night on the town."

"There's nothing to hash out." Occam grabbed a handful of bread from the basket in the middle of the table. "Micha's coming with me when I leave."

June swiveled toward him, alarm rising.

"Now wait a fucking minute," Sam said.

"There's no waiting a fucking minute." Occam scooped up a glob of butter on his knife and slapped it on the bread. "No time like the present." He crammed the bread in his mouth.

"While I appreciate haste," Sam said, "I'm not assured you'll leave him in one piece. I need to know you'll actually let him go when they're done with him."

June spoke up, "I'll go with him."

Sam looked at her. So did Occam, chewing lustily, eyes dancing with bemusement.

"I'll go along," she said. "I'll make sure they don't do anything to him."

"And how will you do that?" Occam asked, launching several soggy pieces of bread from his overfull mouth.

June jerked away from him. "Listen, you disgusting piece of shit. Either you stop acting like a fucking savage, or I'm going to break your fangs off and shove them up your ass. And I don't give a damn who's watching."

Occam laughed. Sam pressed his pink lips in a tight line. Occam didn't speak again until he chewed, swallowed, and gulped down some wine.

"Fine," he said. "Come along. The more the merrier."

"You don't have to do this," Micha said softly to June. "It's me they want."

"And I may need you," Sam said.

"You need me to protect your ace in the hole. Isn't that what the whole thing was about, sending me to the vampires in the first place?"

"Still don't know how you plan to protect him." Occam took another drink of wine.

"I may not be able to affect vampires with my voice," June said, not looking at Occam, "but I can do a whole lot of things you've probably never seen a woman do."

Occam laughed again.

When the food arrived, Occam dug in. Sam crinkled his nose at the fish Occam had ordered for him. Micha picked at his pasta dish. June had gotten some sort of vegetarian stir-fry.

She seethed at the overwhelming ridiculousness of it all, the playacting. Occam pulled out a phone and started texting.

"Since we're going to be spending some time together," he said, "we ought to get to know each other. Little Red, you go first. Tell the class something about yourself."

June stabbed at her vegetables. "Well, let's see. I hate vampires, I'd like to blow Chicago up, and I'd kill for a cigarette right now because you reek of smoke." She popped a piece of zucchini in her mouth and chewed angrily.

Occam laughed, loud enough to draw attention from the tables around them.

"Quit bullshitting, Occam," Sam whispered. "Is this necessary?"

"I have a car coming to pick us up," Occam said. "We have to wait until it gets here." He smiled at Micha. "What about you? Any hobbies?"

"Staying alive," Micha said.

June grew distracted by something—a tingling, burning sensation in her mouth. She peered down at her bowl. Telltale numbness spread quickly to her lips, her throat tightening.

"Oh no." She dropped her fork. "There's something bad in this." She clutched at her throat, a spike of panic shooting through her.

Sam dug into the small handbag he had, one that Cindy had given him. As he did, he let go of Micha under the table, apparently, and Micha blinked back to himself. Occam laughed.

"Sam!" June croaked.

"Fuck!" Sam scooted closer to Micha, and the disguise slipped back over him.

June tried to breathe slowly. Sam pulled out a narrow yellow tube and tossed it over to her. Aaron had supplied them with some necessary medical items.

June uncapped the needle, hiked her skirt up, and stabbed herself in the right thigh. A few seconds later a euphoric rush washed over her, and her lungs seemed to expand beyond their usual size—hurting under her right ribs—and sensation returned to her mouth.

"I brought antihistamine too," Sam said.

"You all right?" Micha reached across the table and gripped her wrist.

"I didn't taste anything in this. There's no sauce or anything...." She picked up her fork with a shaky hand and pushed the vegetables around, examining the dish closer.

Occam had been watching all this with interest. "Food allergies that bad?"

"Yes." June squeezed Micha's hand and released it. She pulled the needle out of her thigh with a wince. "They must be getting worse."

"How long have you had them?" Occam asked.

"All my life. Started when I was a kid." She tossed the needle on the table and pushed her bowl away.

Sam handed her a blister pack of pills.

"Huh." Occam glanced at Sam. "Interesting, isn't it?"

Sam grabbed up the needle and tucked it back in his purse.

"What?" she said.

"Oh, nothing." Occam reached over and grabbed up June's bowl. "Since you're not going to eat this..."

Thankfully, Occam forced them to play his game only a little while longer. He dumped a pile of money on the table, drank down the rest of his wine—straight from the bottle this time—and they left the restaurant. June's lips were still tingly and her tongue thick. Technically, she should visit a hospital after having to take a shot. Technically, that wasn't going to happen.

Out on the street, Occam turned to Sam. "This is where you get off. I'll be in touch with you. Have your little snowflake keep her ears open."

Sam had his arm linked with Micha's. "I don't like this," he said to June. "I don't like both of you going with him."

"I'll keep an eye on Micha," June said. "Someone has to."

"And who will be keeping an eye on you?" Sam asked.

A long black car slid up to the curb, the windows so darkly tinted they were impossible to see through.

"Our chariot has arrived." Occam jerked the lapels of his coat.

June stepped up to Sam. "Listen. I know you want me to go home, but I have to do this, even if it's the last thing I do in Chicago. I'll make sure Occam keeps his word."

"You can't make sure a vampire keeps his word." Sam kept his voice down, the people passing by them oblivious. "He's going to hurt you. He's going to hurt both of you."

"He needs Micha." June kept her voice down too. "He's not going to hurt him. He needs him to do his bidding. And he's not going to hurt me, because he has no need to."

"Then why even go with him?" Sam jerked his free hand upward. "If you think Micha will be fine, why even bother tagging along?"

"He's got a point," Micha said. "I can hold my own."

"Shh." June waved at him. "Call it insurance. Just because I don't think he'll do anything doesn't mean he won't. I'm going to make sure Occam keeps his promise and sends Micha back. If he tries anything, I'll—I'll think of something. I can't use my voice on vampires, but I'm betting their doctors aren't vampires. I'll make sure we escape."

"You're not a bodyguard," Sam said. "You are an idiot, though."

"Yeah, but idiocy seems to be in fashion, so let's roll with it. I'm protecting your bargaining chip, Sam. For the good of the cause, remember?"

"You could get out of here." Worry shone in Sam's eyes, behind the veil of consternation. "You could get back to California. You could leave tonight."

"I plan to get out of here, but I need to make sure Micha comes back first. I can't leave Chicago not knowing that all of you are safe."

"Still," Micha said. "You don't need to put yourself on the line for me again. It's not fair you got tangled up in this to begin with."

"Shut up." She waved at him again. "I need you to do something for me, Sam."

"Hello!" Occam called from the curb. "Impatient vampire here. Needles and urine samples await."

"Tell Diego to take Jason home," she told Sam. "Jason will argue. He'll throw a fit. Tell him I said to go home, get Mom, and take her somewhere safe. Diego won't argue. He'll be pissed at me, but he won't argue."

"What if Jason won't go?" Sam asked. "You should be going with him, June."

"He'll go. Tell him he has to protect our mother. Convince him."

"And you call me a manipulator?" Sam gazed at her, brows drawn down, lips in a tight line. He almost looked like his male self.

"June..." Micha said.

"C'mon!" Occam barked.

June took a deep breath. "Promise me you'll get them out of here, Sam."

He shook his head. "If genetics hold true, I'll have to tie him up and throw him in the car myself."

Sam held Micha's arm until Micha slid into the backseat of the car. Micha turned back into himself when Sam let go.

"Be careful," Sam said softly as June crawled in.

"I will."

Sam bent down, peering in.

"They better come back alive, Occam. I may be in hiding, but I'll come out to bring the entirety of the Paranormal Alliance against the vampires, and it won't be pleasant."

Occam snorted. "All right."

Sam tossed something onto June's lap. His purse. "There's more needles and medicine in there."

"Thanks." She gave him a little wave.

Occam reached out and slammed the door shut. "He talks too much."

As they slid into traffic, Occam settled next to June and sprawled out. June moved away from him, closer to Micha, the purse clutched to her chest.

"I want some different clothes when we get to your house," she told Occam. "I'm not staying in this dress. I didn't expect a slumber party."

"I can help you out of it."

"I'll hurt you." As she lowered the purse to her lap something shifted inside, and she squeezed it gently. The light. "I'll hurt you so bad."

Occam laughed. "We're not going to my house. Unless you two want to be cocktails for my friends."

"Where are we going?" Micha asked.

"Don't want to spoil the surprise."

Chapter 8

They drove for a while, through mostly suburban areas. Micha remained silent, and she pressed to his side, keeping as far from Occam as she possibly could without actually climbing into Micha's lap. She never saw the driver, as a solid partition separated the front and back.

They eventually pulled into the parking lot of a nondescript one-story building, with a sign out front that said "Westside Clinic." The windows were dark, apart from a security light inside the double glass doors of the entrance.

"Hop out kids," Occam said. "We're here."

They got out of the car. Impulsively, protectively, she grasped Micha's hand.

"Oh, how sweet." Occam led them up the walkway to the building. "I didn't realize you two were a couple." He stopped at the clinic doors and drew a set of keys from his jacket pocket. "Explains a lot."

"Does it?" June said. "What does it explain?"

"How Sam uses you so easily."

"He's not using me."

"Gullible." Occam unlocked the door. "Perfect."

"Shut your mouth or I'll punch your fangs out."

They stepped inside, the clinic dark beyond the inner glass doors. Occam punched a code into an alarm pad on the wall.

"You can get all defensive"—a beep sounded and the lock on the inner doors clicked—"but I don't think you're as stupid as you pretend to be."

"I'm not pretending to be stupid," June said.

"No? Well then, it's unfortunate you want to protect the one man we'd like to carve into sushi. But I guess brains and taste don't correlate."

Before June could reply, Micha snarled, "Enough of this bullshit! I had nothing to do with my wife's discovery. Your threats against me are asinine."

Occam walked into the darkened clinic and Micha followed, dragging June after him.

"And so what if you've got a bacterial infection?" Micha continued ranting. "So what if it ruins your fucking 'mystique'? It doesn't make you any less powerful or dangerous. It doesn't make you any less capable."

Only Micha could berate someone with affirmations.

They walked into a waiting room and stopped.

"We don't appreciate normals poking their nose in our business." Occam turned to Micha. He was shorter than Micha and had to look up at him, but didn't seem the least bit intimidated. "It's not anyone's business what's in our blood."

"Not every vampire feels like you," Micha said. "I've talked with vampires who either didn't know what they were getting into or couldn't handle it once they did. They benefit from her discoveries."

"They're the ones who don't deserve to be vampires," Occam sneered. "And they won't be much longer."

"What does that mean?" June asked.

Occam's eyes flashed in the light from the entrance. "You're in a dark, dark forest, Little Red. I hope it's worth having the big bad wolf breathing down your neck. For love, or whatever insipid reason you're here."

Micha placed a hand on Occam's chest and pushed him away. "You reek. Get away from me."

June tightened her grip on Micha's hand. Other vampires could be lurking in the shadows. She braced herself for an attack.

"Don't ever touch me again," Occam said, his voice eerily calm. "Savor that, because if you try it again, you'll leave, as I promised, but you'll do it without hands."

"That's not the promise you made," June said.

"I'll take your tits, too. Tiny as they are."

She glared at him.

Occam led them through the clinic, down a series of hallways. Security lights shone over doorways, providing the only illumination. The building stood silent and seemingly empty.

So when June saw someone, it was a bit of a surprise.

Up ahead, lit faintly by a security light, a figure stood, back pressed against a wall. Occam strode ahead of them, not making any sign he saw the person.

Micha squeezed her hand. "What?" he whispered. He must have felt her start.

She tried to act casual, not giving away his wife's ghost lurked ahead.

As they drew closer to the figure, June inched closer to Micha. Her skin crawled. When they reached the spot where Rose stood, Occam swept by without stopping. The air was colder in that spot, gusting a nerve-rattling chill across June's skin.

As always, Rose stood perfectly still, her expression and eyes blank. She blended into the shadows, as though made from them. She wore the same clothes she always wore, the clothes she had died in.

She whispered as June passed, "It's not meant for you."

To June's surprise, Micha jerked his head around, as though he'd heard her too. June had no idea what her words meant—she never did, until later.

They reached their destination shortly after passing her, and Occam opened a door to the left. He stepped inside and flipped on a light. June winced at the brightness.

"Home sweet home," Occam drawled.

They stepped into a small room with a twin hospital bed in one corner, a tall filing cabinet next to it, and a table, piled with papers. The white walls and green tile floor were stark and dingy.

"Researchers sleep here when they stay overnight," Occam said. "Didn't expect there to be two of you, so you'll have to share. Won't be a problem, I take it?"

"Not at all," she said.

Occam pointed to a doorway across the room. "Bathroom. I'm going to lock you in for the night. In the morning, they'll start the testing. If you need anything—well, you're shit out of luck."

June smoothed her hand down the front of her dress. "Is there anything…"

Occam pointed at the filing cabinet. "They keep stuff in there, probably some clothes. If not, guess you'll just have to stay a pretty princess."

June let go of Micha's hand. "Thanks for your hospitality."

Occam flashed a syrupy smile. "Anytime."

He walked out and closed the door behind him. The lock clicked.

The small bed had a thin green blanket and one pillow. The overhead light buzzed in the silence.

"You heard something out in the hallway," she said to Micha.

"Yes. And something startled you."

"What did you hear?"

"A whisper. I couldn't make out the words, though."

"It was Rose. First time I've seen her in months. She didn't make any sense, as usual. Hopefully she's not still lurking out there. And hopefully she doesn't come in here." She glanced warily at the door.

"I wonder if I've become sensitive too?" The question seemed rhetorical so June didn't reply. "Are you feeling all right? I mean, from the allergic reaction."

"My mouth still feels a little funny." She scratched at her chest. "A little itchy. But the antihistamine is working." She slumped. "Something else I can't eat. I wonder what happens if I become allergic to all the food?"

"Is that possible?"

"Who knows."

She walked over to the filing cabinet, dropped her purse on top, and started opening drawers. She scanned the ceiling. No cameras.

"Sam slipped me the UV light." She kept her voice down, just in case. "It's in the purse."

"Could have used it earlier, when Occam was getting uppity."

"You should watch it, long as we're here. I doubt Occam travels by himself. It's quiet here, but that doesn't mean we're alone."

"Ghosts and vampires. We'll sleep easy tonight."

"As long as they stay out of this room, I don't care. We've been sleeping with the threat of worse."

He was silent for a moment. "June? Thanks. For doing this. I'm glad you're here, even if it's a stupid move on your part."

"Stupid is what I do best."

The room had a single window. A streetlight shone in, but when they turned the light off, the darkness gathered around them sinister and unfathomable. She had Micha next to her for comfort, though, like every other night. She lay with her back to the wall, draped over him, one arm and one leg, her head on his shoulder. She'd found a T-shirt and sweat pants in the filing cabinet. Both were a little big, but better than the dress. She'd put the T-shirt on, but left the pants off.

"I can hear you thinking," she murmured.

"Telepathic now?"

"No. You're just thinking so loud it's burrowing into my skull."

He let out a huff of air.

"Are you worried about the tests?" she asked.

"No, I don't care."

She lay silent a moment and then asked, "Do you think I should have gone home?"

"Yes."

"Would you miss me?"

"It's irrelevant. You'd be safe...safer."

"I hope Jason listens to Sam. That's all I care about, that him and Mom are safe. I'm not worried about me."

"I don't think you can protect me here. You should have gone with them."

"I'll do my damndest."

"Are you protecting me for Sam's benefit?"

She caressed her fingers along his jaw. "No." She turned his face toward hers.

Their lips met, soft and warm. When they broke the kiss, his eyes shone faintly in the light from the window.

"You sure about that?" he asked. "This isn't just to impress Sam?"

She frowned. "Why would it be? You think I'd risk my life to impress him?"

"Would you?"

"No. God, Micha. What are you—"

He rolled toward her and kissed her again, deeper and fiercer. This gesture took her by surprise. He hadn't been so adamantly physical in a long while. He pressed her against the bed. His scent and the weight of his body overwhelmed her, waking her up from the sleepy stupor she'd fallen into.

"Micha," she gasped as he broke the kiss. "We can't mess around here."

He pressed his mouth to her ear, his warm breath making desire crawl up the nape of her neck. "I don't care. Screw them." He slid his tongue down her neck, past the collar of the loose T-shirt to her clavicle.

"Are you sure?" she whispered. "They could be watching us."

"Let them watch."

He lifted his head and kissed her again—his "we're going to have sex" kiss. He forced her mouth open and plunged his tongue in. She wasn't sure if being so taken aback unnerved or excited her. She pushed her tongue against his, exploring the hard ridges of his teeth with the ball of her tongue ring and then plunging deeper into the wet softness behind them. Arousal thrummed in her, spreading through her belly and down between her thighs.

He hooked a finger in the top of her panties. She hadn't mustered the strength lately to tidy up down there, as it was pointless. Neither of them cared if they were dirty and unshaven. Also, they'd done a lot of heavy petting and fooling around lately, but they hadn't had actual penetrative sex in over a month.

Micha sat up and tugged her panties down over her hips. She lifted her bottom off the bed to help him out.

He stroked his fingers up her slit. "You're already wet." His voice had gone to a dark, sexy place.

"You're in a mood." She opened her thighs wider. "What the hell's gotten into you?"

"Might be the last time I get to do this. Let me get undressed."

He pulled off his shirt—he had jeans and a T-shirt on, without the disguise over him. June pulled her shirt off too. Being exposed in a strange, dangerous place made her edgy, but she wasn't about to pass up this rare opportunity. If they were watching, let them watch. She would give them a show.

She sat up and helped him undo his jeans. As she unzipped them she opened her mouth to speak, but he stopped her.

"Don't say anything." He placed a finger to her lips. "I don't want to talk about this."

She didn't talk. She pushed his pants and underwear down instead. He was fully hard, the head of his cock glistening in the light from the window.

She wrapped her fingers around that thick, swollen heat, and leaned over and sank her mouth over him. What she couldn't get in her mouth—a few inches, because she was damn good at this—she used her hand on.

She'd sucked him off a handful of times in the past few weeks, so it was more of the same, and he didn't seem in the mood for it. After a short time, he urged her off. She barely had time to catch her breath before he pushed her back on the bed and crawled on top of her. He kicked his jeans and underwear the rest of the way off.

"We don't have a condom," she said. "Not like either of us has been banging anyone else, but…"

"I told you, this might be the last time I get to do this. I have nothing to lose."

"I have things to lose. Like my childless status."

"Guess we'll have to improvise, then."

He pushed a hand between her legs. She gasped as he pushed his fingers into her, and she got an idea of how wet she actually was. She clenched around his fingers, aching, needing.

"Shh," he whispered in her ear. "Do you trust me?"

"Of course I trust you."

She grunted as he pushed deeper, the pleasure almost too hard and sharp. No more fingers, no more tongue. He'd better give her the cock this time, something real and solid and hard.

"Micha." She gripped his hair. "Don't tease me. You better fuck my brains out."

He pulled his fingers out and she was slick, hot.

"Please," she whispered, close to his lips.

She feared as per usual when they got this far, he would go wishy-washy—roll away, say he couldn't do this right now, he was too distracted, too upset, and she would understand and placate. Instead, he pushed her knees back, and she held her breath. He seemed ready this time, his body at least.

She gasped when the hot bare head of his cock pressed against her. He held still for a moment, hovering over her, and balanced on one arm with his other hand between them, holding his cock to guide himself in. Then he pushed.

He went in smooth and easy. She clenched around him, relieved, ecstatic.

"Micha." She gritted her teeth, twisting the blanket next to her hip. "Oh, fuck…yes…"

He braced his hands on the mattress, his face lost in shadow above her. "You all right?"

She let out her breath as he eased a few more inches in. "I'm great."

He took it easy at first, giving her time to adjust. He had himself angled perfectly, a blunt nudging against just the right spot, and she flattened a hand on his chest to even out his rhythm.

"Don't come inside me," she warned.

"I won't. I promise."

She relaxed and took her hand off his chest. He hooked her knees over his elbows and started pounding into her.

"Ah!" Her pleasure flared, brilliant and intense. "This won't last long."

"You're telling me."

He gave her a double whammy, playing with her clit ring and sucking at one of the barbells through her nipples. He pounded into her, the way he used to, the bed squeaking and thumping against the wall. She had to bite her lip hard to keep from screaming.

Her mind drifted as she gazed up at the darkened ceiling, as he rocked her against the mattress. Her thoughts ran to unbidden, unexpected places. The vision of Sam lying in bed with Muse flashed sudden and bright into her brain. Not Muse next to him, though. Her. In bed next to him, pressed against him.

What? *No, no, no. Stop.*

She squeezed her eyes shut tight. She focused on the feel of Micha's cock pounding inside her, his fingers on her clit. His other hand gripping her wrist above her head.

Sam's hand gripping her wrist on the stairs.

She forced herself back into the moment. "Micha," she groaned, half in guilt, half trying to focus.

Sensation overloaded her senses. His deep, hard thrusts shook her to the core. He knew how to work her ring, teasing her to the edge. The intensity built, higher and higher, stealing her breath, making her claw at the blanket.

"Micha!"

Sam.

She came, clenching hard around him, her body jerking almost convulsively. She yanked at the blanket, yanked at his hair.

"Yes," Micha gasped, dripping sweat across her cheek. "June." He shoved up hard into her and she whimpered.

After another minute of frantic thrusting, rattling the bed frame, he swiftly pulled out of her and stroked himself over her stomach. She released the blanket from her death grip and caressed his sweaty, quivering thighs. Warm fluid splattered her stomach. He groaned and shuddered above her.

She closed her eyes and licked her lips. "Micha…"

When he finished, he rolled off her and collapsed at her side. He left her sticky and wet and sore, and still twitching inside.

"You all right?" She caressed his side. "I needed that."

"Yeah, me too." He panted. "Thank you."

What exactly he thanked her for was unclear, but it didn't matter.

She used the bathroom first, a tiny white closet of a room with a sink and toilet. The walls were dingy, and the air smelled of disinfectant.

She found a rag and cleaned up, refusing to meet her own eyes in the mirror. While tidying up down below, her stomach sank, and anger flared. Micha hadn't pulled out fast enough.

"Damn it," she muttered. "'I promise.' Yeah right. That's what they all say."

She did the math. She was around the end of her cycle, in the clear. Maybe. She should have paid better attention in health class.

How awkward would it be to add Plan B to their supply list this week?

Micha went in after her. She pulled her panties back on but left the pants off. She lay down on the bed, gazing into the darkness, thicker now that she'd been in the bathroom with the light on.

Micha returned, pulled his shirt on, and left his jeans off. They lay on top the blanket, June's side aching and her breath short. He stroked her arm slung across his chest.

"If we make it out of this alive," he whispered, "when this is all over, if we don't feel the same about each other, I want you to know I enjoyed every minute with you."

June turned her head, getting a face full of his hair. "What are you talking about?"

"Relationships formed during times of crisis. They aren't built to last. You and I don't have much in common. We have this, but once it's gone…"

She pressed against him. "Don't get maudlin. Or introspective. Or any of those other big words you like to use."

"I'm just saying."

"Don't say anything. Not everything needs to be said."

Chapter 9

June woke with a start, though thankfully not to Rose, or a vampire—the woman standing at the end of the bed probably wasn't a vampire, anyway. Morning light streamed through the window, making the room appear less stark and more benign than the night before.

The woman wore a white lab coat and thick-framed glasses. She held a clipboard. Her hair was dark and feathery, brushing her shoulders, cut in thick bangs across her narrow forehead.

"I was told there would only be one of you." She checked her clipboard.

Micha stirred. They were still entwined and pants-less beneath the blanket.

"It's a long story," June's voice croaked. She woke most mornings with belated smoker's sludge dredged up from her wounded lung, and this morning she also had a sore throat from the allergic reaction. "Sorry."

Micha stirred again and cracked open his eyes. He opened them wider and blinked at the woman.

"I take it you're the patient?" the woman asked him. She had a throaty voice, not as bad as Muse, but there was something soothing and comfortable about it. "I wasn't actually given a name, just a description—Caucasian male, early thirties."

Micha lifted a languid hand and waved. "Present." He dropped it back to his chest.

"And you are?" she asked June.

"June." She struggled into a sitting position, wincing at the hitch in her side. Giving her identity away probably wasn't smart, but she couldn't come up with a different name on the spot. "Just…June."

"Occam is notoriously bad at keeping us informed," the woman said. "It's a thing with vampires."

"Yeah." Micha rubbed his face. "They definitely lack social graces."

"Yes, well." She tucked the clipboard under her arm. "I'm Doctor Trina Watson. You can call me Trina. I'll be conducting some tests on you this morning." She delved into the pocket of her coat and pulled out a small clear plastic cup with a lid. "I need some urine."

"We just met." June stretched her arms above her head.

"From him." She tossed the cup at Micha. He made a feeble attempt to catch it, and it landed on his chest. "When you've filled it, come down the hallway to the window at the end." She turned and opened the door.

"Okay," Micha mumbled, scrabbling at the cup.

Trina left the room.

"How are you feeling this morning?" June asked.

"Let me get back to you on that one." He sat up with a grunt.

June found the sweat pants and pulled them on while Micha went to the bathroom to fill the cup. The pants were too big, but she used a few of the pins from the dress to keep them from sliding off her hips. She'd lost weight while in hiding, which wasn't a surprise. Her mother would fuss, since she already thought June was too "slight."

Not being able to eat most things without going into anaphylactic shock kind of exacerbated that.

She didn't have shoes, but putting the heels back on was out of the question. She searched through the drawers but didn't find any footwear.

Micha stepped out of the bathroom, plunked his half-full cup on top the filing cabinet, and grabbed up his jeans. He was bleary eyed and off balance. He sat down heavily on the bed, and June reached out and touched his shoulder.

"Sure you're okay?"

"I feel like I do every morning." He dropped his head in his hands. "Like I have a hangover. And I didn't even get to enjoy the drunk the night before."

June rubbed his back while he sat slumped for a few minutes. Finally, he leaned back and continued pulling his jeans on.

Once he was dressed, she kissed the back of his neck. "Come on," she murmured. "Time to play science project."

She tucked the purse into one of the filing cabinet drawers for safekeeping. They wouldn't be dealing with vampires in the daytime.

Micha grabbed his cup. They left the room and walked down the hallway. The clinic was much brighter, the lights on, the sound of voices coming from various rooms, but June still tensed when they passed the spot where she'd seen Rose. The window Trina spoke of was at the end of the hallway, opening onto an office. A woman sat at a desk behind the window, and Trina stood behind her.

"Delivery," June said.

Micha thrust the cup through the window. The woman behind the desk didn't move to take it.

"Good," Trina said. "Hold onto it for a moment."

They stepped back from the window.

Micha scowled. "You'd think after all I've been through I wouldn't have to stand around holding a cup of my own piss."

"Just be happy it's not a body part."

Trina left the room behind the window through a door to the right of it. She held a folder.

"We're going to do some basic tests today," she said. "Normal stuff. Blood work, MRI, X-rays."

"Do the not-normal tests start tomorrow?" June asked.

Trina looked down at June's bare feet. June wiggled her toes.

"A bit unhygienic," Trina said. "Don't you think?"

"All I have with me is a pair of heels. My coming here was a bit of a last minute decision."

Trina adjusted her glasses. "I'll get you a pair of slippers." She turned and motioned for them to follow her. "Come with me."

They followed her down the hallway, June's bare feet slapping on the tile.

"Can I call you something besides Patient X?" Trina asked Micha. "Do you have a name?"

"X is fine," Micha said.

"You know, I have no clue what I'm looking for with these tests. Occam didn't give me any information. He just said he wanted you studied and cataloged."

"How humanizing of him," Micha said.

"I could make my testing more specific if I knew what to look for. Care to fill me in?"

Micha opened his mouth, but then closed it. They couldn't say anything.

"I guess if they didn't tell you," Micha said, "it must be a secret."

"Very well, then." Her voice went high and clipped. "This isn't unusual. I put up with it quite regularly from the vampires."

"I bet you do," June said.

June received a pair of fuzzy blue hospital slippers. They were offered breakfast: coffee, bagels, and fruit. Trina told Micha to eat something before she took blood, so he munched listlessly on a dry bagel. June had some black coffee and a banana. Those things weren't trying to kill her—yet. Trina told her she could tag along for the testing if she stayed out of the way, and if Micha gave his permission. He did.

"Why are you here, anyway?" Trina asked June. She led them to another part of the building.

"Quality control, I guess you could say."

"Are you working for Occam?"

"No. Not in a million years."

"I take it you're a couple? Boyfriend and girlfriend? Married?"

"Let me put it this way," June said. "If I had access to it, my Facebook status would say, 'it's complicated.'"

Micha smirked.

The tests indeed seemed "normal" as Trina indicated. She took Micha's vitals: heart rate, blood pressure, temperature, noting all were slightly elevated. She measured his height and weight. What had he weighed before all this started? He definitely had a few bones sticking out now. She drew blood. She asked him a million questions about his health and family background.

June grew bored and walked around the room, peering at the licenses and credentials on the walls. They didn't comfort her.

When Micha went for his MRI, June obviously couldn't stay with him. She waited outside with Trina in a small room, where two technicians pored over the scans of Micha's brain. She and Trina sat in chairs, side by side, and the lack of conversation eventually became oppressive.

"So," June said. "The vampires recruited you guys to disprove Rose Bellevue's research, I'm told. That's what you do here?"

"That's not all we do here. It's one of many projects."

"But you jump through hoops for them?"

"We don't approve of the Institute's practices, but that doesn't mean everything they've discovered is ripe for the disproving. We've clarified and even mitigated some of their research, but that doesn't mean they're wrong all the time."

"So what happens if you can't do what the vampires are asking?"

"The study is ongoing."

"You'll lie for them?"

"I don't have a say in these things. A governing board oversees all our research and decides what findings we make public. I'm just a researcher."

"Does the governing board like"—June leaned closer and whispered—"bribery?"

Trina pursed her lips. "What are you implying?"

"I'm implying the vampires are shady. I think they'll get what they want from you, regardless."

Trina looked down at the papers on her lap. "June Coffin. You're one of the aural captivators that disappeared."

June's stomach lurched.

"I recognize all the—" Trina made a circular hand gesture, indicating June's ink. "I followed your story. I was really interested in you."

June cursed herself for not coming up with another name. Why couldn't she have said Sally? Barb? Wanda? She kind of looked like a Wanda.

"Aural captivation is an extremely rare skill," Trina said. "I was hoping when you were through at the Institute I could coax you to come visit us. But then everything happened and you…vanished."

"Yes."

"Yet here you are. Don't worry, I won't tell anyone. I get the feeling you're not looking to step back into the limelight."

June relaxed. "Someone actually remembers me."

"I paid close attention. But your story eventually got pushed off to the side and just…died. I always wondered what happened to you."

"My fifteen minutes were up, I guess."

"I don't suppose, even if I asked, you'd tell me how or why you're here, in Chicago still, participating in this strange incident."

"No, I don't suppose I would."

The screens across the room showed a black-and-white composite of the inside of Micha's brain. Where the magic happened.

"And I don't suppose," Trina said, "I could convince you to let me do a work-up on you?"

"No one is ever going to study me again. I'll never even go to the doctor for a check-up."

June worried she'd blown their cover, but Trina didn't seem the type to run to the press. Curiosity glittered in her eyes, behind the lenses of her glasses. She leaned in closer and June tensed.

"Show me how it works," Trina said.

June frowned. "How what works?"

"Your power. Use it on me."

"You've got to be kidding."

"Something simple. Something that won't hurt me."

Doing tricks like a poodle in a circus was far from June's favorite thing. She needed to explain to Trina how dangerous it could be, how one wrong word could be devastating. Trina didn't withdraw, poised eagerly.

June glanced to the side, at the technicians, and then back at Trina.

"Give me your pen," June whispered. Warmth blossomed in her chest and surged up her throat.

Trina's eyes glazed and she reached for the pen in the breast pocket of her coat. She pulled it out and handed it to June. June took it and Trina blinked, coming back to herself.

"Fascinating," Trina whispered.

"I guess so." June fidgeted with the pen.

"What makes the spell break?"

"You complete the action. Unless it's an indefinite request."

"Indefinite?"

"If I told you to lie down on the floor, you'd stay there until I told you to get up. Giving me the pen has a…conclusion, I guess. You give me the pen. You've completed what I told you to do."

"So in theory, you could make me lie on the floor until I, say—died of dehydration?"

June grimaced. "I don't know. I've never taken it that far. I don't want to." Freakin' scientists.

Trina gazed at the pen in wonder. "If you made a demand, and there was a whole room full of people who heard it, would they all do it?"

"No. My own will is involved, somehow. I don't know." She pushed her fingers through her hair and rubbed the back of her neck. "I will it where to go. I kinda just…direct it at a person. So it doesn't affect other people."

"And you could make a person do anything, absolutely anything? Kill himself, or someone else?"

June dropped her hand. "Another thing I've never tested and don't plan to." She handed the pen back to Trina. "Christ, why do all you scientists gotta be so creepy?"

"It's a big part of science, figuring out what can kill you."

"I got an easy answer to that. In this city: everything."

Trina tucked the pen back in her pocket. "I won't tell anyone who you are. I'm just happy to find out you're still around."

"Thanks."

Micha had to go for X-rays next, and it was supposed to take a while, since they wanted to X-ray his entire body, so June wandered off to find something to do. She went to the lounge where they'd eaten breakfast and tried to watch some TV, but after Trina's revelation, she was paranoid about being seen.

She found a small courtyard at the rear of the building, an awning over it and surrounded by a high fence. Benches lined the walls, the space obviously where people went to smoke, as there were cigarette butts strewn all over the concrete floor. The day was warm and breezy, the sun bright.

She tried to relax on one of the benches. In the old days, she would have smoked a cigarette and played on her phone to pass the time. With no distractions, her mind wandered. What was Sam doing? Had Diego and Jason left the city yet? Was Muse lurking nearby? She sent out a mental "hello," and assured her everything was cool.

Talking to imaginary people. She was going insane.

The door to the courtyard opened and June tensed. Trina stepped out. She'd taken off her lab coat and had on a white blouse and black dress pants. She clutched a pack of cigarettes.

"Are you following me?" June joked.

"Sort of." She sat down next to June on the bench. "Figured you'd find your way out here. It's a good hiding spot."

"Must not be that good, you found me."

Trina shook a cigarette out and offered June the pack. "You smoke?"

June envisioned grabbing the pack and cramming them all in her mouth. "I quit."

"Good for you." She sounded genuinely complementary. "I've been trying. I know how bad they are. What's your secret?" She lit up with a little red disposable lighter.

"I got shot." June poked her side. "In the lung."

Trina frowned. "I think I'll just try nicotine patches."

"Patches wouldn't work for me. Unless I put them on my tongue."

Trina took a drag and blew the smoke out the corner of her mouth, away from June. "Getting shot does seem like a habit changer. Who shot you?"

"A vampire."

Trina flicked the ash to the side. "Not a friendly bunch, are they? Why did a vampire shoot you?"

"I guess I deserved it." June propped her right foot on her opposite knee and bounced her fuzzy blue slipper. "How long do we have to stay here?"

Trina shrugged. "Depends on how long it takes to do all the tests Occam wants. Not more than another day." She narrowed her eyes. "So he isn't your boyfriend?"

"Why is that everyone's foremost burning concern?"

"I'm trying to assess your reasons for acting as his watchdog. You said you're not working for Occam. If it's not because he's your boyfriend, you're doing it for someone else. Someone who isn't the vampires."

"Maybe he needs a watchdog. Lots of crazy people out there."

"So who are you working for?" She took another drag off her cigarette.

"My friends None-Of-Your-Business and I'm-Not-Telling-You."

Trina blew the smoke out. "So much secrecy. We do independent research at the request of lots of various groups, but they don't often like to tell us their reasons."

"I'm not asking anything of you. Occam is asking. I'm just making sure Occam returns Patient X in one piece. To us. To the people I'm not working for. No one asked me to come."

"I'm not stupid, you know. I'm well aware that's Micha Bellevue. Rose Bellevue's missing husband."

June groaned. "Jesus Christ, are you Sherlock Holmes or something?"

"No, like I said, I'm not stupid. I think everyone who's seen him here knows. The vampires strongly suggested we turn a blind eye to anything we 'suspect.' I suspect they've given the governing board lots of money. We have standing orders to keep our mouths shut, or else."

"I'm sorry you're in that position. But in that case, you probably shouldn't complain so loudly about it."

"I don't like being pandered to."

"Then get a new job."

Trina turned her gaze away and took another drag.

"It won't help you to be plucky," June said. "I've seen what happens to the plucky people."

Trina smashed her cigarette out on the bench half smoked. She pushed it back into the pack and stood.

"I'll try to be a good little girl and stay quiet," she sniped. "And you can keep guarding your not-boyfriend. And when this is all over, you can leave, and we'll pretend it never happened."

"Don't take your shit out on me. Your issues were going on long before I got here."

Trina turned and walked briskly to the courtyard door, her heels clicking on the concrete. She went inside and the door swung shut behind her.

June abruptly sat forward, inhaled the lingering smoke on the air, and slumped back with a sigh.

"Goddamn it."

June was even more worried they'd be outed now. Trina had better be right, that the vampires were passing funds under the table in exchange for silence. They had also better be of the mind that snitches got stitches.

She sat on the bench for a while longer. Cars passed on the nearby street, birds twittering, the breeze whistling softly through the fence slats. The day was almost too warm, like Sacramento. Would she ever see the California sun again?

She was getting up to go back inside when someone cleared his throat and she nearly pissed her pants.

She'd been pretty sure—no, absolutely sure—she was alone out there. She wasn't.

Occam sat on a bench in the corner adjacent to her, where the building met the fence. He wore a wide-brimmed hat, sunglasses, and a long sleeve shirt.

He lifted an arm and waved. He also had gloves on. "Hi!"

June glared. "I thought I was safe from vampires during the day."

"There's nothing dangerous about being predictable."

Chapter 10

June sat back down, making sure to keep a comfortable—for her—distance between them.

"What do you want?" she asked.

"Just wanted to talk to you."

"Why didn't you wait until dark?"

"It's no fun if you're not surprised." He flashed his fangs. "Are you surprised, Little Red?"

"I shouldn't be, I guess. Isn't the sunlight hurting you, though?"

"It hurts a bit, when I'm directly in it. It weakens me, makes me sluggish and uncoordinated. I suppose that's to your advantage."

"Only if you came here to kickbox. I thought we were talking?"

"Yes, we are."

June spread her arms and shrugged. "There's nothing to report. They're doing tests on him. I think they're planning more, because they told me we might be here another day. I don't have any news."

"I'm not here to talk about him. I'm here to talk about you."

June eyed him warily. His eyes weren't visible behind his glasses, but his stare was tangible.

"What about me?" she asked. "I'm not very interesting."

"I wouldn't say that." He folded his gloved hands on his lap. "You seem quite intelligent, to start with—which is why I can't understand what makes you trust a man like Sam Haain so implicitly."

Of course, he would show up to continue their argument from the night before.

"It's not so much 'trust.'" She sat back against the wall. "He's been the only one who could help me."

"And you help him in return."

"I kind of owe him."

"Sam is weak. He used to have a respectable amount of power, but it started going downhill when he decided to play diplomat and accept Aaron Jenkins's offer of peace. He's even weaker now, in hiding. If he had his old power, he would have cleared his own name by now. He wouldn't need Micha to be his Get Out of Jail Free card."

"He still has his supporters."

Occam chuckled. "Don't you ever wonder how the self-proclaimed smartest man in the city overlooked a huge, glaring issue that if exposed much earlier, might have kept this whole mess from happening in the first place?"

"What are you talking about?"

"How did a man who had operatives inside the Institute not know Eric Greerson was corrupt?"

She flashed back to Sam and Eric rescuing them in the elevator at the Institute. Sam said he'd overlooked Eric. He'd told June before Eric was an ignorant figurehead, nothing more.

"It's because," Occam said, "his operatives inside the Institute were giving him false information."

June stared at him.

"Not all of them, of course. He's got a few loyal ones in there, ferrying him information, stealing things for him. They got him the research on the serum, obviously. But some of them have been on Robbie's side for years. They were telling Sam that Eric was docile and stupid. Robbie's quest isn't a new campaign, and his supporters aren't paltry. This has been going on for years. Robbie had the perfect scapegoat, blaming it all on the SNC, trying to break the treaty."

June furrowed her brow. "That doesn't make sense. Robbie wants to bring down the Institute as much as Sam does. He was looking for Sam's approval doing all that stuff. Why would he hide what Eric was really doing? They both want the same thing."

"Yes, Little Red. Why would the Big Bad Wolf hide in Grandma's nightgown?" He rolled his head against the wall to look at her. "Think hard, now."

June's stomach sank. "He... He wanted to do it himself..."

Occam gave her a thumbs-up. "Robbie wants the Institute to crumble, but on his terms. He doesn't want to be Sam's minion, or even his partner. Robbie wants to be in charge. He wants to run the Paranormal Alliance the way it should be run—according to him."

"And we've seen how Robbie takes care of business."

"So we have."

"He thought keeping information from Sam gave him an advantage?"

"And it did, didn't it?" He sounded reverent, impressed, the way a psycho might be impressed with Hitler's military skill. "Robbie was the perfect snake in the grass: unobtrusive, outwardly loyal, a good little lapdog. He let Sam have his crumbs, so he wouldn't suspect what was really going on, and they were things that would help Robbie in his quest too. He's also physically powerful. His power makes him very, very dangerous."

"But I hear it's killing him. He won't be able to run things forever."

"A man like that has a contingency plan." Occam sat forward. "Robbie's real downfall, if he isn't careful, will be his insanity and zealousness. Sam may be adamant and a bit off his rocker, but he never used violence and schemes like killing his own kind to get what he wanted. Sad, because I would have enjoyed watching that. If Sam wants to bring him down, he'll have to be as crazy as he is. Crazy people are dangerous. Crazy people don't care. Sam has to stop caring."

Occam was quite articulate. Having a conversation with him might actually be pleasant, if he wasn't himself.

"How do you even know all this?" June asked.

"Vampires observe. It's what we do. Observe, and listen, and spy, and laugh at the way people throw themselves on the fire. That's precisely the reason we don't get involved, unless it benefits us. But knowledge is power. We have so, so much to hold over your stupid little heads."

"Do you know where Robbie is right now?"

"Perhaps."

"You should tell Sam."

"I don't owe Sam anything." He slid down the bench, closer to her. "And what good would the knowledge do him? He's not hiding from Robbie right now."

She subtly recoiled. "You know about Sam's brother, Thomas? How he was killed?"

"Oh, yes. Vampires executed his murderers. Kevin Kramer paid blood and money for that hit. He didn't pay enough for silence. But Aaron Jenkins did. We're still benefitting from his annual payments. We don't get involved in your politics, but we like your dollars."

"I was told four men were involved in the murder, but only three were killed." She paused. "Was Robbie the fourth man?"

Occam chuckled and got to his feet.

"I wasn't involved in that situation. I had my own concerns at the time, climbing my way up the vampire ladder, so to speak."

He walked over and stopped in front of her. She gazed up at him, tense. He reached out and clamped his hand on her shoulder, and she cringed.

"Why didn't they kill Robbie?" she asked.

Occam delved into his shirt pocket. "You presume too much, Little Red." He held something out to her. "A gift."

She narrowed her eyes at the object in his hand: a tube with a stopper in the end, filled with a dark red fluid, like blood.

"What's this?"

"Something to soothe over any bad feelings. I want you to like me, June."

"I don't think that's gonna happen."

"I promise it's very useful. It's only the base, though. It needs a special ingredient to work."

She continued eyeing the tube. "What is it?"

Occam waved it in front of her face, back and forth, as if trying to hypnotize her. "It's one of the key components for a special brew we like to call the Oracle of the Dead."

She shrank back. "I don't want that."

"You may have need of it, someday. Although, as I said, it's not activated. The Oracle of the Dead is made from vampire blood, but it takes another kind of blood to make it work—the blood of a powerful paranormal human."

She didn't take it. She wanted to fling his hand off her shoulder, where he was still resting it casually.

"Three drops." He turned the tube over, making the blood gurgle down. "It has to come from someone with significant power, like Kevin's grandmother had. Like Robbie has." He tapped the glass. "Of course, Kevin's grandmother was sleeping with a vampire."

"I don't ever want to see that thing in action again."

Occam released her shoulder and grabbed her hand. He plunked the tube in her palm and wrapped her fingers around it. The glass was cold.

He leaned down, so close his scent, noxious and offensive, invaded her nostrils. "You might need it," he whispered. "From me to you, darling."

She snatched her hand out of his grip.

Occam stood upright. He adjusted his sunglasses and hat. "I must be off, before I'm too weak to function. Wouldn't want you to have that great an advantage. It was nice talking about you."

"We didn't talk about me at all…"

Occam vanished. The door to the building hadn't opened, neither had the gate in the fence, but he was suddenly no longer in the courtyard. He'd either disappeared into thin air or vaulted the fence, somehow without her even seeing him move. Her skin crawled.

She held up the tube, fighting the urge to smash it on the concrete.

"Thanks a lot," she muttered. "Happy birthday to me."

* * * *

June opened the door to the room she and Micha had slept in, hoping to hide out where vampires couldn't find her, and nearly jumped out of her skin. A little white figure sat on the bed.

"Damn it, Muse." June quickly closed the door. "What are you doing here?"

Muse quirked an eyebrow. "You called out to me."

"So you *were* around."

"Of course. Sam has me watching over you."

"How did you get in here?"

"Maybe I'm a ghost."

June cringed. Her mind flew to Rose lurking in the hallway.

"You saw Rose?" Muse perked and scooted over. "Sit." She patted the bed.

June walked over and sat down beside her. "I don't know what she wants."

"What all ghosts want, I'm sure. To be understood. In her case, avenged."

"If she deserves vengeance." June sighed heavily. "Nothing is happening. Micha is just going through tests. I told you that in my head message."

"I know. I thought you might like to know what's going on back at the house."

June perked up. The corner of Muse's mouth jerked and then her eye.

"Diego took your brother home," Muse said.

June nearly melted in relief. She nearly burst into tears.

"Thank fucking God." She rubbed her face. "If they can get Mom to go into hiding with them, I'll feel even better."

"They weren't very happy with you. Not at all."

"I don't figure. Jason can be really hardheaded, but I know his weak spot. He'll do anything for Mom."

"Very clever of you."

"It's better this way. Now Jason is one less thing I have to worry about."

"You could have left with them, you know. Sam wanted you to."

"I know." She stood, too full of nervous energy to sit still. "I know what Sam wants, but he doesn't always know what's good for him. I think there's more I can do here. Isn't that why he helped me in the first place? So I could help him?"

"You were supposed to be a peaceful way to plead his case to the masses. I don't think that's going to happen now." Muse's face was placid. "You're too wrapped up in things here, aren't you? Wrapped up in emotions?"

June turned away. "I care about people here, yes, if that's what you're trying to force out of me."

"Nothing wrong with caring."

"Nothing wrong with not caring, either. People seem to forget that."

They were both silent for a moment.

"Occam visited you," Muse said. "I see him in your head."

"Yes. So eager to talk to me he came out in daylight."

"Element of surprise." She snorted. "Vampires like that. He gave you something?"

June opened her hand. She turned around and held the tube up. "He said it's just the base."

Muse's face was now marred by random twitches. Her hands jerked in her lap.

"I saw this used, once," June said. "I don't want to use it. There's nothing I want to ask a dead person."

"Only family members can make inquiries about each other. It's a very blood-based bit of magic. So unless there's something you desperately need to know about a family member, it's of no use to you."

"Then why'd he give it to me? Why does he think I'd need an oracle?" She furrowed her brow. Rose's words seemed to whisper in her ears again. *It's not meant for you.*

Muse opened her mouth, but suddenly, a loud ringing filled the air. June started and nearly dropped the tube. Muse jumped to her feet.

"Fire alarm?" Muse yelled over the noise.

"We better hope!" June dashed to the door.

Was it a burglar alarm? Had Muse tripped it? Probably not. Burglar alarms weren't generally armed during business hours, and it would have gone off as soon as she entered, anyway.

"Get out of here," June told her. "Before someone sees you."

June left the room and rushed down the hallway. Gray smoke billowed from a doorway at the other end. People were yelling. A man had a fire extinguisher. He ducked under the roiling cloud of smoke and sprayed white foam through the doorway.

The acrid scent of burning plastic filled the air, and she clapped a hand over her mouth and nose as she approached the room.

Inside the doorway, Micha sat on the floor, slumped over with his head in his hands. Trina bent over him, coughing and waving the smoke away.

"Micha!" June ducked under the smoke and knelt beside him. "What happened? Are you okay?"

"He's all right," Trina said. "I don't think he's hurt."

Micha lifted his head. He was pale, his expression both stricken and angry. His eyes glistened.

"I couldn't control it," he said. "I couldn't stop it—" He coughed as the smoke wafted over them.

"Let's get out of here." Trina tugged at Micha's arm. "Come on."

Micha got to his feet, June helping him as well, and they walked to the waiting room. No one was around and all the doors were open. They'd evacuated the clinic.

"We can't let anyone see him," Trina said. "Or you. We'll stay right here until it's safe to take you back to your room."

Micha sat down in a chair.

"What happened?" June asked.

"The same thing that happened in the penthouse," Micha said, "when I burned your arm. It got out of control. I couldn't stop it."

"Pyrokinesis." Trina sounded awed. "Very rare. More rare than aural captivation."

June ignored her and sat down next to Micha. "It's all right. You didn't mean to do it."

Micha dropped his head in his hands again. "I can't take this anymore."

June reached out and rubbed his knee.

"I'll get you some water," Trina said. "If anyone comes in, go back to your room so you aren't seen."

She left, and June continued rubbing Micha's leg. Smoke drifted from the hallway. Approaching sirens filtered in from outside. Micha tensed and she stopped rubbing.

"We better go hide our shameful selves." She sighed and stood up. "Since we're obviously the bad guys here."

Chapter 11

The next day June accompanied Micha to all his tests and kept a close eye on him, in case one of his powers got out of hand again. The researchers didn't have too many more hoops for him to jump through, however, and shortly after noon, Trina informed them they were done testing him.

"So how do we get out of here?" June asked. "Should we just hop on a bus? Call a cab?"

"I'm supposed to call Occam after sunset. He'll come get you."

"Great. I'd rather take my chances out in public."

The rest of the day was long and boring. June sent out mind messages, in case Muse still lurked nearby. They watched TV, ate food they were given, and she eventually convinced Micha to go out into the courtyard with her. He glowered at the sunlight, sitting slumped on a bench. She couldn't blame him for being despondent. She was mad enough to resent the weather as well.

As evening fell, the tension built while they waited for their vampire taxi.

Micha wanted to sleep, saying he felt weak after having so much blood drawn. June suspected he just wanted to hide, but she left him in their room and went to watch TV again. She wished she had Cindy's laptop so she could read her favorite blogger, the one who continued to insist Micha had been kidnapped by the CIA. She'd commented on his posts a few times, not to correct, but to fuel his paranoia.

She kept sending out a message: *The tests are over. Occam is coming to get us. Get here first so the creepy bastard doesn't take us home with him and touch us inappropriately.*

She eventually couldn't sit still any longer. She walked down the hallway, heading back to their room. The light coming through the door to the courtyard, at the end of the hallway, was murky blue. Maybe Trina was out having a cigarette. June could say good-bye to her and inhale her second hand smoke one last time.

Her new scientist friend wasn't outside, though. A door to June's right opened and Trina stepped out.

"Hey," June said. "Just the smart broad I was looking for."

Trina's eyes were wide behind her glasses. She clutched a folder.

June's stomach did a flip. "What?"

"We got some of Micha's test results back."

"Oh, God. Should I sit down for this?"

"What the hell is he?" She lowered her voice to a whisper. "Where did he come from?"

June raised her eyebrows. "His mother's uterus? And as far as I know, he's a man. Why, did you find alien DNA?"

Trina brandished the folder at her. "He's got multiple paranormal hormones and the receptors for them. Four individual kinds we've isolated so far."

"Yeah, I kinda knew that."

Trina took a step back.

June shrugged, not sure what else to say, what she could say. "That's kinda why he's here."

"Do you understand"—Trina lowered her voice to a whisper again—"this is unprecedented?"

"Is it?"

"There are people with groupings of powers, though they're uncommon. But no one has more than two powers. No one that's ever been studied, anyway."

"I guess there's a first time for everything."

"This isn't possible." She stepped closer to June. "Medically speaking. Don't you understand? He couldn't have been born like this. He couldn't have formed that many hormones and receptors on his own. Where did they come from?"

"I'm not allowed to tell you that."

"He claimed he was a normal. I remember that from the stuff I've read about him. When this gets out, it's going to be the biggest scientific discovery in the paranormal community."

"I'm sure that's the point."

"You can't let Occam keep this a secret."

"I don't think he intends it to be."

"We have to tell people." She clutched a hand to her chest, eyes going wide again. "I could write a paper about this. Finally get a big publication."

June rubbed her forehead. "I know this must be super exciting for you, but it's a delicate situation. I'm not the person who makes the decisions here. You'll have to—"

Behind them, a door opened at the other end of the hallway. They both looked in that direction. Two women in lab coats were striding toward them, one tall and the other short, walking close together.

So close, in fact, they were touching.

Trina narrowed her eyes as they approached. "Excuse me. I'm sorry. Who are you?"

The taller woman stepped ahead of the other, and suddenly both vanished. In a blink, they turned into Sam and Muse.

"Where's Micha?" Sam asked.

"What the—" Trina backed up. "Who are you?"

"Don't panic," June told her. "They're friends of mine." She jerked her head in the direction of their room. "Down there. I take it you heard my call?" she said to Muse.

Muse nodded. Sam grabbed June by the arm and pulled her down the hallway with him.

"Thought we'd get the jump on Occam," he said. "Somehow, I don't trust him to just drive you back to our house and drop you off. Sorry we couldn't get here sooner. We had to get a car from Aaron."

"I'm just glad you got here ahead of the vampires." June's heart was tripping—not from merely the rush of adrenaline, but from Sam showing up in such boisterous fashion. She didn't like being the damsel in distress, but sometimes it was nice to be rescued.

"Hey!" Trina rushed after them. "Are you glamour generators? You can't just walk in here and do what you want, you know. This is a scientific facility!"

"And I love scientists," Sam said over his shoulder.

"Right here." June pointed at the door of the room.

Sam let go of her arm.

For a few breathless seconds June thought they might actually get out of there before Occam showed up.

Then the door to the courtyard flew open, bouncing off the wall next to it and slowly creeping back. A figure stood in the doorway.

"Naughty boy, Sam," Occam said. "Trying to break our agreement."

Occam wasn't alone. Zack and Belle stood behind him, looming like shadows.

"The tests are done," Sam said.

Muse slid up beside him.

"You said you'd return him after the tests," Sam reminded him.

"I said I'd return him as soon as our agreement was filled. Our agreement was, I turn over your evidence along with Micha's tests to the FBI. Then Micha does as I ask. That's when the agreement ends."

"That was not the agreement," June said. "You promised you'd let him go."

"Did I? Whoops. I made an amendment."

Occam stepped into the hallway. The other two followed. Zack smirked over Occam's shoulder at June, malevolence glittering in his eyes.

"What's going on here?" Trina demanded. "Occam, you know you're not supposed to be in here."

"He's coming with me," Occam said. "You can take June if you want. Though, she might want to come with me too. I'm interesting and you're boring, Sam."

"We didn't agree to this," Sam said.

"We didn't not agree to it."

"I can't trust you not to harm him. I know how you operate. You might not do anything with the evidence and just mount Micha's head on a spike and parade it around the Nocturnal District."

Occam laughed. His minions tittered behind him. "Don't give me ideas. Don't worry. You have my word."

June stepped around Sam. "He's coming with us. You're not taking him anywhere."

Zack and Belle shot forward. Despite being farther from the door to Micha's room, they managed to get there first. June lunged at them, as did Sam, and grappled with them. Zack sneered in June's face.

"Want some more of this?" he breathed at June.

Tingles washed over her skin.

She gripped his face and slammed his head back against the door. The door swung open, and all four of them tumbled inside.

"I'm calling security!" Trina yelled.

"Tell her not to," Sam told June. "We can't be seen here."

"Don't call security!" June's power rushed out of her like a warm wind.

Micha was sitting up on the bed, his back against the wall. Zack and Belle broke free and blocked Sam and June, keeping them from getting to him. Occam drifted into the room.

"Restrain him," Occam ordered. "If he won't come along peacefully, we'll drag him."

"Stay away from him!" Sam rushed at the bed.

Zack tried to clothesline him with his forearm, but Sam ducked.

Metal flashed at Sam's hip when he ducked and his shirt rode up. June lurched forward and grabbed the gun out of his belt. She whirled around and aimed it at Occam.

"Tell them to back off," she said. "Right now."

Occam, filling the doorway like a noxious gas, rolled his eyes.

"Do you know how many times I've been shot? Go for it. You won't hit a major organ, trust me. You're not that good."

Suddenly, a small fist appeared between Occam's legs and slammed up into his groin. June flinched. Occam spilled forward with an angry yelp. Muse stood behind him, fist balled.

"Nut shots still work," Muse said.

A scuffle ensued. Sam took Zack down, slamming him to the floor. Belle jumped on top of Micha on the bed.

"You!" June aimed the gun at her. "Get off him!"

Belle reeled back, but not because of June's command. She shrieked and scrabbled at her face. Micha had the light in his hand, a bluish glow emanating from it. He had his head turned, shielding his own eyes. Belle fell off the bed.

"You bastards," Occam hissed. He was already back on his feet. "You're using a weapon against us? Against your allies?"

Sam, still struggling with Zack, snarled at him. "Allies? Are you fucking kidding me?"

June was about to start shooting everyone, but Occam swiftly reached out and grabbed Muse by the hair. She shrieked as he jerked her across the room.

"Back off, Sam." Occam pulled Muse around in front of him. "And you, Little Red, put the gun down."

Sam quit fighting and Zack slumped against the floor. Belle was curled in a ball next to the bed. Zack rolled over and scurried away from Sam and to her side.

"I'll twist her head off." Occam gripped Muse's chin with his other hand. "Literally, Sam."

Muse breathed through her nose, clutching Occam's wrist. Sam, still kneeling on the floor, glowered at them.

Sam waved at June, and she lowered the gun.

"You." Occam jerked his chin at Micha. "Get up. There's a car waiting. And that light is coming with us, but in my hand."

"Let her go," Sam said. "You can take him."

June gaped at him. "Who the hell are you to decide whose life he gets to mess with?"

"He won't kill Micha." Sam looked at her, eyes intense and dark. "He needs him. He will kill her."

"He can't twist her head off." June clutched the gun at her side. "Being a vampire doesn't give you superhuman strength, I know that much."

"Doesn't take superhuman strength," Occam said. "Done it before." He nodded to Zack. "Get that thing out of his hand and bring it to me."

Micha inched across the bed.

"If he flashes him, Sam," Occam warned, "you'll take this little one home in a bag."

Zack stood up and approached the bed. He held a hand out. Sam nodded at Micha, and Micha handed the light over, glaring at Zack.

"Good," Occam said. "Come along now, Micha. I have a much nicer room waiting for you."

June turned to Micha, her stomach in knots. Micha crawled slowly off the bed. Zack went back to his sister and helped her to her feet.

"Micha," June said. "Don't let him mess with you. We'll get you out of there, I promise."

"I'll be all right." He walked toward Occam. "They haven't killed me yet."

June swallowed, blinking back tears. Occam was right; she wasn't that good of a shot yet. She might hit Muse, or miss him altogether. She would bring more pain down on them if she fired and missed.

Zack led his sister out of the room. He handed the light to Occam in passing.

"I can't believe you would do this, Sam." Occam brandished the light at him. "That you would bring something like this here."

"I find it hard to feel guilty when you're threatening to twist my bodyguard's head off."

Occam walked backward out the door, pulling Muse with him. Micha followed him out, his steps slow and shuffling. Sam got up and followed them, and June did as well, still clutching the gun tight. Trina, in the hallway, had flattened herself against the opposite wall. She watched as they passed, her lips pressed in a tight line.

Occam continued walking backward down the hallway, out the door, through the courtyard, and out the gate in the fence. Micha, Sam, and June followed into a parking lot on the other side. The black car from the restaurant was parked nearby, the engine running. Zack and Belle got in. Occam motioned for Micha to get in as well.

Micha stood for a moment outside the open back door of the car. His eyes gleamed, his face stony. June gritted her teeth, continuing to fight back tears. She would not let Occam see her cry.

"Get in," Occam ordered. "No sad good-byes today."

Micha ducked down and got in the car. Muse struggled in Occam's grip. A rivulet of blood trickled down her forehead.

"Let her go," Sam said. "Occam!"

"I won't forget this." Occam held up the light. "Shame on you, Sam."

Occam let Muse go—flung her, in fact, toward Sam. Occam leaped into the car before Sam caught her. June jerked the gun up, intending to shoot the tires.

"Don't!" Sam grabbed her arm. "If they get out of that car, at least one of us is going to die."

The car sped off across the parking lot.

June screamed in rage.

Trina stood at the gate. "Oh my God," she gasped. "Jesus. Sam Haain. I knew I recognized you!"

Sam let go of Muse, and though she wobbled, she stayed upright, clutching her head. Her blond hair had turned bright red.

"Give me that," Sam said, holding a hand out to June.

June hesitated, but then handed over the gun. Sam clearly didn't want her to do anything crazy. Because she definitely wanted to do something crazy right now.

Instead, Sam did something crazy. He turned around and aimed the gun at Trina. She blanched.

"The game has changed," he said. "I'm not giving Occam the pleasure of winning. He's getting a standoff instead."

Chapter 12

Sam drove the car Aaron had supplied them with, Muse slumped in the passenger seat. June sat in the back with Trina.

"You can't kidnap me." Trina was a fuming ball of rage. "Just take this!" She picked up the folder from her lap. "This is what you want, not me."

Sam drove on in silence.

"This is outrageous." Trina huffed and dropped the folder back on her lap. "It's not like they can't just order another round of results. These aren't the only copies of his tests."

"Precisely." Sam glanced in the rearview mirror. "That's why we need you. Now it becomes a criminal matter. Now the police become involved. Now the project is put on hold, and Occam doesn't get the results."

June sat forward. "As long as he doesn't get the results, Micha doesn't do his part, and Occam doesn't give him back."

"He doesn't kill him, either. Because he needs him. As I said, it's a standoff."

"When does it end?" June held her hands up.

"When he gives Micha back and I turn the information over and let her go. Remember, I'm the smartest man in this city. Still."

Trina folded her arms. "I'll tell them who kidnapped me. I'll make sure everyone knows."

"So tell them." Sam shrugged. "They haven't found me yet. You don't know where I'm hiding."

June sat back and rubbed her eyes. "She will once we take her there." She wiggled her toes, brought back to the fact she was still in someone else's sweat pants, T-shirt, and wearing fuzzy blue hospital slippers.

"That's why we're not taking her there," Sam said. "It's not safe to go back right now, anyway. If your friend could find us, other people can. I'm sure Occam knows where we are now, too."

Megan Morgan

Sam took them to a motel—not as fancy as the place he hid them out when June first met him, just a nondescript no-tell motel along the side of the road. They already had a room booked.

The room was at least clean, with two double beds, a TV, a tiny bathroom, drab brown carpet, and nauseating floral wallpaper.

Muse sat on one of the beds with her head in her hands. Sam knelt in front of her.

"You should have your father send a doctor," Sam said softly to her.

Trina, though still seething, offered some advice. "Get a rag and clean the wounds first. Scalp wounds bleed a lot, but they're usually superficial."

"Occam really twisted someone's head off?" June asked.

"In a manner of speaking." Sam gently touched Muse's hair. "The head didn't actually pop off, but there was an internal decapitation. So I'm told. I wasn't there for it, but apparently Occam got in a fight and ended someone quite dramatically."

June shuddered. "You can just...do that to a person?"

"If you're determined enough." He turned his attention to Trina. "I need you to put some restraints on her, June."

Trina widened her eyes and backed away.

"He means mentally," June said. "I hope."

Trina tossed the folder on the bed and clamped her hands over her ears. She scurried backward and hunched against the wall, hands so tight over her ears her arms shook.

Sam stood. "She can't stay that way forever." He walked to the bathroom.

June sat on the bed next to Muse and waited, racked with guilt. Sam returned with a wet rag and started cleaning up Muse's head.

After a few minutes, Trina slid down the wall, whimpering, and took her hands off her ears. "Oh God," she choked out.

June picked her words carefully. "You will not try to escape this room as long as we're keeping you here." Her power flowed across her tongue, wrapping her speech. "You will not make any phone calls for help, or cry out to anyone outside, or hurt anyone in this room in an attempt to break free."

Sam had Muse's head in his lap, dabbing her scalp. "Tell her not to destroy the evidence, either."

"You will not try to destroy or dispose of the results." She eased her power back. "I think that covers it."

Trina slumped against the wall, staring at June with glazed eyes. June needed to gargle an entire bottle of mouthwash to wipe that sin away.

"I hate this." June got up. She had nowhere to go, though.

"Thank you," Sam said quietly.

As Trina suggested, Muse's wounds were superficial. Sam disguised himself and went out to get supplies and food. When he returned, he rubbed antibacterial ointment on Muse's head and wrapped her in a bandage, so she looked like a little vanilla ice cream cone. Trina sat in a chair by the window and didn't speak, watching them with a dull, depressed gaze.

"We'll see if Aaron can get us a better hiding spot tomorrow," Sam said, as they were making sleeping arrangements. "Of course, I'm hoping by tomorrow evening Occam will want to negotiate."

"I hope his negotiation doesn't involve sending us Micha's head in a bag," June said.

Sam and Muse took one of the beds. Muse had already fallen asleep on it after taking the painkillers Sam brought her. She twitched and shuddered in her sleep. Trina refused to get in the other bed with June, and June didn't blame her. June gave her a pillow and blanket, and she curled up in the chair. June got in bed but didn't expect to sleep.

She lay there, staring at the light from the bathroom stretched across the ceiling, the soft breathing around her a small comfort. Muse's breath hitched with each shudder in her sleep. The occasional car passed on the street. Once, footsteps passed by the door, and June held her breath until they were gone.

Eventually, she checked the clock. Ten after midnight. So many hours before dawn.

She pushed the covers back and quietly got up. She padded to the bathroom and closed the door to a crack.

She leaned, both hands on the sink, and stared into the mirror. The overhead light was harsh, picking out lines on her face she didn't know she had. Her eyes shone vivid green. Sam's words from months ago came back, when he'd told her vividly colored eyes betrayed strong powers. She couldn't hide them. They gave her away at every turn.

She sifted her fingers through her hair. Her light roots were a couple inches long, the black dye job on the rest faded. She placed her hand back on the sink and tilted her head. She looked old and tired. Her thirtieth birthday was coming up in a few months, though she had no reason to care. Where would she celebrate it, if she celebrated at all?

Would she even be alive to celebrate?

A movement caught her eye, and she jerked her head around. The door inched open and Sam peeked in.

"You all right?" he murmured.

"Define 'all right.'" She stepped back and motioned him in. "Come in, so we don't disturb the girls."

Sam pushed the door open, slid inside, and closed it behind him. His tired face was full of lines as well. His hair had gotten longer too, now past his shoulders. His eyes were intensely dark, but not preternaturally so, just natural dark brown.

"I couldn't sleep," she said. "You know how it goes. I felt rotten, doing that to Trina."

"Good."

She arched an eyebrow.

"It means you still have morals."

She shook her head. "I'm gonna let her have the bed. It's the least I can do. I'll just...sleep in here, I guess."

With that, she turned and stepped into the tub. She sat down on the cold, dry porcelain and stretched her legs out. She slumped against the sloped back.

"I haven't slept in a bathtub since college." Sam sat down on the side of the tub. "Comfy?"

She folded her hands on her stomach. "You know what they say, you do your best thinking in the bath."

"You shouldn't think too much. The more you think, the worse you'll feel."

"This feels like before, when Jason was trapped inside the Institute. Only now, I'm worrying about Micha and Jason. And Diego. And my mother."

"Life is just waiting for the next thing to worry about." He stood, but instead of leaving the room or sitting down on the closed toilet lid, he stepped into the tub as well.

June drew her legs up, frowning at him. Clearly, he wasn't kidding and fully intended to get in the bathtub with her, so she scooted to the side to give him room. He settled down on the other end. Being much taller than she, once he stretched out, he placed his bare feet next to her shoulder.

She had no choice but to drape her legs over Sam's hips. "This is absurd."

"Yes, it is." He winced and wiggled around. The taps were on the wall above him, but the faucet had to be right in the middle of his back. "I think we could use a little absurdity right now."

Being tangled up with him so intimately was weird, but not bad. Not bad at all.

"Are we going to stay here all night?" June asked.

"If that's what it takes."

She didn't ask what they were trying to achieve. She wasn't sure they would get to it, either.

Sam got out again and retrieved blankets and pillows from the room. She got out so he could make a thin mattress of sorts on the bottom of the tub with the blankets, except for one, and then they got back in. She was more comfortable than she would have expected, once she snuggled under the last blanket with a pillow behind her. Sam tucked a pillow between his back and the faucet.

They lay staring at the grungy tile above the shower. The outer room was quiet. Everything was quiet. So much, she heard someone cough in the room next door.

"What would you be doing right now if none of this had happened?" Sam asked.

She shrugged under the blanket. Sam's foot rested against her arm, shifting restlessly.

"I guess I'd still be tattooing people," she said. "Running my shop."

"It's something to own your own business."

She nodded. "Diego and I finally got our shit together and rented the building a couple years ago. It's a small space, but it works. And the apartment above it was open, so I rented that too and I live there. Then we took a couple artists on, and it's been going all right. We're covering the bills and turning a little profit."

"Is that all you ever wanted to do?"

"I guess. I was always an artist. Jason had his acting. I had my art. If I wasn't tattooing, I'd be doing something artistic." She paused. "I miss it, you know? Holding the gun. Putting ink under skin. Drawing isn't quite the same."

"I'll bet."

"What about you?" She stretched, shifting her knees across Sam's hips. "What would you be doing right now if none of this had happened?"

"Raising hell, I suppose." He waved vaguely. "Keeping the Paranormal Alliance on track. They have multiple chapters and run their own meetings, but once a year we have a big get-together and discuss the year ahead. That's coming up in a few months."

"Maybe you'll get to attend."

He snorted. "Do you know your darling Micha once called our gathering a 'meeting of the militia?' He insists were going about things the wrong way, even though we do the same things he does. We develop educational programs. We give to charities. We have outreach programs. But apparently we don't operate to his benevolent specifications."

"He really called you a militia?"

"If we were a militia, we would have taken over this city a long time ago."

"What do you do besides run the Paranormal Alliance? From what I hear, you've got some political influence. You obviously have money. Does that all come from the Paranormal Alliance? Or do you have a real job?" She couldn't believe she hadn't asked these questions before now. Somehow, discussing their personal lives seemed strange, in the midst of everything else.

"I'm actually a politician. I come from money. Groomed for the Ivy League, and that's where I ended up. Did damn well, too. By the time I got out of college I was in that circle of influence, the upper echelon of Chicago. I actually rubbed elbows with our illustrious President. I was planning to run for mayor, eventually."

She lifted her head and stared at him, stunned, and sort of awed, too.

"Surprised?" he asked.

"Yes." She dropped her head back. "And no. I can see you as a politician. So what happened? Why aren't you mayor now?"

"The thing about being in politics is you see way too much of the plight of the common man. You might think politicians don't care about the people they represent, but good ones do. It's just that sometimes it can get overwhelming, especially when the problems are coming from all sides, and some of them—most of them—are things you can't do anything about."

She listened, intrigued.

"My career was really getting started around the time the Institute opened. That was a hot subject then, hotter than it is now. The paranormal plight was on everyone's lips. I wasn't the only paranormal politician at the time, but I was the one most open about it, so a lot of the issues came my way. And I saw things. I saw the oppression and mistreatment. I saw the misrepresentation. I was harassed myself of course, but I didn't care as much about that as I did about seeing others abused and mistreated."

He sounded a lot like Micha, but she refrained from pointing that out.

"I had an intimate view of the inner workings of the Institute at the time, since they schmoozed with the city as much as possible, sliding their way in. I knew something wasn't right. I could see it. I could feel it in my gut. But when I started asking questions, people didn't like that. The founders of the Institute were powerful people. They had money and influence. Some had celebrity status. They were known and loved. They could fund bribes, buy their way in, apply the necessary charm. Their corruption started long before the doors ever opened."

"And that didn't sit well with you."

"Not in the least. There was a big movement at the time amongst the paranormal people to stop the Institute from opening, but it was faltering and weak. I'm good at organizing, so that's what I did."

"And thus the Paranormal Alliance was born. Wow…"

"Of course I knew my enemies would want me out of my position when I made that move, so I prepared. I'm good with money too, so I did a lot of investing. I made sure I could pay the bills and fund the organization before I quit my job. I've written a couple books since then, gotten a lot of attention around the world with paranormal people. They've kept my bank account full."

"A humanitarian and a scholar." She wasn't mocking.

"They call us zealous, and radicals, and we've gotten a reputation, but what of it? We help our own. We don't do things violently, even though we could. I couldn't leave politics completely of course. That's why I still hold a few positions. I'm like you, with your art. I itch for it. Micha claims they only tolerate me because of affirmative paranormal action, and that I strong-arm my way into everything. I say he can choke on my dick."

She wiped a hand over her mouth to hide a smile. "There's so much bickering, when you guys all ought to be on the same side. Like you and Aaron. You guys all hate the Institute, so why are you fighting each other? You're like rats in a cage, chewing each other's legs."

"It's not as bad as it used to be. We're starting to band together. But I'm never going to like your boyfriend and his holier-than-everyone attitude."

She tried to kick him in the side but succeeded in merely squeezing him with both feet. "I told you, quit calling him that."

"Pardon me, your fuck friend."

"Why do you keep bringing that up? Are you jealous?"

He adjusted the pillow behind him. "You wish."

"All this makes me realize I know so little about you. Are you married? Or have—someone? Like, is Muse…"

He narrowed his eyes. He had one arm on the side of the tub and drummed his fingertips against the porcelain.

"What?" She frowned. "It's a simple question."

"I'm not married. Nor have I ever been."

"All right." She searched her brain for another subject. "You told me before you're part Israeli."

"My grandfather came from Israel, yes. In nineteen forty-eight, to escape the Arab-Israeli war. He came to Chicago and started his own business, a printing company. He met my grandmother, an American woman, shortly after. She worked at her father's shop nearby. I've heard that great love story so many times." He made a disdainful face. "How the sunlight fell on her hair and blah, blah. His parents didn't like it because she wasn't Jewish."

"Your grandfather is Jewish?"

"A Hiloni Jew, yes. Which means he's not religious. Most Israeli people are Jewish, of various sorts. My father was raised up in the culture, but he abandoned it when he got older. There are parts of Judaism that still believe people with paranormal powers are influenced by dibbuk, evil spirits. My mother is a shapeshifter. They met in college. He couldn't abide by the idea that the woman he loved was evil."

"So I take it your father and grandfather don't get along?"

"They've had their differences over the years, but my grandfather was always proud of him, or at least it seemed that way. My father is very good at business. He's also involved in politics. I think that's why my brother and I—" He stopped short. "We were raised in it, and it's what we became."

"Your brother was a politician too?"

"He was working toward it." He patted his hand on the tub. "Like I said, we had money growing up. It got me the education I needed. My mother and father are in New York now. My father took a CEO position there. My grandmother is gone, but my grandfather is still here. He's tried to get me back to my roots before, even though my mother is a gentile and so I'm not considered Jewish." He drew a deep breath. "I never really accepted that culture anyway. It never accepted me."

"Yeah, I know the feeling of being an outcast."

The bathtub was a strange place for existential angst, yet here they were.

"I didn't grow up with money," she said. "Quite the opposite. After my parents divorced, my mother was always working. All I really had was Jason, well…I mean…" Her mind went to Katie, to the tattoo on her arm rather than any concrete memory. She hadn't told Sam about her dead little sister, but maybe someday she would, if he wanted to talk about his brother. "I was never really alone with Jason. That's the thing about having a twin, even a fraternal one."

The light over the sink buzzed. Her hand rested on her chest, her heart beating beneath her fingertips. The hard surface of the tub hurt her side, but the rest of her body was comfortable. Sam flexed his toes against her arm, and that tiny movement drew all her attention away from herself and the demons screaming in her head.

"So are we gonna sleep in here?" Sam asked.

"I'll be damned if I feel like moving."

Chapter 13

June opened her eyes. Muse stood over the tub, hair sticking up around the bandage, hands on her hips. She arched an eyebrow at June.

"Oh, man." June lifted her head and winced, her back and neck stiff.

Sam snored faintly at the other end of the tub. He'd turned onto his side, giving her more room. She'd slid down, her legs bunched to one side. The blanket had become twisted around both of them. Sam's pillow was skewed, his hair hanging over the edge of the tub. She had never seen his face look so relaxed.

She squinted up at Muse. "Seemed like a good idea at the time. That's how most of my experiences sleeping with guys are."

"I'm shocked." The corner of Muse's mouth jerked. "He rarely sleeps so soundly."

June sank back down in the tub. "If you gotta pee, go ahead." She grabbed the shower curtain and dragged it across the front of the tub. "There you go. Privacy."

June extracted herself from the tub shortly after, slowly and painfully. Sam woke with a start when she stood up.

"Morning." She wobbled as she got out. "God, my ass hurts."

Sam snorted and slid down in the tub, dragging his pillow with him. He settled on the bottom and pushed his pillow into the corner. "I've heard that before." He snuggled under the blanket.

"Behave." She reached up and jerked the shower curtain fully closed.

Trina had moved to the bed during the night. June tried to apologize again, but Trina still wouldn't speak to her.

Muse called her father to ask for his assistance in finding them a new place to hide. June told her to ask him to bring her some proper clothes, especially shoes. She couldn't run from bad guys in fuzzy blue hospital slippers.

"He'll get us somewhere safer," Muse told Sam after the phone call. "Someone is coming to get us at noon. We're supposed to leave the car here, and someone will pick it up."

Sam was rumpled and bleary-eyed, and it was strangely charming. He was always so put-together, even for as long as they'd been in hiding.

"Good." He ruffled his hair. "I'm going out for food. I'm starving."

June was too, and grateful Sam had spent enough time with her to know to bring back something she could actually eat. She was also glad they had a shapeshifter with them so they didn't starve.

Trina remained silent through the morning. She refused to eat. Waves of anger radiated off her.

"Is someone going to miss you at home?" June finally asked her. "Do you have kids? Are you married?"

Her eyes flashed. "So now you care?"

"I always cared. This is a crappy situation, and I'm sorry."

"I have a boyfriend. He's going to kick your ass."

"You can thank Occam for this," Sam said. "If he'd kept his word, I wouldn't have to do this."

"Look at it this way"—June cut Sam off before he made it worse—"we won't hurt you. Micha may not be so lucky. At least you ended up with the good kidnappers."

Trina huffed and fell back into stony silence.

Sam had brought back newspapers, so they could find out if their escapade the evening before had come to anyone's attention yet. They also turned the news on TV, but the reporters were just going on about more threats to the Institute from both SNC and Paranormal Alliance members. They also reported on a strange side story about a telepathic woman who had gotten pregnant and lost her powers as a result.

"That's weird," June muttered. "Like the baby sucked them out of her or something?"

Trina spoke up. "It's not unheard of. It's happened before. The baby's DNA can alter the mother's DNA. That's true of any pregnancy." She rubbed the bridge of her nose. "I really need a cigarette. It'd be nice if you could go get me some. Since you're the good kidnappers, and all."

"Smoking is a terrible habit," Sam said from behind a newspaper. "Just ask June."

Trina glared in his direction. "Maybe you can shoot me then, so I can quit too."

"My gun is in my bag," Sam said. "Don't feel like moving."

"Look, I really am sorry." June sat on Sam and Muse's bed, trying to give Trina her space. "We've been in this situation for months. We've gotten desperate."

Trina folded her arms. "What's really going on with Micha? Why does he have all those abilities?"

Sam lowered his paper. "Micha was a normal, but he fell victim to the Institute. They're trying to turn normal people into paranormal ones."

June raised her eyebrows at him.

He shrugged. "We need at least one scientist to know what's really going on. We need help."

Trina screwed up her face. "How could they even do something like that? How is that possible?"

"It's a long, complicated story." Sam returned to his paper. "They made a serum, and Eric Greerson injected Micha with it. Now he has a bunch of different powers. He's one of us now. Hooray."

"He can't control them, though," June said.

"So..." Trina unfolded her arms and sat up straight. "That's why you and Aaron Jenkins killed Eric Greerson?"

"Not really." Sam turned a page. "That was more self-defense."

"So the Institute is as corrupt as they say." Trina stared across the room.

"Even worse," June said.

"What does Occam want with Micha?" Trina asked. "I thought vampires kept to themselves?"

Since Sam didn't seem to mind her knowing the details, June went ahead and filled her in. "We have documentation on the serum. Micha is a guinea pig. We want the Institute to be investigated, but we need medical proof for Micha. Occam was our link to you guys. In exchange, he wants Micha to tell the public his wife's research is false."

"And how did you get involved in all this?" Trina asked.

"The Institute took my brother hostage. Remember the press conference back in January? That was Sam's idea, trying to get them to bring him out. We weren't at the Institute at the time, like they said—or at least, I wasn't. But things went downhill from there."

Trina frowned. "Why didn't you leave with your brother once you got him out?"

Sam dropped the top of the newspaper down, revealing his face. "Yes, June. Why didn't you leave?"

June glared at him. "It's complicated."

"Is it?" He continued staring at her.

"Yes, it is."

"Wow." Trina blinked a few times. "This is a lot of new information."

"Yeah," June said. "Some days I still can't believe it myself, and I lived it."

At noon, a long black car with tinted windows, much like Occam's car, arrived to pick them up. This was apparently the preferred transport for clandestine travel. Aaron was inside. He looked a little thinner than the last time June had seen him, four months prior. He was dressed impeccably as ever, though.

"Father," Muse said. "I didn't know you were coming. Isn't this dangerous?"

"I have news," he said. "I wanted to deliver it in person."

"Sounds ominous," Sam muttered.

After they pulled into traffic, Aaron spoke. The partition was up between the front and back of the car.

"The police are investigating what happened at the clinic last night," he said. "Your little kidnapping scheme."

"It was the only thing I could think to do at the time," Sam said.

"You'll be relieved to know the only thing they caught on camera was everyone leaving the building. Thankfully, the clinic isn't the Institute, and they turned over untouched footage without a hassle. Well, I say thankfully, but perhaps unfortunately. They saw you, Sam."

"Of course they did." Sam sounded unperturbed.

"And you," he said to June.

June shrugged. "So they know I'm still around? They're interested in me again?"

"I suppose they're interested in all of us. There's a problem, though—a wrench in your works, Sam. They didn't record the fight with Occam, as there weren't any cameras in that area. And because Miss Watson left with you, with the files, they came to the conclusion it was some sort of inside job."

"What?" Trina said sharply.

"I held a gun on her," Sam said.

"Yes. But they think it was for show. They think Miss Watson was working with you to get the test results out of there."

"That's outrageous!" Trina clenched her fists in her lap. "How could they think I had something to do with it? My reputation is spotless."

"I do admit it sounds staged," Aaron said. "Micha leaves with Occam. The rest of you leave behind him. It's clear you weren't supposed to be in the clinic, Sam, nor was Occam. There's nothing to prove you and Occam had a struggle inside. It looks like a heist."

Megan Morgan

Sam groaned. "Shit."

"Don't despair just yet, though," Aaron said. "There's more."

"Do tell," Sam said.

"The police wanted to know what was taken out of there. So the clinic gave them a copy of the test results."

"Then they know what's going on." June's stomach did a flip-flop.

"Yes," Aaron said. "Word through the wire is the FBI was called in on the investigation."

For a moment, they were silent. Sam sat up straight. "So the Feds are involved now. Just like we wanted."

June's spirits lifted. Maybe this was all about to end without any more stress on their part.

"Yes, but"—Aaron held up a finger—"Micha's test results only show he has paranormal powers. They don't show where they came from."

"They need the information we stole from the Institute," Muse said. "We have to get it to them."

"It's at the house." Sam's shoulders slumped. "We can't risk going there right now. I would bet my right arm Occam is watching the place. He's going to be one pissed off vampire when he finds out his plans are ruined."

June swallowed. "I hope he doesn't take it out on Micha."

"We have to figure out a way to get in the house," Sam said, "without anyone noticing."

"Looks like our first order of business is a brainstorming session," Muse said.

The car took them to an apartment building in a quiet residential neighborhood. Aaron explained it was another one of his secret places, and they would be safe there, providing they didn't go outside. In reality, this was the third place Aaron had hid them out, and they were still no closer to being "safe."

"I'm running out of places to hide you," Aaron said. "Try not to get yourself into any more trouble."

"Have Ethan get in touch with me," Sam said. "Don't tell him anything. I want to speak to him myself. I'm going to see if he can get some of his connections to dig around and find out what the FBI is doing with the test results."

The building parking lot was surrounded by a high fence, so they weren't exposed as they got out of the car. As June stepped out, a solution to their dilemma struck her. She whirled around. Sam was crawling out of the car behind her and he furrowed his brow.

"Oh my God," she said. "That's it. Ethan!"

"What?"

She could barely get words out in her excitement. "That day we talked to Ethan in the diner, downtown. You faxed him the documents. He has a copy."

Sam stared at her, his mouth dropping open. "Holy shit. Why didn't I remember that?"

Muse climbed out behind him. "You have a lot on your mind. Trust me, I know."

"I could just—" Sam held his hands out, eyes glittering. His next words were clearly "kiss you," but instead he grabbed June's head and did just that: a firm kiss, right on the lips.

He let go of her and she stumbled back, mouth tingling, cheeks hot.

"We have to get in touch with Ethan." Sam bent down and spoke into the car to Aaron. "Call him for me, tell him where we are. Tell him to come see me at once."

"We'll eventually have to answer to someone," Aaron said. "Even with the proof in hand. But this might get us on the right track." He leaned over and looked out of the car. "Good thinking, June."

"Thanks," she mumbled.

They walked toward the building, Sam leading the way. He hadn't had so much bounce in his step in months. "If Ethan does this for us, I'll finally let him into the Paranormal Alliance."

"He'll be thrilled, I'm sure," Muse said.

June followed them, licking her lips, cheeks still hot.

The apartment they were to be sequestered in was a small two-bedroom, a little cramped but much bigger than the hotel room. The place was furnished—simple, bland, but everything was clean and comfortable.

Aaron, as usual, promised he would have someone bring around groceries and supplies. They were the most pampered fugitives in history.

They turned the news on. June wished Occam would send Sam a message, preferably one that wasn't accompanied by any of Micha's severed body parts.

"My back still hurts from that tub," Sam complained as they sat on the couch.

"Mine too," June said. "Guess that wasn't our most brilliant idea."

"It was enlightening, though."

"Was it?"

Sam didn't reply. He picked up the remote and started flipping through channels.

"How's Muse's head?" she asked.

Muse had gone off to one of the bedrooms for a nap, Trina to the other. June had reinforced her commands so Trina wouldn't try to escape from the apartment, either. At least they had privacy there, so Trina could get away from June and brood in peace.

"She'll be all right, I think. Though I'm still going to cut Occam's balls off and feed them to him."

"Would they grow back?"

Sam knitted his brow. "I don't really know. I mean, they can survive and recover from grievous injuries, quickly even, but I don't know if a severed body part would completely grow back. Vampires have never been part of the Paranormal Alliance. There's very little literature and texts on them. They like their mystery, after all."

"Maybe we can do some experiments on Occam and find out. You know, in Rose's memory."

"I'm sure she'd be pleased."

Sam finally found a news station where the reporters were talking about their adventure the day before. The "medical record heist at Westside clinic," as they were calling it. They showed captured footage and pointed out Sam and Micha. Trina's kidnapping did seem put on, especially since everyone else seemed to go along with the event in peaceful fashion.

June's identity remained unconfirmed, as they only got the back of her head.

"They still don't care about me." She flung her hands in the air. "I'm still a ghost."

"It's for the best. Being anonymous is good. I wish I had that luxury sometimes."

"Maybe stop kidnapping people, then?"

Sam, of course, was the one the reporters were excited about. A host of Paranormal Alliance members got in front of the camera to proclaim whatever Sam had "heisted" from the clinic would certainly, ultimately prove his innocence.

"My darlings." Sam nearly swooned. "They're still on my side."

They flashed back to the news studio, where a woman concluded, "Researcher Trina Watson may have assisted in the theft, and at this time is still missing. Police are on the lookout for all individuals involved in this incident."

"They don't seem to know who Occam is," June said.

"Old vampires tend to keep their identities secret." Sam got up. "My followers are still out there. And they're right. This will clear my name, provided we can get the evidence in the right hands."

"And clear Micha, too. Show them once and for all he wasn't involved in his wife's death. Or kidnapped by the CIA."

"I hope Occam is watching this." Sam walked off to the kitchen.

She looked back at the TV. "I hope Occam doesn't feel negotiation is beneath him…"

* * * *

Later in the afternoon, a visitor arrived. June had seen Ethan only once since they'd gone into hiding at the penthouse Aaron initially kept them in. He was still slick and obnoxious and eager to do Sam's bidding.

"Aaron told me to bring you these?" Ethan held up a folder and handed it to Sam. "I made sure to get everything you sent me."

Muse had joined them in the living room. She and June stood back while Sam rifled through the papers in the folder.

"Good, good," Sam murmured. "Do you think you can deliver this to the people investigating what happened at the clinic yesterday? The ones who now have Micha's medical records?"

Ethan raised his eyebrows over his glasses. "You mean the FBI?"

"I know it's a risk. You might have to implicate yourself. They might ask if you know where I am. Are you willing to stand up against questioning? For me?"

June expected Ethan to leap around like an eager puppy, maybe hump Sam's leg, but he hesitated instead.

"I don't have the pull I used to." He pushed his glasses up his nose. "I'm not sure I have that kind of access these days."

"He writes for a tabloid now," Muse muttered from the corner of her mouth to June.

"All you have to do is take this to them." Sam held out the folder. "You can get it to them anonymously, of course, though I'd hate for someone to intercept it. I'd prefer it be put right in their hands by someone I trust. Otherwise, I would have mailed it to them long ago. It's sensitive information, and we have a lot of people breathing down our necks."

Ethan took the folder and drew a deep breath. "All right, Sam. This is the most important thing you've ever needed someone to do. I understand that. If you think I'm the man for the job, clearly I am."

"I'll make you a full member of the Paranormal Alliance. Hell, I might even make you an officer or something."

Ethan's demeanor shifted to the tail-wagging June expected. "That's all I've ever wanted, Sam. Even now, with you in exile, it's the greatest gift you could give me."

June wrinkled her nose.

Ethan tucked the folder under his arm. "I've spoken to people at the FBI before, when I was following stories. I'll make a few phone calls."

"You're absolutely sure you're willing to put yourself on the line like this?" Sam asked.

Ethan beamed. "Of course."

"Make sure they know this is connected to Micha's medical records."

"I certainly will." Ethan left.

Sam started pacing. He raked his fingers through his hair and clutched it.

"So, what?" June said. "Is there some sort of gauntlet you have to go through to get into the Paranormal Alliance? Do you have to put yourself in danger?"

"There's only one test." Sam stopped and jerked his head at Muse. "Her."

"Some people can't be read by telepaths," Muse said. "Ethan is one of them."

June nodded. "Ah, I get it. So he has to prove his loyalty instead. Is it like how you can't read Robbie?"

"Robbie is too powerful to be read." The corner of her mouth jerked. "He's different. He can put up walls I can't climb over. Ethan is simply wired so I can't read him. It happens."

"And when you can't be read by Muse," Sam said, "I don't trust you until you can prove I should."

June recalled the day they met on the pier, the way Muse read her mind to make sure she wasn't dangerous. *Did Sam trust me then, or did it take a while?*

"So what is Ethan?" June asked. "His power?"

"Pyrokinetic," Sam said.

June blinked a few times. "Like Micha's sister. Like…Micha."

"They're rare." Sam started pacing again. "But being special isn't good enough reason to trust a person. Muse, I trust. She's the only person in the world I trust completely."

June had once scoffed at the idea of Muse being Sam's "bodyguard." Now she couldn't imagine a better person to have in charge of their safety.

Muse could certainly hear that thought, and June's cheeks warmed.

Muse scratched delicately at her head. "Surface thoughts are sometimes loud and hard to miss. So thank you for the compliment. I'm going to take these bandages off and wash my hair. They're driving me mad."

June went to check on Trina. She was curled up on the bed in the second bedroom.

"Sam sent someone with the information to the FBI," June said from the doorway. "This should all be over soon."

Trina lifted her head. June couldn't tell for certain, but she looked like she might have been crying.

"And then we'll all be arrested." Trina spoke thickly.

"You won't be in any trouble." June stepped into the room. "You were kidnapped. We'll make sure they know you weren't helping us."

Trina propped herself up on one elbow. Her hair was pulled back in a sloppy ponytail and she'd taken her glasses off. Without them, she appeared younger and more vulnerable.

"Forgive me if I don't believe you." Her voice turned icy. "I don't know what's really going on here. You could be planning to dump me and let me face the music on my own."

June walked over to the bed. "Can I sit?"

"Could I stop you?"

"Retract your claws." June sat down on the edge of the bed. "I'm trying to be on your side."

"Except when you're playing with my mind."

"You asked me to, just the other day."

Trina huffed and rolled onto her back.

"Come on," June said. "You think I enjoy this?"

"I don't get it." Trina folded her arms over her chest. "Why didn't you go to the police a long time ago and explain what happened? Why didn't you—an innocent bystander, by your account—get the hell out of here and away from all this while you still could?"

"I told you. It's complicated."

She snorted. "I don't think it's complicated at all."

"Isn't it? Enlighten me."

"You're in love with Sam."

June widened her eyes, so big she must have looked like a startled lunatic. "I am not in love with Sam."

"Yes, you are."

"No."

"That's why you're not committed to Micha."

June rolled her eyes. "I'm not committed to anyone because we're all in mortal danger. This isn't exactly a romantic cruise we're on."

"Feelings are feelings; they don't follow rules. They happen when they happen. You can't control them."

"Who are you, Dr. Ruth?"

Trina sat up. "No. I'm a woman. Women understand each other."

"Yet strangely, I'm not getting you at all."

"I'm also good at reading people. I don't need to be a telepath to figure things out. It's important in my job to understand motivations. You might think it's all clinical, but understanding other human beings makes my work easier. Emotions and paranormal powers are strongly linked."

"Awesome. But I'm not in love with Sam. How are you even getting that?"

Trina eyed her closely, in a way that made June want to bolt from the room. "You admire him. You feel indebted to him for helping you. And at the same time, you really like him as a person."

"Have you met Sam Haain? Do you like him as a person?"

"I've only known him for a day, and he held a gun on me and kidnapped me."

"He does shit like that all the time."

"Yet you find it attractive."

June stood up. "I'm not here to have a whirlwind romance with anyone. I'm fighting for my life. That takes a lot of my focus."

"So why are you involved with Micha?"

"I don't know." She waved a hand. "That's complicated too. It's comforting. We've been through a lot together. Feelings are feelings and stuff. Didn't you just say that?"

"And if this all ended tomorrow, and you were completely safe, what would you do? Would you still be with Micha? Would you walk away from Sam?"

"We're not gonna be safe tomorrow." June walked to the door. "Why do you give a crap? I thought you hated me."

"Just passing the time. I'm bored."

"I'll get you a crossword puzzle book or something. Just—shut up!"

Their groceries and supplies arrived. June also got some new clothes and was finally able to change out of her hospital slippers. They continued watching the news as night fell. Sam's name was on everyone's lips. Eventually the words "extensive manhunt" flashed across the screen.

"We're in trouble." June was curled up on one end of the couch. "They're actively looking for us now. They know we're in Chicago."

"I'm not worried." Sam sat next to her. He had a cup of microwave noodles and held a steaming forkful over the container. "Ethan will have the information to the FBI by morning. They'll have proof of what's going on."

"If they do catch us," Muse said on the other side of him, "do we do the cyanide capsules, as discussed?"

June gasped.

Sam glanced at her. "It was a joke." He crammed the noodles in his mouth.

She picked up a pillow from the couch and flung it at him. "Neither of you are fucking funny!"

Paranormal Alliance members were still adamant Sam was innocent. SNC members threw their opinion in as well, which was the same. At least someone believed in them.

As the night wore on, June's nerves grew thinner and more stretched.

"There's no word from Occam yet." She fidgeted. "We have to make sure Micha gets pulled out of the flames before this fire gets out of control. I wish he'd get in touch with us."

"He will," Sam said.

"When, exactly?"

As if June had said a cue, her question was answered. Sam was right: vampires were good trackers. Occam proved this by showing up at their living room window—their second story living room window—and letting himself in with a hammer applied directly to the glass.

Chapter 14

"You moved today and put me off your scent," Occam said as he climbed in the window. "Otherwise…" He leaped over the pane and landed with both feet on the floor. "I would have had this in your skull by now." He spun the hammer in his hand.

Sam stood glaring, broken glass strewn on the carpet in front of him. June did the sensible thing and backed away.

"I knew you'd find me," Sam said.

"Did you?" Occam continued spinning the hammer, eyebrows raised. "You pissed me off, Sam."

"You pissed me off too, Occam."

"Everything could have gone smoothly." Occam pushed a hand in his pants pocket.

June stiffened.

He pulled out something small and shiny gold. "Everything could have gone according to plan, but you had to go and complicate things."

Without looking at her, Occam tossed the object at June. She flinched, jerking a hand up to catch it.

Then she saw what it was. "Oh my God."

Micha's wedding ring.

She lunged at Occam, blind rage clouding her reason. Muse grabbed her arm.

"Don't play into it." Muse's grip was surprisingly strong. "If he'd really done something to him, he would have brought a body part."

June still panicked. Her side ached, as it always did when she got stressed out.

"This could have been simple, yes," Sam said. "But you and your harpies decided to take Micha hostage. You made this difficult, Occam."

"I'm only assuring his part of the deal is upheld." He kicked a shard of glass toward Sam. The piece bounced off the tip of Sam's shoe and skittered away. "You've messed things up worse than you know."

"By kidnapping a researcher and bringing attention to Micha's tests results?" Sam snorted. "No, Occam, I call that cutting out the middle man. Or, the middle vampire."

"There're two parts to that, isn't there?" Occam said. "Micha's test results, and the documentation on the serum."

"Which I've just sent to the FBI, actually, via one of my Paranormal Alliance members. You know, the ones I'm so out of favor with?"

This should have been a smack in the vampire's smug face. However, after a momentary pause, Occam started laughing. "It wouldn't happen to be the reporter I saw leaving here earlier, would it?"

"So you've been spying on us." Sam put his hands on his hips. "Not surprised."

"I love your genius, Sam Haain. You're almost as smart as you are attractive."

"You are the foulest creature in this city," Muse said.

"And your master is the stupidest," Occam replied. "He's stuck his foot in it so deep, the alligators will chew his leg off in no time, and he doesn't even realize it."

"What are you talking about?" June asked.

Occam turned his attention to her, his eyes blazing and bloodshot. "I told you, Little Red. Vampires observe. We know everything that goes on in this city, every little secret you try to hide from each other." He looked back at Sam. "Everything the Institute does. Everything your insipid organizations get up to. All the inner machinations you could only wish to know. We're much older, wiser, and more powerful than any other paranormal being. You should respect us."

"Are you going to jerk off all over the floor, too?" Sam spread his arms, indicating the glass.

"Always so quick to ridicule, Sam. So quick to jump. We vampires know the value of waiting. We can afford to. Patience is a virtue." He flashed his fangs. "We will watch you destroy each other. Then we'll step up and take our rightful spots as owners of this city without ever having to lift a finger."

"So why are you messing with Micha?" June asked. "That isn't being neutral."

"Because he benefits us. That which benefits us is our concern."

"What he has inside him will shut the Institute down," June said. "Don't you want the Institute shut down? Send him back to us and let us do this."

"I don't care what happens to the Institute." He strolled over to her. She took a step back. "In the end, if he won't do what we want, he'll become our plaything. We've already had some fun with him." He smirked at her hand, where she was clutching the ring.

"Take me instead," she pleaded. "I'll be your insurance policy, until he tells them Rose's research is fake. I'll stay with you until it happens."

Occam tilted his chin up, eyes glittering with interest.

"Please," she said, lowering her voice. "Take me with you. Send him back."

"No." Sam stepped forward. "You're not going anywhere, June." He glowered at Occam. "What did you come here for? To kill us? To make me pay for my insolence?"

Occam turned toward him, the movement fluid and creepy. "Why yes, I was going to kill you."

Muse circled around Occam, her eyes hard little pinpoints as she focused on him. He seemed to be ignoring her.

"But now I've decided," Occam said, "that would be no fun. I wouldn't get to watch you, and Aaron Jenkins, and the Institute all tear each other to itty-bitty shreds while we lap up the blood. While we sit back and wait for our turn in the spotlight."

"Always looking out for number one," Sam said. "And as if you could kill me."

"Sam." Occam chuckled. "Do you really think I didn't bring some friends with me? Even when you think a vampire is alone, we never are. But like I said, I'm not going to kill you, now that I'm clear on what you've done. I came here to take you down and found you digging your own grave."

June's stomach clenched. Occam's words from yesterday popped into her head—how he seemed to know where Robbie was, how he claimed Sam's operatives had been working against him inside the Institute.

"What are you talking about?" June asked. "What do you know?"

Occam turned back to her. "Oh," he whispered, sounding pleased and reverent. "There we are, finally. I knew you were the smart one."

"What's going on?" June held his gaze.

"I wouldn't be neutral if I told you."

"Don't get sucked in, June," Sam said. "He's lying."

The taunting glint in Occam's eyes and the smile curling his lips said otherwise.

"You should let her go with me," Occam said, speaking to Sam but still looking at June. "She wants to."

"She's not going anywhere with you," Sam said.

"There are many sides to this," Occam said to June, "the poor, plighted paranormal people's side, the Institute's side, the fanatic's side. The right side to be on is no side at all. That's where the smart money is. And I think you're a woman who likes to invest wisely, aren't you, June Coffin?"

Maybe Occam had some Siren in him.

"Enough of this." Sam stepped forward, the glass crunching under his feet. "She's not going anywhere with you, Occam."

"I'm not in any hurry." Occam waved a languid hand. "I still have a few strings I can pull her toward me with. If one doesn't work, another will. What strings do you have, Sam? You'd better tug hard before you lose her."

The whisper of metal on metal sounded behind Occam. Muse had drawn her curved blade, the one she'd sliced Robbie's face with at the press conference.

"How fast do you think the other vampires can get up here?" she asked. "Faster than I can open your throat?"

Occam didn't move or react. Nor did vampires instantly fill the room. Occam bowed his head, laughing quietly.

"She hasn't got much time left," he said, looking sideways at Sam. "What will you do without her, I wonder? But then, you haven't got much time left, either."

Occam spun around, jerking his arm out to block Muse's blow as she brought the knife down in a swift arc. The blade stopped inches from Occam's throat.

Occam grabbed Muse by the arm, holding the knife, and spun her around, so she ended up behind him, and flung her at Sam. He caught her and she snarled, the two of them stumbling back.

"You're all doomed." Occam rushed to the window.

Muse charged after him again, knife lifted.

June yelled, "Stay!" Her power vibrated the air.

Muse stopped in her tracks, wide-eyed, teetering in place. She dropped her arm and gawked at June.

Occam was half out the window, one leg still inside. He paused as June ran over to him.

"Give me your word," she said, "that you'll bring Micha back in one piece."

"Why should I?"

"Why shouldn't you? Once he's benefitted you, he's nothing. Throw him back to us. Let us all eat each other. Don't get involved in this war."

Occam stared into her eyes.

"Your word," June said. "Give it to me, Occam. Please."

Why was she asking this of a vampire? Why did something inside her whisper to try it, that it might work?

"Occam…"

"Very well," he said. "In one piece." He looked her over. "I found something I want more than him, anyway."

With that, he dropped out of sight.

For a moment, June stared at the blank spot where he'd been. Then she turned to Muse, who was still standing in place.

"You can move now," June said.

Muse sagged, like a soldier coming out of attention. "What the hell are you doing!" she railed at June.

"Saving our asses. You put that blade in him and fifty vampires would have been up here carving us into bite-sized pieces. Do you think he was bluffing about that?"

Sam gripped Muse's arm. "You shouldn't have done that, June."

"Someone has to do something sensible." June gnashed her teeth. "Act like the smartest man in the city, and stop taking stupid chances!"

Sam strode over to her. "What the hell was he talking about?" He got in her face. "About me digging my own grave? You seemed to know."

"I don't know." She gestured at Muse. "Read my mind! I'm telling the truth. It's something about Robbie, I think. He knows where he is. Occam visited me at the clinic and was talking all this cryptic shit about how Robbie is more powerful than we think."

Sam looked at Muse. She nodded slowly, uncertainty in her eyes. Doubt was a new look for her, and it didn't suit her.

"We have to be careful," June said. "I think we're in danger. But Micha will be all right. Or at least, he'll come back with everything attached. Occam won't break his word to me."

"You trust a promise from a vampire?" Sam asked.

"Yes. He wants my favor."

Sam turned away. "This is ridiculous." He walked across the room, kicking at the glass, and stalked into the kitchen.

"Everyone all right?" Trina asked, peeking around the corner from the hallway. She flinched as Sam slammed something in the kitchen.

Muse tucked the knife in her belt. "No." She turned and stalked off to the kitchen as well.

Trina crept out.

"We should let you go," June said to her. "Something bad is going to happen, and you shouldn't have to be involved in it."

Trina stopped in front of June and looked down at the ring in her hand. "You should come with me."

June closed her fingers around the ring and swallowed.

"But I understand," Trina said. "It's complicated."

* * * *

June couldn't sleep—not just because she let Trina have the bed and was curled up in a chair in the corner of the bedroom. She could have been stretched out on the most comfortable bed in the universe, the mattress stuffed with the feathers of angels, and she wouldn't have slept. Her mind kept pulling out ideas about every horrible thing that could possibly happen to her body, in various ways, at the hands of various people. When it tired of that, it moved on to picturing these things happening to people she cared about.

She got up and walked out to the living room.

A light was on, and Sam sat in a chair by the broken window. He was sprawled, elbows on the arms of the chair, fingers steepled beneath his chin. June padded to the couch and flung herself down on it. She stretched out.

The TV was off, the room silent. The lack of reporter's voices was refreshing.

"Keeping watch?" she asked.

"I guess."

Pieces of glass still littered the carpet. Sam had kicked most of it into a pile by the window, but small shards still glinted in the thick weave. One of them could have found a broom and swept it up properly, but housekeeping was low on everyone's list of priorities.

"Normally," June said, "I'd tell you to quit worrying and get some sleep, but I think there's a lot to worry about."

She twisted Micha's ring on her finger, too big for anything but her middle finger without it slipping off. She wouldn't keep it anywhere else, for fear of losing it.

"You've actually never told me that," Sam said.

"What?"

"You said 'normally' you'd tell me that. But you've never actually said that to me."

She shrugged. "Seems like something you're supposed to say in these situations."

The night outside the broken window was quiet, apart from the distant sound of traffic. Were any vampires lurking out there, watching them? Probably.

"Occam wants you," Sam said.

"Yes."

"He wants to make you a vampire."

She tensed. "You think so?"

"It's obvious."

She rolled her head to the side, to look at him. "You've known that for a long time, haven't you?"

He narrowed his eyes. "What?"

"You and Aaron sent me to talk to the vampires because you knew if they took offense to your begging, they'd have me as a consolation prize. So no skin off your back, either way."

Sam lowered his hands. "That is not the reason we sent you."

"Bullshit."

"Aaron suggested something like that could happen, but it wasn't a desired outcome for either of us. I never wanted you to be made into a vampire. Neither did he."

"I was a tactic with a built-in insurance policy." She sat up. "You sent me to be snacked on."

"No, I didn't." He lurched forward. "If that were the case, I would have let you go into Old Town by yourself. But I went with you, didn't I?"

"Really? You swear you didn't send me to be turned into a vampire?"

"I swear to you, June."

"What do you swear it on?"

He pressed his lips together. "Seriously?"

"Seriously. Because right now, I'm not sure I can trust you."

He stared at her, face sagging. He blinked a few times. "Why do you think you can't trust me?" He lowered his voice.

"Because you keep telling me you're the smartest man in the city, but there's all these things going down, all these things you didn't notice before, and they're putting us in danger. You didn't cover your ass as well as you thought you did."

"So you don't trust me because of the situation I've been thrust into? Because people are working against me? How the hell is that my fault?"

She swung her legs off the couch. "You missed everything leading up to this. You missed Robbie. He was right under your nose."

"Yes. A charlatan. A powerful one. Who I didn't know about because he made sure I didn't." He got to his feet. "Stop blaming me for something that was out of my control. Do you think you could have found a snake hiding in the grass? Do you think a man like Robbie lets anyone know what he's up to before he's damn good and ready?"

"I just want to believe I'm not expendable to you."

Sam walked over to the couch. She shrank back as he leaned over her, clamping his hands on the back of the couch on either side of her head. He bent down, his hair sweeping around his face, and stared into her eyes.

"I did not set you up." He spoke low and succinctly. "I did not send you to the vampires with the idea they could use you as a teething ring if things didn't work out. That's why I went to Old Town with you, to make sure you were safe."

She gazed up at him, plastered to the couch. "You swear it."

"I swear it on my life." He paused. "I swear it on Muse's life."

She breathed slowly, in and out through her nose.

"And I didn't use Micha as a bargaining chip," he said. "He's the most valuable player in this game."

She squeezed her right hand into a fist. The ring was cool against her palm.

"I know you care about him." The corner of his mouth jerked, the way Muse's did, an involuntary tic. "I'll do everything in what little power I still have to get him back for you."

She sank against the cushions.

"Occam's a lot scarier than the Institute," he said. "Micha would be safer behind their doors." He lowered his head. His hair obscured his face. "If the vampires fought the Institute, that place probably would have crumbled a long time ago."

"Maybe." She turned her face to the side. "Or maybe their power does come from their neutrality. Maybe without it, they wouldn't be what they are. I mean, picking a side means picking a cause, and your own cause gets drowned out by that."

Sam lifted his head.

"I wish they'd like our cause." He pushed away from the couch and stood in front of her.

"What is Occam?" she asked. "Is he a leader? Is he in charge?"

"Vampires don't really have that kind of structure in their society. The oldest most obnoxious ones just manage to boss the other ones around."

"So he's the biggest loudmouth."

"I guess. Like everything else about them, they tend to keep the exact details from outsiders." He locked eyes with her again. "He's right about Muse, though." A hint of desperation edged his words. "She's losing her dexterity. If she were in her prime, Occam wouldn't have dodged her like that, and he wouldn't have been able to grab her at the clinic. She's not reacting fast enough. Her perception is muddled."

June held her tongue. She had tried to comfort people before and failed. The smartest thing she could do when someone was baring their anguish to her was keep her mouth shut.

"I don't know what I'm going to do without her," Sam said.

She looked down at her clenched hand.

"When I met her," he said, "I underestimated her, like everyone does. She was different then. She was young. She was…full of passion, the same drive I had in me. Now she's tired, jaded. She's seen too much. We both have."

Muse had once told her Sam wanted a poster child for his cause, someone to let the masses look upon and feel sorry for. Maybe what he really needed was a partner, since his current one was dying.

She tried to pull something out of her brain that wouldn't make her sound like an idiot, nor belittle Sam's anguish. She kept it simple. "I'm sorry."

He snapped out of his reverie. "Let's not preemptively grieve. We have lots of other things on our plate right now. This is really not your worry."

"I happen to like her too."

"You should try to get some sleep. Isn't that what you're supposed to say?"

She sat up. "Sleep? What's that? I haven't had much lately."

"We can get in the bathtub, if you like."

She rubbed her face. Her eyes stung. Her head hurt. "What good would sleep do, anyway?"

"It'll make the morning come faster."

"What amazing thing is supposed to happen when the dawn arrives, exactly?"

"I'm trying to be optimistic here. You could at least play along."

She opened her hand and gazed at the ring on her finger. "I'm not sure I'm any good at optimism."

He kicked a shard of glass on the carpet. "You any good at poker? I found a deck of cards. We can do that instead of sleeping."

"Too bad we don't have any money." She smirked. "I'd clean you out."
"I do have my clothes."

Chapter 15

June lay in bed next to Trina, a tentative truce between them allowing June to enjoy half the bed. Despite the world's belief to the contrary, she hadn't been in bed with another woman since she was a kid, hiding out in her mother's room pretending she had a nightmare. Right now, she wanted her mommy more than ever, wanted to curl up next to her. She wanted her mother to stroke her hair while she read one of her romance novels.

She'd never admit this childish longing, even to Jason. Especially since in their eighth year, Jason had found out over breakfast she spent the night in their mother's bed. He called June a "scaredy-cat butt baby." June hit him in the face with a bowl of Cheerios, milk included. June's loving, comforting mother then turned into a bitch, putting her in time-out for an hour.

She didn't need any more scenes like that.

Morning seeped through the window across the room, casting dull light into the shadows. Trina breathed slow and even beside her, beneath the covers, June on top. June was still too wired, too tense to sleep. She'd learned to function on minimal rest, ever alert, waiting for the next bad thing to happen.

She twisted the ring on her finger. Worse than not being able to sleep, worse than waking up next to a woman who wanted to smother her with a pillow, was not waking up next to Micha after having him there, every morning, for months.

Where was he this morning? How was he feeling? Was he restrained? What did vampires do with human prisoners during the day?

She slipped the ring off and lifted it to the light, the gold gleaming faintly. Real gold, not cheap painted crap that would turn someone's finger green. Micha had kept wearing it, despite his anger and outrage, and she never questioned him about it. Maybe he, like her, held out hope things weren't what they seemed.

Something moved in the corner of her vision. Something familiar.

She sat bolt upright before her mind fully processed what she'd seen. However, when she looked into the shadows on the other side of the room, nothing was there.

She knew what she'd seen, though. Rose.

Trina stirred, mumbling in her sleep, and settled down again. June's heart thumped in her ears.

No ghost. Maybe she was imagining things. Maybe the lack of sleep was catching up to her.

She slowly lay back down, still vigilant, scanning the room. The night June had first seen Rose, when she'd awakened in Sam's hotel suite to find the lost spirit standing over her, was the beginning of a nightmare. Everything Rose said eventually made sense, but she could have just sent messages via Ouija board or something. June didn't need to see her.

She held the ring up again and turned it in her fingers, trying to guess the size. Micha had some thick fingers. She knew that all right.

Like a punishment for her inappropriate thoughts, Rose appeared, whole and vivid, at the end of the bed.

June jerked upright again and scrambled back against the headboard. By the time she plastered herself to it, Rose had disappeared once more.

"What are you doing?" June said into the empty room. "What's going on?"

Trina stirred again and rolled over, her back to June.

This time it couldn't be her imagination. Rose had been standing right there, clear as day. Clearer than she'd ever been.

"What the hell?" June whispered.

After a few minutes, in which Rose didn't reappear, June looked down at the ring, frowning.

She pinched the ring between her thumb and index finger and held it aloft, pointed at the end of the bed.

Like a projector flickering on, Rose appeared.

She looked as she always did: pale, lifeless, still. However, this time she stared at the ring in June's hand, instead of at June. The air around the bed grew chilly.

"Holy shit," June whispered.

She could apparently summon Rose at will now, using the ring. This would be useful if it meant she didn't show up any other time, only when June wanted her.

"Can you hear me?" June asked. "Can you understand what I'm saying?"

Rose lifted her blank gaze to June's face, her eyes seeming both unseeing and all observing at the same time. This was the first time she responded in a manner suggesting sentience, and it was super creepy.

"They got Micha," June said. "But I'm gonna get him back. Can you like, see if he's okay?"

"Beware of what he's offering," Rose said, in her airy, nerve-jangling, whispery voice. "He has more to use against you than you realize."

Still being all weird and cryptic. But then...

"Occam is a clever vampire." Her voice changed, growing almost companionable, almost human. "Many vampires are. They enjoy toying with non-vampires. I found that the most difficult part of working with them."

June nearly dropped the ring. "You're actually communicating with me. You understand me."

"I'm attached to you. I can't leave your side to find out if Micha is all right."

"Why are you attached to me?" June sat forward, still scared, but eager to get this opportunity. "Is it because I was there with you when you died? Or is it because I'm...with Micha?"

"You're the only hope I have of leaving a good name in this world. You have to find out the truth, about what I was forced to do at the Institute."

"Lady, I got enough problems without avenging the dead."

"You must learn the truth." She drifted closer, passing through the bed, a wave of cold preceding her.

June shrank against the headboard again.

"You must discover how I was a means to their end," Rose said.

"Why don't you just tell me what they did?" June's voice shook. "Cut out the middle man and save me a bunch of work."

She drew closer, and June panicked. She scrambled off the bed with a yelp. In the process, she dropped the ring on the floor. Rose vanished.

Her flailing woke Trina. She rolled over and lifted her head.

"What are you doing?" Trina's voice was thick with sleep.

"Nothing." June's heart pounded and her side ached. "I just had a bad dream."

Trina sagged against the bed. "Oh." She tugged the blankets up around her chin. "Man, it's cold in here."

June snatched up the ring and placed it on the bedside table. "Yeah, it is."

She didn't have a hope in hell of going back to sleep, so she went out to the living room and turned on the news, trying to calm her nerves—the irony of the news calming her down was not lost on her. The morning air flowed cool through the broken window.

June gradually relaxed. She'd left the ring in the bedroom, not wanting a repeat performance. Somehow, even though Rose was much more forthcoming now, June had a ton more questions than answers.

About a half hour later, Muse padded out of the bedroom she and Sam were sharing. She wore a white T-shirt, too big to be one of her own, and her white leggings. June tried not to wonder if she and Sam had sex—those surface thoughts were easy to read, after all.

"Didn't wake you with the TV, did I?" June asked.

"No. I can't sleep."

"Join the club."

Muse went to the kitchen. June joined her after a few minutes. Muse was making coffee.

"I'm sorry about yesterday," June said. "About throwing a spell on you. I was just trying to protect us."

Muse glanced up, the corner of her mouth jerking. She looked back down at the coffee she was spooning into a filter. "I acted rashly. You were right to do what you did. Occam isn't a pleasant creature. He tends to bring out the worst in me."

June leaned against the counter, her back to it, gripping the edge. "How much do you know about ghosts?"

"Rose appeared to you again."

"Yes."

"No one knows much about ghosts, not even the people who study them. Ghosts are cryptic. Sometimes they seem completely purposeless. There are different types, but they're all a mystery."

"What types of ghosts are there?"

"Well, let's see." She scrunched her face up. "There are residual ones, which are like recordings on the fabric of reality, I guess you'd say. They're not real so much as memories, and you can't interact with them. They're the annoying ones who open and close doors and walk up and down the stairs every day at the same time."

"And the ones who aren't just annoying memories?"

Her eye twitched. "That's what you're dealing with, an intelligent one. A clinger, actually."

"Yeah, she's clinging all right."

"You saw her die. That's probably what made her latch onto you."

"Why me? There were other people there. Hell, she could have latched onto Jason."

"You're wishing a ghost on your brother?" She opened the cupboards above her head and took out a coffee cup. "You want some?"

"Yeah, sure. And no, I'm not. But what's so special about me?"

"It's hard to say. Ghosts don't follow rules. It sounds like she has unfinished business. Ghosts with unfinished business can be persistent."

"Can they get attached to objects?"

Muse side-eyed her. "Like Micha's ring, you mean?"

"I'm sure you can see everything that just happened in my head." June let go of the counter and turned toward her. "So come on with it."

"Something that was personal to her, something they had an emotional connection to—yeah, she could be controlled by it. Makes it easier to communicate."

"That's the first time she's ever spoken to me directly. She responded to my questions. She used whole sentences."

"So you've had a breakthrough. Congratulations."

"Just what I want." June rubbed her forehead. "Awesome."

Muse was silent. She dumped a bunch of sugar into her cup.

"Is sugar and caffeine good for you?" June asked. "I mean with your… thing."

Her face was calm and smooth, but then her mouth jerked to the side, violently, and she bared her teeth. June was struck with a quiet mixture of horror and pity.

"I'm coming apart." Muse added more sugar to the cup. "I'll drink whatever the hell I want. I don't have enough time left to worry about crap like that."

"I just thought you might be more comfortable without anything agitating it."

She snorted wetly, a lot like the sound the coffee maker produced as it percolated.

"When Rose visits you"—grimness tinged Muse's voice, a tone she'd used once before, when they were trapped in a tiny, featureless room at the Institute—"does she seem self-aware? Like she knows what's going on around her?"

"Not really, not before today. She looks and acts—dead. She's just a shell."

Muse picked up her cup and turned away. "I see." She went to the refrigerator and pulled out a carton of milk.

"I don't think"—June hesitated—"it's a good way to spend the afterlife. Not everyone becomes a ghost, right? I think actually finding peace would be the better option."

Muse kept her back turned to June.

"You just told me," June said, "we don't understand ghosts. So maybe death isn't as bad as we think, either. We're just afraid because we don't know."

Muse turned around. "Well, it's something we all have to do someday, isn't it? Some of us sooner than others." She flashed June a tight smile.

"Maybe. But for all of us, it could be sooner than we know."

"That's not very comforting, is it?"

June sagged. "I guess not."

June went back to the living room and sat down in front of the TV. Muse remained in the kitchen. The silence was heavy and sad.

Muse brought her a cup of black coffee a few minutes later. June took it from her trembling hand. Was the tremor produced by her condition or her state of mind?

"How did you know I like it black?" June asked.

Muse snorted and sat down beside her. "Really?"

"Guess it's a surface thought, huh?"

"As soon as you saw me brewing coffee your preference popped up, like a bubble on the surface of a lake. You're not even aware of it."

What other things popped up to the surface? Much more than June wanted to know about, probably.

"I'd like to learn how telepathy works," June said. "It seems interesting."

"I've had it all my life, and I doubt I could explain it. You can either do it, or you can't."

They sipped their coffee and watched the morning news. In the middle of a story about a carjacking, the screen suddenly cut away and a perky newswoman popped on.

"Breaking news," the woman said, with barely-contained excitement. "Members of the Paranormal Alliance—the group led by the infamous Sam Haain—have convened for what appears to be an impromptu meeting, perhaps a protest, in Jackson Park, between South Lakeshore and the East Lagoon. We'll get cameras out there and bring you first-hand coverage as soon as possible."

June looked at Muse.

"A meeting?" Muse said.

"A protest."

"We need to wake Sam up."

Chapter 16

June ran to the hallway. She almost knocked on Sam's door, but pushed it open instead. No time for politeness.

The room was muted in shadow, sparsely furnished like the other bedroom. Sam lay on one side of the double bed, on his stomach, in jeans and shirtless. Despite the news, June stopped short. The sinuous, dusky curve of his back and the span of his broad shoulders occupied her attention for a moment. He had his face turned away, and his hair scattered across the pillow, one arm dangling off the bed.

"Sam." She touched his shoulder. His skin was warm and damp with sleep sweat. "Sam, wake up. Something is—"

Sam slept so close to the edge of the mattress with one arm dangling off it for a reason, apparently. Lightning fast, he snapped his head up, grabbed the shotgun on the floor—unnoticed by her until that moment—and flipped over, pointing the barrel at her.

She backpedaled, hands up. "Jesus Christ! It's just me. Damn!"

He lowered the gun and dropped it on the bed next to him.

"Are you out of your mind?" he snarled. "Sneaking up on me in my sleep? I could have blown your head off!"

"I wasn't sneaking up on you!" She pointed toward the living room. "Something is going on. You need to get out here."

He sat up, placing a hand on the gun. "Is it Occam again?"

"No, I don't know what it is. You don't have to bring your gun. It's on TV."

"I'd love to shoot the TV."

He didn't bother with a shirt and hurried out to the living room after her. She got an eyeful of his sculpted chest and flat, tight abs. His body was nice as hell, his skin tanned and mostly hairless. She stifled her hormones. Bigger things were going on right now.

Muse stood in front of the TV, hands clasped to her chest. The newscasters were nattering back and forth.

"The Paranormal Alliance is gathering in Jackson Park," Muse said. "Some sort of meeting or protest. They're getting cameras out there."

"Why didn't I know anything about this?" Sam demanded.

"Probably because you're in hiding?" June said.

"Aaron should have known something was about to go down and informed me, though."

"Maybe my father didn't know anything," Muse said. "Maybe it's spur-of-the-moment."

Sam pushed his hair back from his face. "Get me some coffee."

June looked at Muse, unsure whom he was addressing. Muse didn't move.

"Yes, master." June scowled and walked to the kitchen.

Twenty minutes later, news crews finally arrived at Jackson Park. In that time, Sam sucked down two cups of coffee, and Trina emerged from the bedroom and sat on the arm of the couch. They were all silent, except for Sam occasionally swearing under his breath at the reporters to get on with it.

The first shot of Jackson Park showed a grassy field full of people. Some were holding signs. They were shouting. A reporter named Jack Johnson told the viewers the Paranormal Alliance was gathering for an unknown reason, in an ominous tone suggesting everyone should pack their children in their minivans and get out of the city before the miscreants blew it up.

He pulled a person over for an interview. June perked as a woman with vibrant red hair stepped into the frame.

"Cindy!" June said.

"That's my girl." Sam clenched his fists.

"My name is Cindy Preston," she told the viewing audience. "We're here today to protest on behalf of Sam Haain and demand the police investigate the incident at the Institute, which has led to his current state of persecution."

"So well-spoken," Sam said.

"I have a feeling she practiced that," June said.

"You're here today to demand justice for your deposed leader?" Jack asked.

"Sam Haain is not an assassin." She put her hands on her hips. "He's not a boogeyman. He's not some cold-blooded killer. He was set up. The Institute has been doing terrible things to paranormal people and conducting dangerous experiments. It's time someone investigated this properly."

"What does the Paranormal Alliance intend to do here today, Ms. Preston?"

"We intend to stand here and shout until someone listens. We're going to protest. We're going to raise hell. We're not leaving until someone tells us they'll do something about this mess."

"Do you have any idea of the whereabouts of Mr. Haain, Ms. Preston?"

"Hopefully he's not in this hellhole of a city." She advanced on him, dwarfing him with her Amazonian size. "Wherever he is, I hope he sees this. I hope he sees the support we're giving him. We don't believe in the image you guys are trying to portray."

Jack was slowly backing away from her. "You don't believe he participated in the murder of Eric Greerson?"

Cindy grabbed the microphone. "This city is full of lies! Half the idiots in charge wouldn't know the truth if it took a shit on their faces!"

Jack tried to wrestle the microphone from her. "Ms. Preston, we're on air. Don't be vulgar."

"You haven't seen vulgar yet!"

The scene switched back to the studio, where the female newscaster sat with a tight-lipped expression.

"Good lord." June slapped a hand to her forehead.

Sam laughed.

"We now have some more information," the newscaster said. "Paranormal Alliance members are telling us this protest was organized via e-mail, social media, and text messages overnight."

They flashed back to Jackson Park, where another reporter stood with a much more benign-looking woman: young, clean-faced, her dark hair pulled back in a ponytail.

"I know her." Sam scooted to the edge of the couch. "Vanessa Bree. She's the secretary of our South Chicago charter."

"What we're hearing," the news reporter said, "is that you were contacted via e-mail about this last night?"

"Yes," Vanessa said. "I heard about it on Twitter before I got an e-mail, though. They were telling us all to meet here, that we were going to do something about the way they're treating Sam. We just want them to investigate what happened."

"Who was sending the e-mails?" the reporter asked.

"I don't know. We have officers. It probably came from one of them. People were talking about it on Facebook and Twitter."

"Do you believe Sam Haain is innocent?"

"I do." Her posture was tense. "They need to do a real investigation. The Institute has done some bad stuff, and most people don't even know about it. Sam's a good guy. He's not a killer. We want someone to find out what's going on instead of taking the Institute's word for everything."

Sam leaped off the couch, fists clenched in the air. "Yes!" He circled the couch. "Finally. I knew they wouldn't sit around and take this crap forever."

"What will this accomplish, though?" June asked. "This isn't the first time they've held a protest since you vanished. So far it hasn't helped anything."

"It's perfect timing," Muse said. "With Ethan taking the information to the FBI."

"And if we can make Occam hand over Micha," Sam said, "it'll be all the pieces coming together at once."

The news was eager to cover the events. The crowd grew bigger over the hour. More members were interviewed. The reporters wondered about the possibility of someone of import addressing the situation.

Sam stood in front of the TV, instead of sitting. He'd put his shirt on, which was a pity, and had another cup of coffee, which was dangerous given his already hyper state. June debated taking a shower, but she didn't want to be naked and wet if something went down.

"They should riot," June said. "You know the Powers That Be only care when their pretty things start getting smashed up."

"We're not violent," Sam said. "Despite what Robbie led people to believe." He whirled around to face Muse. "I know what I need to do. Contact your father."

Muse frowned at him. "Do you think that's safe right now?"

"As safe as it's ever been."

Muse widened her eyes. "Sam, you can't."

"What's your plan?" June asked. "For us non-telepaths in the room?"

"I have to go," Sam said. "To the protest."

June boggled. "Don't you think that's—oh, I don't know—crazy? I know the party is about you, but that doesn't mean you're invited."

"I'm a shapeshifter. No one will know I'm there."

"There's a little problem with that," Trina spoke up. She'd been silent through all of this. "Some glamour generators can see the imperfections and abnormalities in your glamour. If there are others there, they'll know you're not who you appear to be."

So Occam wasn't as special as he claimed to be—other shapeshifters could sniff their own kind out, too.

Sam turned on Trina. "First, we don't use PC science-speak in this house."

"This house?" June said.

"I'm a shapeshifter. There's very few of us. There's only six registered with the Paranormal Alliance and almost five hundred members total. The odds of running into another one are slim. And even if I do, I know what they look like, and I can avoid them."

"The entire Paranormal Alliance probably isn't there," Muse said. "So there's that, too. But Sam, I don't think this is a good idea. At all."

"I can't just sit here."

"Let my father send in some people to snoop around."

"Your father's people aren't as good as I am. I'd rather you don't go with me, either. I don't want to put you in danger."

Muse's whole face jerked and twitched. "I like that idea even less," she said. "You going without your bodyguard?" Her gaze hardened. "Is this because of last night? What I did to Occam? You think I'm becoming careless?"

Sam's words flashed into June's head, about Muse's perceptions and agility being off. Muse snapped her gaze to June.

"Shit," June gritted out.

"Fine." Muse drew herself up. "Go. Have fun. I'll stay here and guard everyone. That's all I'm good for now, in my weakened state."

Sam sighed. "Muse, I need to know what's going on, and the less people I put in the line of fire, the better. I'll be back before dark, I promise."

"I'll go with you." June stood. "You'll need somebody to watch your back, if not her."

"I just said it's dangerous." Sam held a finger up to June. "That's why I'm not taking her. Did you just miss that entire conversation?"

"Yes, but you can disguise us, and if you have to let go of me or something, people are less likely to recognize me. They'll recognize her on sight. She's always around you." She took a deep breath. "Sam, you can't do this alone. And if you go by yourself, we're all going to be worried sick. Please, let me come with you. Just like when we went to Old Town. Watching out for each other, remember? I trust you, you trust me? This is not the first dumb quest out into public we've taken."

He was silent, his eyes shining in the light coming through the window. The ghost of their conversation, about trust and Sam's intentions with her and the vampires, hung heavy on the air.

"Fine," he said. "If you really want to risk your neck again."

Muse turned and stalked off to the hallway. Sam's decision had to burn. June would make it up to her later, if Sam didn't. She tried to project thoughts in her direction that she just wanted to protect Sam, and she wasn't trying to slight her.

"But no shenanigans, Sam," June said. "You don't do anything crazy. I've survived this long. I'm not letting you get us killed, or worse, arrested. We go there, check it out, and come right back."

The bedroom door slammed. Trina still sat on the arm of the couch, eyeing June, eyebrows raised.

"I'll be lucky if I get killed or arrested," Sam said. "Because what Muse is going to do to me when I get back will be much worse. I hope you're happy."

"I'm not."

* * * *

June's skin itched with anxiety every time they went outside. They took public transportation, hand in hand, as they'd done to get to Old Town. Aaron could get them a ride when they needed one, but moving alone, in secret, was much safer. Sam was once again a woman—apparently, a fetish for him—buxom, with long dark blond hair and wearing a flowery halter dress. June was a ginger-haired man dressed like a hipster, complete with thick-framed glasses and tattered skinny jeans.

They got as close as they could to the park and walked the rest of the way. The sun made her sweat, rivulets creeping down her spine under her fake clothes.

"I notice the SNC never protests on Aaron's behalf," June said. "I wonder why that is?"

"The SNC is a splintered group. Most of the members have waffled on their loyalty ever since Aaron made his treaty with me. They're also a slightly more, shall we say, civilized bunch."

"And your group likes to raise hell. You know what they say, though. The squeaky wheel gets the most grease."

"In this case, the loudest mouth gets the most dental work."

She squinted at him. "That doesn't make any sense."

"Doesn't it? I guess you haven't seen the hits we take."

When they arrived at Jackson Park, noisy, angry people packed the place. News cameras and reporters were everywhere.

"This is chaos," she said. "Should we really do this?"

"Chaos is a great cover."

They weaved through the crowd, passing through a broad tree-filled area and across a bridge next to a marina. The wind off the water dried some of her sweat, and if not for the jostling crowd, it might have been a pleasant stroll through the park with her pretend girlfriend.

"I'm keeping an eye out for other shapeshifters," Sam said. "If I drag you off in another direction, just go with it. I don't recognize a lot of these people."

They passed by a series of tennis courts. Beyond, the real action was taking place in a vast open field. People were gathered as if at a musical festival, but they weren't passing around joints and singing songs.

"We need to find out some stuff," Sam said. "But I can't ask people questions because I don't sound like a woman."

"You know, you could have made yourself a man. Just saying."

He waved a hand, as if she suggested something silly. "I need you to ask people things. Pretend we just wandered down here to see what was going on."

"Wait." June stopped. "I don't sound like a man, either."

"You sound more like a man than I sound like a woman."

"Are you kidding right now? Why don't you just freakin' change our genders!"

"I can't do that here. People would see."

She gritted her teeth.

"Seriously," he said. "You have kind of a throaty voice. No one will know. It's loud here."

"What should I ask?"

"First, find out who organized this."

Maybe they'd run into Cindy and get all their questions answered, without having to risk their necks by talking to a bunch of strangers while they both sounded like the opposite gender. Her voice was not that throaty.

"How do I know which people are in the Paranormal Alliance?" she asked.

"I'll tell you."

Sam nudged her toward a group of people crowded around a news camera. A reporter was interviewing someone and people were waving signs in the background. June stood on tiptoe. She turned to the man standing next to her.

"Hey"—she added some bass to her voice, an instant comical failure— "what's going on here? We were passing by and saw a crowd."

The man was tan and blond, wearing sunglasses. He frowned at her. "We're with the Paranormal Alliance. We're trying to get justice for Sam Haain."

"Oh," she said. "Yeah, I always thought he was innocent. The news can't get anything right."

Before she could ask anything else, the man pushed forward, yelling. He was swept up in the commotion.

"Never mind." Sam tugged her away. "We'll find someone else."

"It'd be really nice if we ran into Cindy."

June grudgingly let her tall girlfriend drag her around. She talked to a few more people, but got the same answers the news had given: the members wanted the truth uncovered; they wanted someone in an official capacity to address the crowd; they'd found out about the protest on the Internet.

"I wish I could find one of my officers," Sam said. "This seems like something they'd put together."

They traversed the field, listening in on conversations, observing people act up in front of news cameras, taking in the scenery. Police lined the edges of the crowd, watching everything with hawk-eyed glares. A makeshift stage had been erected and people were gathered around it. Several people were in the process of rigging up a PA system.

"Someone's going to speak," June said. "Maybe the mayor will show up."

"I hope not. I can't stand to listen to that man talk. You should hear him at formal dinners."

The sun got on her nerves. Sam had given himself sunglasses but neglected to grace her with a pair. Would not-real sunglasses actually work? The logistics of shapeshifting creeped her out. She could feel the clothes she wasn't actually wearing against her skin. She could touch and move them.

"Stop it," Sam muttered.

She plucked at the T-shirt she was "wearing."

"Don't make it obvious."

"But how does it... I mean, how can I—"

"I'll tell you later. Just act casual."

The teeming crowd around them increased the temperature. Sam's hand grew slick in hers.

"How long are we going to hang out here?" she asked.

"Until something happens."

Megan Morgan

She scanned the crowd. Her stomach lurched as she spotted a head of flaming red hair close to the stage.

"Cindy!" She pointed. "I'm pretty sure that's her."

Sam stretched over the crowd. "This is going to be tricky. Don't let go of my hand."

They picked their way through the crowd, struggling not to break contact. Luckily, Cindy didn't move.

They stepped up behind her. June touched her arm.

She turned, sunglasses obscuring her eyes, the brightness of her hair brilliant against the sun-washed whiteness of her skin. She wore a yellow sundress.

"Cindy," June said. "It's us."

"Us who?"

June resisted the urge to pinch her. "You don't remember your old friends? We had some good times. Like that one time I stayed at your place. And that one time in the parking garage."

She stared blankly.

"How's Dipity?" June asked.

Cindy flinched. She opened her mouth, eyebrows climbing over her glasses. "Holy shit." She lowered her voice to a whisper. "What the hell are you doing here?"

"Oh, you know," Sam said, "having a good time."

Chapter 17

"Come over here." Cindy jerked her head to the side. "Away from all these people."

They worked their way out of the crowd and to the right of the stage. Cindy led them around the side of a van that people were unloading PA equipment from.

"You shouldn't be here," Cindy whispered. "It's dangerous."

"Yeah, I tried to tell him that." June shrugged. "So did Muse."

"I wouldn't miss my own party," Sam said. "This is marvelous."

"Someone is going to 'address our concerns.'" Cindy peeked around the van. "Word is it's the FBI. Doesn't matter, though. If they don't say the right things, these people will riot."

"Yes, they will." Sam spoke proudly.

"You don't want to be here if that happens," Cindy said. "You could be exposed."

"I wouldn't bother trying to talk sense into him." June shook her head.

"I'm not worried about it." Sam renewed his grip on her sweaty hand. "We won't get caught. I want to hear firsthand what the FBI has to say, what they intend to do about this. I'm guessing this is all because the Paranormal Alliance found out from the clinic heist that I'm still around. It gives them hope."

"Exposing yourself wasn't the brightest idea," Cindy said. "They're hunting for you now."

"Let them hunt. They haven't found me yet."

Cindy huffed. "You should be scared, Sam. Hell, I'm scared. I didn't want to come here alone. I tried to convince Kevin to come with me. I thought out of respect for your brother he might help defend your name."

Kevin was Cindy's ex-husband, not a fan of Sam's or paranormal people in general. He was, however, Sam's brother's best friend—when Sam's brother had been alive.

"Thomas was more like Kevin than he was me," Sam said. "I doubt he'd be here to defend me, either."

June had a lot of questions about Sam's brother and their relationship—questions she couldn't ask right now, and unfortunately, would probably never be appropriate to bring up.

"Did the officers organize this?" Sam asked.

"I'm not sure," Cindy said. "A lot of chatter took place online last night. Everyone got e-mails. I'm not sure who they were from, though. I didn't recognize any officer's e-mail addresses, so maybe it was just some angry members."

"It's heartwarming." Sam puffed out his chest. "If only I could get up there and thank everyone myself."

"Try not to let that sweeping emotion cloud your common sense," June said.

"Maybe they're trying to lure you out." Cindy fretted. "We all want our leader back. We want to hear the story from your own mouth."

"But that would be a bad idea." June spoke pointedly. She wished Cindy wouldn't give him ideas.

Sam stepped back, pulling her with him. He looked behind the stage. "What's he doing here?"

Behind the stage was a familiar face wearing glasses, a man with slicked-back hair and a suit.

Cindy peeked around the van. "Ethan Roberts? He's not working for the newspaper anymore, right? They fired him?"

Ethan stood with several other men. He didn't have a camera, indicating he wasn't covering the story for his tabloid.

June shrugged. "You did tell him he could be part of the group now, Sam."

"I told him if he took the files to the FBI, I would let him in." Sam stared across the distance at Ethan. "He's not an official member yet."

"Maybe he did get them to the FBI," June said. "Maybe that's why he's here, because they're about to show up."

Cindy clutched her hands beneath her chin. "Sam, they might be here to clear your name!"

"We don't have Micha, though," June said. "Occam kidnapped him."

Cindy curled her upper lip. "Freakin' vampires. What does Occam want with Micha?"

"He's being spiteful." Sam turned back to them. "Don't worry, we'll get him back."

"I hope he doesn't hurt him," Cindy said. "Vampires don't have a lot of morals."

"He won't hurt him," June said. "He promised." The ring was in June's pocket. She couldn't leave it at the apartment and risk losing it, no matter how much she hated the new superpower attached to it.

"A promise from a vampire," Cindy said. "Yeah, that would ease my mind. We better get back out in the crowd, before we draw attention to ourselves."

"If anything happens, I'll get in touch with you as soon as I can," Sam told Cindy. "Watch your back. And don't do anything stupid on my behalf."

"Aye aye, captain." She saluted him. "Nice style, by the way. I think I used to have that dress."

"You did." Sam fluffed the skirt.

They slipped back into the crowd. People wandered back and forth across the stage, checking cables and setting up a microphone.

"I'm sure part of Ethan being here is he just didn't want to miss this," June said. "Especially since you're letting him into the club."

"I'm wishing I'd brought Muse now. No offense, but she's better with a knife, even in her current state."

"If you'd brought her, you would have missed the opportunity to hold hands with me again."

Sam smirked. Despite his feminine features, it was his own characteristic. "I think you like this more than you let on."

She entwined her fingers with his and squeezed. "Maybe I do."

The PA system was ready to go, but no one from the FBI took the stage. Instead, several people in succession made passionate speeches and got the crowd pumping their fists and shouting. June and Sam stood a few rows back from the stage and to the side. Cindy stood in front of them, up against the stage. Sam listened raptly, chin titled up, as each speaker went on about how wonderful and innocent and heroic he was.

June tried not to spoil the fun by rolling her eyes or grumping.

"That's our treasurer," Sam said when a stocky dark-haired man approached the microphone. "He a windbag. He'll have plenty to say."

He did, and was emotional about it, romanticizing Sam to the hilt as the others had. The rhetoric made June's stomach ache, especially since she hadn't eaten breakfast.

"Maybe we should get out of here," she said after Treasurer Windbag left the stage. "I don't think the FBI is coming. We can watch coverage on TV, in safety. Besides, my hand is turning to mush." The sweat had wrinkled her fingertips.

Sam slid his hand up to her wrist, their skin gliding together. "There. Now hush."

"Sam."

His eyes went wide behind his sunglasses.

"Samantha," she corrected herself. "I think we should go."

"Just a few more speeches. If no one interesting comes out, we'll leave."

The whole thing was like attending one's own funeral, only slightly less creepy.

Midway through the next speech, movement behind the stage caught June's attention. A group of people were gathering back there. Her spirits lifted. Maybe the FBI was about to throw down.

"What's going on back there?" Sam stood on his tiptoes.

"Probably more people who want to talk." June sighed.

She skimmed the crowd, seeing if anyone looked as bored as she felt. A familiar face popped out for a split second, and she quickly looked back at the spot. She had to be imagining things.

She wasn't.

Roughly thirty yards away in the tight-packed crowd, a man stood, staring at them. He wore a hoodie despite the heat, the hood pulled up and shielding his face. His eyes were bloodshot and watery.

"Sam." She scrabbled at his hand. "Someone's watching us."

The man moved toward them. The speaker on stage had finished and other people were coming out. Sam was focused there, but he looked at June, and then around.

"Occam," she whispered. "To the left."

Occam pushed up next to them and stopped. His eyes were rimmed with red, his skin flushed.

"I know you're in there," he taunted.

"What the hell are you doing here?" Sam whispered.

Dread welled in June's chest. The intensity of Occam's gaze chilled her to the bone beneath the blazing sun.

The blazing sun. A vampire was out in broad daylight. He didn't even have the benefit of shade, like at the clinic. Why?

"Get out of here," Occam said. "Or you are going to die."

Occam looked to the stage. A new speaker was walking out.

"Ethan," Sam said. "Get the hell away from us, Occam!" He pushed at him. Occam barely budged.

Ethan strode up to the microphone, the stage filling up with people behind him.

"Hello, faithful members of the Paranormal Alliance!" Ethan said into the microphone. A cheer went up.

"Sam, we have to go." She dug her nails into his hand. "We have to get the hell out of here."

"Wait," Sam said. "This could be it."

Occam pushed in front of them. "You can leave with me right now." He held a hand out to her. "I can glamour you, too."

"You're all gathered here today to defend Sam Haain," Ethan said. "A good man, an innocent man. A man persecuted and disparaged by the Institute. The Institute wants to harm all of us. Too long they've been allowed to operate. Too long they've been allowed to mistreat and abuse us."

June flinched as Occam spoke close to her ear. She hadn't seen him move.

"Sounds like a familiar speech," he whispered. "Where have you heard this before?"

People were shouting around them.

"Oh God," she breathed out. "Sam, Robbie's here."

The people onstage were forming a tight-packed wall, shielding someone behind them from view.

"And we have proof!" Ethan said. "We have proof of what the Institute has been doing, and we've given it to the FBI. Their secrets are exposed."

"Come with me," Occam said. "I can protect you, June."

He clamped a hand on her wrist. A tingling sensation rushed over her skin and her vision rippled.

"Stop," Sam said. "Let go of her. You're going to expose us!"

Another rush of tingles swept her body, making her nauseous. "Quit pulling on me, both of you!"

"You can't fight my glamour, Sam," Occam said. "I'm a vampire. And I'm much stronger than you."

"Since your brave leader has abandoned you," Ethan said, "you need someone who can lead you in a righteous surge against the Institute. Someone who isn't afraid to fight fire with fire. That man is here today."

The group behind Ethan parted. As Ethan stepped aside, shouts of confusion and horror rose from the crowed. A gangly man, clothed all in black, stepped forward. His hair hung past his collar, straight and chestnut, his skin nearly reflectively pale. Thanks to Muse, a long, dark scar traversed his face, starting on the left side of his mouth, distorting his lips, slashing across his nose, skipping his right eye, and finishing on his forehead. His eyes were milky white and seemed to glow in the sunlight.

"Many of you know who I am," he said. "For those who don't, my name is Robert Beecher."

Panic shot through the crowd. Police rushed the stage.

"Don't be frightened," Robbie said. "Those of you who haven't come to me already, you now have the choice to do so."

"No!" Sam screamed, as June started forcefully pulling him away. "I can't believe he—Cindy!"

Cindy was pushing her way toward them, her sunglasses knocked off, her face blanched.

"Run!" June shouted.

"Your time to run is up." Occam still had her wrist.

The police were abruptly thrown back from the stage, as if they'd hit a force field.

"No one is leaving here," Robbie said, calmly. "Unless you leave with me."

Screams were rising farther out in the crowd. Something else was happening. Flames erupted in several places, shooting up like fiery geysers. June didn't understand, but when she did a second later, horror blinded her. The columns of flame were people.

"He's got a bunch of pyros with him." Sam let go of her wrist. "Holy shit."

They could get out in the commotion, if they kept moving. They had to. People in the crowd were turning on others, attacking them, as if Robbie had flipped a switch and activated his murderous army. The traitors were among them, ready to force a conversion.

"Oh my God!" Cindy reached them. "Sam, we have to get the hell out of here!"

"I only want you to listen to me," Robbie said, speaking over the panicked commotion. People were trying to run. More flames erupted. "I want us to unite together against a common enemy. I only want our safety."

Occam grabbed June, wrapping his arm around her neck and jerking her chin back.

"What the hell?" She struggled against him.

"The only way we're getting out of here now is if we look like we're on his side," he said in her ear. "Tell Sam to grab that girl and come on."

"Sam, grab Cindy!" June called out. "Make it look real, or we're going to die."

Sam was gaping at the stage, immobile. Cindy leaped on him, grabbing him around the chest.

"Glamour her, Sam," Occam said. "Wake up, boy."

Cindy changed into a dark-haired woman. Sam remained his female self.

"Where are we going?" June wheezed out.

Occam had a fierce grip. "I've got a plan B, since you were too stupid to run when I told you to."

He dragged her through the tumultuous crowd. She couldn't keep track of the other two. Robbie was still speaking, but his words were drowned out by screaming and shouting.

A pillar of flame erupted nearby, and the crowd surged, pushing against them. The heat gusted over her, screams filling her ears.

"Fucking pyros," Occam snarled.

Occam's body was unnaturally hot, his hands nearly burning her skin. His movements were sluggish and uncoordinated, though he was still plenty strong.

"The sun is burning you," she said.

"Yeah, well, you know." He huffed close to her ear. "Vampire."

They escaped the crowd and stumbled into an area where news vans were parked. Shots rang out, finally answering the assault. June flinched.

Occam let go of her and pulled open the back doors of one of the vans.

"Get in." He pushed her.

Belle and Zack were in the back of the van, wrapped in hoodies like Occam. June scrambled in between them. She looked around. Thankfully, Fake-Cindy appeared, dragging Sam. They jumped inside, Cindy changing back to herself in a blink. Occam jumped in too and swiftly pulled the doors shut, plunging them into darkness.

Their collective frantic breathing filled the space for a moment, until the engine started, the floor of the van vibrating.

"There's no way we'll just drive out of here," Cindy said, her voice bouncing off the walls.

"The hell we won't," Occam said.

The van lurched into motion, wobbling, creeping along. Screaming rose over the sound of the engine.

"Did you steal a news van?" June asked.

"It only looks like a news van," Occam said. "I can make things look different, remember?"

"You can glamour objects?"

His answer, and everything else, didn't matter at the moment as they sped up, the van rocking and jolting. A sharp ping sounded on June's side of the van. She jumped.

"The bullet proof plating is real, though," Occam said.

She reached out in the darkness, searching for Sam. His labored, hitched breathing helped her find him. She grabbed up his still-sweaty hand and squeezed it. He was trembling.

"It's all right," she lied. "It's going to be all right."

The going got smoother. They picked up speed. The sound of the panicked crowd vanished in the distance.

"Holy shit," Cindy suddenly said. "You guys are vampires, aren't you?"

Chapter 18

As they stumbled out of the van, June squinted painfully against the sudden onslaught of sunlight. This must have been how vampires felt. After a moment of letting her eyes adjust, she got her eyesight back. They were in a garbage-strewn dilapidated neighborhood.

"Where are we?" Sam asked. "We can't stay here. We have to go back to the apartment!"

"We're staying right here," Occam said. He was huddled down into his hoodie.

Sam grabbed Occam by the shoulders. "Muse is back at the apartment. Ethan knew where we were."

June sucked in a breath. "Trina."

Occam threw Sam's hands off him. "You're an idiot. You think they didn't go to the apartment before any of this even went down, to try to grab you? I'm sure they would have loved to parade your head around on a spike. The perfect topper for their coup cake."

"Fuck!" Sam spun around to June. "We have to do something. We have to find Robbie."

"You will," Occam said. "When night falls. Now, you better get inside before someone recognizes you and you end up with a whole new set of problems."

Occam led them into a sagging two-story house with nearly every window boarded over. Inside they faced near-darkness, but vague shapes of furniture hovered in the gloom. The smell of mildew hung thick on the air. The floor was sticky.

"Must you hide out in the nastiest places you can find?" June asked as they ascended a precariously creaking flight of stairs.

"Nasty places are good places to hide from the sun." Occam's voice was sluggish. "Vampires hang out communally. We don't have one home. We drift around to wherever we deem safest."

"So you're the homeless of the supernatural world," she said. "And you were worried about Rose Bellevue ruining your mystique."

Occam laughed.

He led them into a room and turned the lights on. The place actually had electricity. The room held two bare beds shoved against opposite walls and piles of ratty sheets, blankets, and God knew what else heaped on the floor. The windows were covered. On the opposite side of the room was another closed door.

"This is where we keep humans, when we have them," Occam said. "You can call it the guest suite, if you like."

"Where you 'keep humans,'" June said. "Nice."

Occam's skin was red, like a sunburn. Zack and Belle hadn't come upstairs with them.

"We're not staying here." Sam raked his hands through his hair, nearly vibrating. "Robbie just killed half the Paranormal Alliance and took the other half under his foul control, and you want me to sit still?"

"It would be in your best interest," Occam said. "This is the safest place for you right now. You're next on Robbie's to-do list. He's looking for you."

"He's right, Sam," Cindy said. "I can find out what's going on, though. I can try to find out where Muse is."

"You're in danger as well," Occam told her. "You didn't drink his Kool Aid. I'm sure right after Sam on his to-do list is everyone who got away."

"Why are you doing this?" June asked. "Why did you save us? I thought neutral parties didn't get involved."

Occam pushed his hood back. His eyes were bloodshot and the skin around them inflamed. "Except when it benefits us."

She took a deep breath. "You knew what Robbie was planning, didn't you? You didn't warn us about it, though."

"What?" Sam's eyes turned wild. "You knew this was going to happen, Occam?"

"Of course I knew," he said calmly. "Robbie has been soliciting our help since he revealed himself this past winter. He's been telling us his plans. Trying to gain our sympathy and support."

Sam seethed, fists clenched, shaking.

June slowly put the pieces together. "You don't care if he comes into your territory, because he can't do anything to you with his power."

"He's been terribly long-winded, though." Occam waved a hand. "He's going to shut down the Institute. He's going to make sure all supernatural people get the respect they deserve, yadda yadda. He tried to impress us with the number of people he wooed to his side. He tried to show us how strong he was with all the secret connections he had. He even tried to pay us at one point." He smirked. "Not enough."

"And you kept this from me?" Sam looked like he was about to explode.

"I'm not your friend, Sam, or your ally. And what would you have done anyway, in hiding? On the run? He was working behind your back for years and had many people in his pocket. Even if you were out in public and still in charge, what could you have done to stop him?"

June reached out and gripped Sam's arm, trying to steady him.

"So why did you get involved now?" she asked. "If you didn't care what Robbie did, why did you save us?"

Occam took a step toward her. Even in the damp mold-scented room, his smell preceded him. "I didn't save all of you. They were incidental. I saved you."

June shrank back.

"You wanted me to save them too. So I did."

"I don't care about your little fucking crush, Occam," Sam said. "I've got huge fucking problems. I can't stay here, waiting for Robbie to do something else."

"Go, then." Occam shrugged. "I only brought you here because June wants you safe."

June turned to Sam. "He's right. Robbie is out there. He's everywhere. If you want to be able to do anything, you have to stay off his radar."

"God only knows what he's doing right now," Cindy said, her voice nearly a whisper. "What he's already done."

Sam gnashed his teeth. "This is a nightmare. Those were my people, my friends!" His voice cracked. "I swore I'd always protect them."

"Protect us from people like the Institute." Cindy gripped his shoulder. "Not from our own kind, Sam. We didn't think we'd need you to."

June resisted the urge to throw her arms around him and hold him. She was shell-shocked too, sickened, disheartened, but if they succumbed to their terror and grief right now, they wouldn't be able to think straight. Not thinking rationally would give Robbie the opportunity to swoop down on them like the demon he was.

She had an idea.

"Do you think Robbie will come back to you?" she asked Occam. "Come back and try to persuade you again?"

"Oh, yes. He'll definitely give us one last opportunity to join him. He'll be proud to show off his biggest and bloodiest achievement. I mean, if that doesn't convince us, what will?"

Sam turned away, wrapping his arms around himself.

"Sam," June said. "Robbie will come back to the vampires. Which means, if you want to confront him, we have to stay with them."

He turned around. His face was blank and pale, his gaze distant. His eyes welled with unshed tears, his clenched fists trembling against his biceps, as if ready to pummel someone.

"I'm going to kill him," he whispered, venom in his voice. "I'm going to rip him to shreds, slowly, so he feels every bit of it."

"Good luck," Occam said. "Let me know how that works out."

Sam clenched his jaw and turned away again.

"I have to sleep," Occam said. "I have to recover from the sun." He leaned toward June. "You'll make sure neither of them does anything to us?" He jerked his head at Sam and Cindy.

June frowned. "Uh, sure..."

"I'm not going to mess with you, Occam!" Sam said. "You're not my priority right now."

"Good." He shambled toward the closed door on the other side of the room. "For behaving yourselves, you get a prize." He pounded on the door, making the wood shudder. "Hey! Get down here."

A moment later, the distinct thumping of someone's footsteps descending stairs sounded from behind the door.

The door opened a crack, then wider.

June gasped. "Micha."

Micha stepped out. "June! Guys!"

She rushed over to him. He didn't appear beaten up—a little pale, and he was still wearing the same clothes as when he'd been abducted, but otherwise he seemed fine. She threw her arms around him and clung. He smelled bad, but she didn't care. He hugged her tightly in return.

"You're all right," she whispered against his shoulder. "They didn't hurt you." She looked around at Occam. "Thank you."

"I'm not a liar," Occam said.

She drew back and kissed Micha, hard. His mouth tasted like— popcorn?

"Aw," Occam said. "On that happy note, I'm off to sleep the day away."

Cindy came over and gripped Micha's arm. "I'm so glad you're all right." She frowned. "You are all right, aren't you?"

Occam had already left the room. Micha looked around at them. "Yeah, I'm okay. Are...you guys okay? What are you doing here?" He fixed his gaze on Sam over June's shoulder. She couldn't look at him right now.

"It's been a really bad day," June said softly. "You better sit down for this."

They sat down together on one of the beds. The mattress was lumpy and stained—with what, who knew?—so she didn't sit back much farther than the edge. Sam sat on the bed across from them, back against the wall and legs stretched out in front of him, arms folded over his chest. Cindy sat beside him Indian-style.

The story was hard to tell, but June told it. Sam and Cindy didn't contribute.

"Damn," Micha said, quiet and grim. "He finally struck."

"We knew this was coming." Cindy broke her stupor. "We didn't know what, but we knew he would come out of hiding eventually, and in a big way."

"I can't believe he's got so many people on his side," Micha said.

"This is my fault." Sam spoke dully. Though his face was passive and sagging, the desperate, pained light in his eyes was hard to stomach. "If I hadn't abandoned them, if I hadn't gone into hiding and I'd stayed visible to give them some reassurance and hope…"

"You wouldn't have given them much hope from prison," June said. "Which is where you'd be if you hadn't gone into hiding. Listen, Sam. This isn't something Robbie cooked up in the few months you've been missing. He's been planning this for a long time. He indicated that at the press conference when we saved Jason, remember?"

"Right," Micha said. "He admitted he's been killing paranormal people to keep them away from the Institute. He's been at this for a while."

Sam closed his eyes. "And me being out of the picture gave him the perfect opportunity to strike."

"He would have struck eventually, no matter what." June sat forward. "Sam, people like him don't plan stuff like this for years and then just drop it because they can't find a good moment to make their dreams come true. He would have had his day, sooner or later."

Cindy reached out and touched Sam's knee. "She's right." Her voice was soft. "You couldn't have stopped him, Sam. He's been working against you for who knows how long, poisoning people's minds."

Sam opened his eyes. "I just wish I knew where Muse is."

"Muse is a tough bitch," June said. "I can't see Robbie getting her so easily. Besides, she's telepathic. I'm sure she knew they were coming."

"Unless Robbie came alone," Sam said. "She can't read him, remember? Or Ethan. If they came together, alone, they could have surprised her."

June rubbed a hand over her mouth. Robbie would do terrible things to Muse and Trina if he got his hands on them. Her brain formed plenty of grisly possibilities.

Sam unfolded his arms and clenched his fists against his thighs. "How long are we going to sit here and do nothing?"

"What can we do?" Micha asked. "Where would you go, Sam? You'd stumble right into his arms."

"You heard Occam," June said. "Robbie will come back and brag to the vampires about what he's done. He'll come to you. You don't have to go looking for him."

Sam sat up, away from the wall. "What the hell is it with Occam courting you, anyway?"

She flinched. "I don't know. I guess he thinks I'd make a good vampire. Lucky for us right now, I'd say."

He pushed himself to the edge of the mattress. "He's very actively interested in you. So much so, he put himself in jeopardy today, going out in the sun. So much, he was willing to save all of us, because it was 'what you wanted.'"

"I don't know! Beyond making me a vampire, I don't know what he wants with me. He's kind of his own man, you feel me?"

Sam narrowed his eyes at her.

"Don't look at me like that." She pointed at him. "I have no idea what he's up to. I just met the man last week, and I really wish I hadn't. But then, you and Aaron thought it was for the best, didn't you?"

Sam got to his feet. "Occam is more dangerous than Robbie, remember that. Robbie has a cause, something greater than himself to answer to. Occam just serves his own selfish purposes."

She got up as well. Sam stood in front of her. His gaze was pained but angry, his lips in a tight line.

"I know this has been a really tough day," she said. "But you can't go running out there looking for Robbie. Not if you want to survive long enough to do something about him. There is nothing we can do but wait."

"I've been waiting for months!" he practically yelled in her face. "All my waiting has led to this!"

"This isn't your fault!" she yelled back at him. "Pull yourself together for a few minutes and think. Be the smart man I know you are—the one who saved Jason, the one who got us out of the Institute. Are you still that man, or are you going to let grief dull your edge?"

Sam didn't speak. The house was silent around them, as if listening for his response.

"I need to know," she said, "if you're still the smartest man in this city."

He hesitated, but finally spoke. "I'm still the smartest man in this city," he said. "I am."

"Good. Then I still believe in you. Fix this. Without getting any of us killed."

She turned away. Micha gazed at them, one eyebrow arched.

"I can find out what's going on." Cindy stood. "I can at least find a TV and watch the news."

"Occam was right," Sam said. "It's not safe, even for you. A resourceful man like Robbie, I'm sure he has a mental list of dissenters, if not a physical one."

"I'll be careful." Cindy stepped up beside him. "Maybe I can find out what's happened to Muse."

"I'm not ordering you to do anything." He sat down heavily on the bed. "If you want to go, then go. Don't get yourself caught, or killed."

"I'll come back as soon as I can." She started toward the door. "I'll use the GPS on my phone to figure out where we are right now and go from there."

"We're somewhere near the Nocturnal District," Micha said. "I recognize the area."

Cindy slipped out the door.

Silence fell. June fidgeted. Maybe one of them would say something so she didn't have to keep carrying the conversation.

"Wanna see my luxury suite upstairs?" Micha asked her.

"Yeah. I think he could use some alone time right now." She nodded at Sam and stood.

Micha did too.

"We'll be right upstairs, Sam. Promise me you won't leave." If he needed to cry, she would give him the space to cry without losing face.

"I'm not going anywhere," Sam said. "But I swear to fucking Christ if I hear you having sex up there, I'm coming up and punching both of you in the face. I really want to punch the hell out of someone right now."

She grabbed Micha's wrist. "Yes, Dad."

"I mean it!" he called after them as Micha led June up the stairs beyond the door.

"He sounds a little jealous," Micha muttered.

"I think he's kinda high-strung right now."

Chapter 19

The stairs led to a loft-like room, small, obviously meant to be a bedroom, though the only semblance of it being so was a mattress on the floor in the corner. Blankets were spread over the mattress, no pillows. A single window, over which ratty curtains hung, looked out on the street and allowed enough light to reveal the unappealing décor. The carpet, perhaps beige at some point, was stained and filthy.

"By vampire standards," she said, "these are pretty luxurious accommodations."

"You hungry?"

"I'm goddamn starving."

Micha grabbed something from a pile in the corner opposite the "bed." A heap of food sat there: bags of chips, candy bars, other assorted bags and boxes of junk. He held a bag out to her, and she now understood why his mouth tasted like popcorn.

"Apparently vampires have forgotten what kind of food humans need to survive," he said. "It's the thought that counts, I suppose."

She took the half-empty bag of popcorn, the kind with no hulls, soft and squishy and more like Styrofoam than food. "Does this have butter on it?" She peered into the bag, grimaced, and thrust it away. "Yes. Do you have anything in your stash that won't make me vomit in a few minutes?"

"Dig through and find something. Mi prison, su prison."

She riffled through the pile. She cringed when a cockroach ran out and skittered across the carpet. "Splendid. Tell me they at least let you use the bathroom."

"Yes, though the plumbing is questionable here."

She searched carefully—anything sealed would probably be uncontaminated. "What have they been doing to you here?"

"Nothing. Just holding me. Some vampires were messing with me the night they brought me here, but Occam ran them off. Other than that, he came to see me yesterday and told me if I didn't come up with a convincing story that Rose's research was false, he'd make the rest of you pay."

"Ah-ha." She stood up, a bag in hand. "Corn chips. No gluten."

"I thought I might be able to escape. Maybe slip out during the day. But I didn't want him finding you and hurting you."

She ripped the bag open. "He found us anyway. Sam says vampires are really good at sniffing people out."

She threw all politeness to the wind and stuffed a handful of chips in her mouth. She was starving.

"So," he said, "the FBI have my results, and now they have the information on the serum?"

She nodded, chewing.

"Then they're about to expose the Institute." The light from the window washed out the color of his eyes—much like Robbie's eyes, in her still-horrified memory. "They'll uncover the truth. They might even discover Sam and Aaron only killed Eric in self-defense."

"We got bigger problems right now," she said around the wad of chips. She swallowed and grabbed another handful. She attempted to eat them one at a time this round.

"You don't have to do anything else, you know. For me. Or for Sam. Your brother is safely away from here, and the Institute is about to be blown open. You could get out of here. Your part in this is over."

"I suppose I could. But now I find myself worrying what might happen to you poor bastards."

"You think you can change what's going to happen to us?"

To keep herself from shoving her face in the bag, she set it on the windowsill. "No. But I can stick around and see you safe."

He walked over to her. "What if we're never safe? Is this the kind of life you want, all this hiding and running?"

"At least it's exciting. Like I'm in an action movie."

He slid his arms around her. She pressed against him, gripping his shoulders.

"I was scared they'd hurt you," she whispered. "Or killed you." She drew back. "When Occam showed up at our place last night, he gave me your wedding ring."

"Is that what he did with it? Should have known he would use it to torment you. He took it from me yesterday." He paused. "I don't know why I still wear it, to tell you the truth."

"Maybe part of you still wants to believe she wasn't setting you up."

He drew back from her, looking out the window.

Megan Morgan

She stuffed her hand in the pocket of her jeans. "Something…strange happened." She drew the ring out. "When I hold the ring up, I can summon Rose."

"Summon her?"

"Yeah. It calls out to her or something. But she's not like she usually is. She seems more aware."

He furrowed his brow.

"Doesn't make her any less creepy, though." She shuddered. "I hate ghosts."

"Do it. Summon her now."

"What?"

"I want to see."

She cringed. "You've never been able to see her when she appears."

"Maybe it'll be different. Maybe I'll be able to see her if she's connected to the ring."

"If that were the case, why hasn't she appeared to you before now? You've been wearing the ring."

"Ghosts can't hurt you." He gently gripped her arm. "They might be freaky, but they can't do anything to you."

"Being freaked out is something."

"I want to see."

Could a living person have a fistfight with a ghost? Not that she assumed Micha to be the kind of guy to punch his wife, but he might be the kind of guy to punch her betraying, treacherous spirit.

"Damn you for being so good looking." She sighed. "You're the only person who can get me to summon a ghost."

He smiled. "Only for a minute, I promise."

She turned around. She picked the farthest corner and took a deep breath. Silently cursing Micha, herself, and whatever entities might be listening in, she lifted the ring, holding it between her thumb and index finger.

Nothing happened.

Micha hovered behind her, so close his body heat radiated against her back, his breath passing over the nape of her neck.

She was about to lower the ring, when something flickered in the corner. She widened her eyes and then lurched back when Rose suddenly appeared, full-bodied and staring at her with her empty dead gaze.

"Damn it," June gritted out. "Still not used to that."

"She's here?"

"She's in the corner," she whispered. She had no idea why she was whispering. "You can't see her?"

"No." Disappointment laced his voice. "It feels colder, though. Like it did in the hallway at the clinic."

Rose remained in place, staring.

"Well, if you can't see her, might as well get rid of her..."

Before June could lower the ring, Rose stepped forward.

"Gah." June backed up against Micha's chest.

"What?" Micha asked.

Rose spoke, her voice toneless. "If you ask the vampire the right questions, he will not lie to you."

June's skin crawled. "You mean Occam?"

"Is she talking to you?" Micha asked.

"She said if I ask the vampire the right questions, he won't lie to me."

"What questions?"

Rose took a few more slow steps forward. June backed up farther, pushing at Micha. He took a few steps back, allowing June to cower like the mouse she was.

"He knows your enemy," Rose said. "He knows him better than anyone."

"My enemy?" June said. "Robbie?"

Micha stepped around June. "Ask her if she knew what Eric Greerson was going to do to me."

Rose flicked her gaze from June to Micha.

"She's looking at you." June grew slightly more fascinated than scared. "She's aware of you."

Micha moved toward the corner.

"She's not speaking," June said. "She's just looking at you."

"Rose, are you there?" His voice had a high uncertain pitch.

Rose continued staring.

"She's not speaking. Can we stop this?"

He walked back to June and plucked the ring from her fingers.

"I don't think—" June shook her head.

Rose vanished.

"She's gone."

Micha held the ring out defiantly. A chill lingered on the air, making the hair on June's arms stand on end.

"It's not going to work, Micha. I believe you when you say ghosts can't hurt you, but I don't think it's a good idea to keep pulling them from their...rest, either."

He lowered the ring. "I just want to talk to her and ask her if she knew. Can you ask her? Next time you see her?"

"She's never responded to anything I ask until today. She just comes and tells me cryptic things and then disappears."

He thrust the ring at her. "Take it back."

"I don't want it." She held her hands up. "It's yours."

"It might come in useful. You might need to talk to her at some point."

"I don't want the power to summon a ghost."

"Occam gave this to you for a reason."

She frowned. "To freak me out, to make me think he hurt you."

"No." He took one of her hands. "He didn't force it off my finger. He asked me for it, no threats, no mocking."

"What are you talking about?"

He placed the ring in her hand and closed her fingers around it. "I think he knew what it would do. He meant to give it to you, so you could see Rose."

"That doesn't make sense. He doesn't know I can see her."

"I think Occam knows a lot more about what's going on than we realize."

Reluctantly, she shoved the ring back in her pocket. "I'm tired of this shit," she murmured.

"So am I." He stroked her hair down the side of her face. His hand was soft, warm. Alive. "I'd do anything to be back in my apartment above Michigan Avenue, sitting at my desk and looking out at the skyline. Answering a thousand e-mails, worrying about my workload the next day." He dropped his hand. "But I can't have that. I probably never will again."

"I know how you feel. I don't know if I'll ever see my crappy little apartment above my shop again. Or get drunk on a Saturday night with Diego in our usual dive and fight with his stupid roommate." She paused. "I don't know, though, if I could go back in time and never come here, if I'd do it. I'd miss out on the good things I found in Chicago, too."

"Surely, meeting me was not worth losing your normal life."

"My normal life wasn't that charming, either." She smiled. "Besides, I wasn't talking about you. I meant Dipity."

He grinned and glanced at the mattress. "Want to snuggle on my awesome bed? I kinda missed sleeping with you next to me."

"Only kinda?" She tugged him toward the mattress. "Sam said no sex."

"Sam can go to hell."

She bit her lip. "I think he's already there."

They lay down on the mattress. The thing was as uncomfortable as it looked and smelled as well, though Micha's scent was superimposed on top. She lay tangled up with him, his heart thumping against her arm. Their legs were entwined, shoes off.

Micha propped himself up so his face was above hers and kissed her.

When she closed her eyes, the churning crowd in the park swam in her head—the frightened faces and Robbie's blank white eyes, surveying the crowd with cold calculation. The flames erupted all over again.

She also envisioned Sam downstairs, the pain in his eyes, the tension in his face. He was traumatized, probably thinking of doing something stupid, despite his promise not to leave. She should be down there to stop him, talk to him, whatever he needed. What the hell was she doing right now? Once again seeking comfort from Micha instead of being there for him.

Micha moved to kissing her neck. He tugged at the collar of her T-shirt with his teeth and placed a hot kiss on the bare skin of her shoulder.

She shifted against him, battling between the desire for comfort and the need for solitude.

"You all right?" he murmured. "You want me to stop?" His breath had gone shallow, his hand stiff on her side.

"I'm fine. And yeah…it's just. It's not a good time."

He settled back down beside her and rubbed her hip. "I get that. I'm sorry. I just missed you."

"I missed you too," she murmured.

They were quiet for a few minutes.

Finally, he whispered, breaking the silence, "I think we can still work out."

She didn't reply. After a moment, he lifted his head and kissed her temple. He rested his hand on her chest, over her heart.

"Maybe," she said.

She lay still, listening to his breath until it turned slow and shallow. The house was horribly quiet. Sam wasn't moving around down below. She didn't hear him crying, either.

She carefully sat up and grabbed her bag of chips off the windowsill. She was still hungry.

Chapter 20

June had dozed off, and woke to muffled voices. Evening had fallen, and the room was steeped in shadows. Micha lay pressed against her side, snoring faintly. For a moment, her brain convinced her they were back at the house and she was waking up next to Micha as she did every night. Reality followed swiftly, however. Funny how hiding out in that house was comparatively better than what she was enduring now.

She strained to hear the voices. They were coming from downstairs—Sam and Cindy.

She untangled herself from Micha and sat up. Her mouth was dry from the chips.

Micha stirred and lifted his head. In the darkness, she could barely make out his face.

"I think Cindy's back," she said. "I wonder what time it is?"

Micha sat up. June stretched and groaned at the stiffness in her muscles. Today had been vigorous.

"Did they give you any water?" she asked.

"There's a plastic jug over by the food. I think it's safe. I haven't gotten dysentery yet, anyway."

She got up, wobbled over to the corner, and sought out the jug. The water was warm, but it felt heavenly, parched as she was.

An angry shout sounded from downstairs, making her jump and spill some down her front.

"Hey!" Sam's voice. "Get down here."

"We're coming!" June yelled back. "Give us a minute."

"We don't have minutes," Sam snarled.

She hoped he was just being dramatic and something else terrible hadn't happened.

She and Micha went downstairs. She winced at the light. Cindy was there. She sat on the edge of one of the beds, brow scrunched up and tears in her eyes. The constant pit in June's stomach opened wider.

Sam was pacing.

"You're probably hungry." Micha thrust a bag of chips at Sam. "I'm sure the vampires didn't feed you."

Sam glared at him. "Feed me? Like I'm a fucking animal?" He snatched the bag, though.

"By their standards, we all are," Micha said.

Sam tore the bag open.

"What's going on?" June sat down across from Cindy, on the other bed.

"It's awful," Cindy choked out. "It's all over the news. They're calling it the 'Massacre In the Park.' Eighty-three people. That's how many they've confirmed dead. Not all were Paranormal Alliance members, but most were."

"Oh, wow." June sat tense, her heart pounding painfully under her ribs. "Damn. I'm sorry."

Sam sat down beside Cindy, cramming chips in his mouth.

"I talked to some people I trust," Cindy said. "They're all scared he's coming for them. Some are packing up and getting out of Chicago."

"Maybe we should do the same," June said.

Sam swallowed and licked his lips. "We're safer than most. We at least have the advantage that he doesn't know where we are." Finally, he was talking some sense.

"What is the news saying about Robbie?" June asked.

"No one knows where he is." Cindy shook her head. "There's a huge manhunt going on. They won't find him. His followers will protect him."

"We need to be the ones who find him." Sam stood. "If he's coming to the vampires, I hope he comes quick. What if he starts killing more people to draw me out?"

"So I take it you didn't find Muse?" June asked Cindy.

Cindy wiped at her eyes. "I went to the apartment building. I didn't go inside, though. I sat in the parking lot and called out to her with my mind. Nothing."

"I wish we hadn't argued today," Sam said. "I wish I'd brought her with me." He glanced at June. "Both of you. I don't want you dead, either."

"He won't kill her," June said. "She's too important to you. Robbie will use her. He'll dangle her to try to get you to come out." She took a breath. "I hope to God he at least let Trina go. She's of no use to him."

Sam scoffed. "They definitely killed her. She's of no use to him, precisely."

June jumped to her feet. "She was innocent! She didn't deserve to be tangled up in this, and she sure as hell didn't deserve to die."

Sam turned to her, eyes glittering. "Neither did those people in the park. But a lot of innocent people died, because that's the way Robbie wanted it. A lot more innocent people will die."

"You didn't have to kidnap Trina to make a point to Occam. You weren't responsible for what happened to those people today, but if she's dead, that is your fault. Occam wouldn't have hurt Micha even without us taking Trina."

Sam grabbed her arm. "You know him so well, don't you? Why don't you go suck your vampire boyfriend's cock and get us some information?"

She slapped him across the face before she could stop herself. "You're an idiot! You're smart, but you never think!"

Micha jumped between them. "Hey, hey." He held his arms out, keeping them away from each other. "It's not the time for this."

Sam rubbed his cheek, glaring at her.

June backed off. "I know what it feels like to get mixed up in shit you never wanted to be involved in. To be an innocent bystander and get sucked in without warning. But you don't take it out on the people who care about you!" She turned and stalked toward the door.

"Where are you going?" Sam called.

"To suck my vampire boyfriend's cock!" She flipped him off and left the room.

"Don't leave the house," he yelled.

"I'm not as dumb as you!"

The hallway was dark. She inched her way down the stairs. She had no idea where to go. She just needed to get away from that room for a few minutes or she would beat the hell out of Sam. She was trembling with anger, with grief. Would Trina's family ever know what became of her? Would her boyfriend search for her? Would her body turn up?

Below, the house was dark and silent. She walked through what seemed to be a living room, the shapes of furniture looming in the darkness. She searched for a light switch or lamp.

"Won't make a difference," a voice said behind her. "No bulbs."

She jumped and gritted her teeth. "Damn it, Occam. Why can't you say hello like a normal person?"

A low laugh. "I'm not a normal person."

Now that her eyes were adjusting, she could make out a figure sitting on the couch a few feet away.

"Are we alone?" she asked.

"How forward of you. Are you coming on to me, Little Red?"

"I just want to make sure I'm not about to become a vampire juice box. Are your friends lurking nearby?"

"We're alone." The figure shifted. "Come join me for a chat."

"Sure, why not?" She walked to the couch. "Have you just been sitting down here waiting for me?"

"I knew you'd come looking for me eventually. I heard the fighting upstairs just now. I figured at least one of you would storm off."

She sat down, well away from him. His smell drifted over nonetheless, not entirely repulsive this time, cigarettes and a faint hint of—cologne? Was he sprucing himself up for her?

"I didn't come looking for you," she said. "I just...had to clear my head."

"Trouble in paradise?"

"Paradise." She huffed. Rose's words rattled around in her head. Since she had him alone, she might as well ask some questions and see if they were the right ones.

"You've had a rough day," he said.

"No kidding." She sat back. The couch was lumpy and sagging. "Can I ask you a few things?"

"I was hoping you would."

She tucked her hands between her knees. "I could start with the obvious, like where's Robbie and what's he planning, but you wouldn't tell me that, would you?"

"Maybe you overestimate my knowledge, or my ability to care where Robbie is and what he's planning."

"Robbie didn't come to you just once, asking for your help." Faint voices drifted from upstairs. She hoped no one came down to look for her. "You said he showed up multiple times. That got me thinking."

"Did it?" His tone was light but curious.

"You're neutral. It seems like everyone in this city wants to harness your abilities for their cause, but everyone fails. So if you told Robbie no, you meant it. He'd know you meant it. Even a man like Robbie wouldn't think he's such a special snowflake if he just kept pushing, you'd finally come around to his way of thinking."

"But?"

"But...he kept coming back."

"Yes."

"He wants something else from you. More than just a vampire army."

"Oh, he wants a vampire army." His voice floated on the air. "But you're right. He wants something else, too. Something more important. Something he can't stop trying and trying again to obtain."

"What is that thing?"

"Robbie is ridiculously powerful. Few telekinetics in history have been able to move a person, or affect human flesh, and none of them to the extent he can. There's never been a man more supernaturally powerful, at least not one we can remember. But there's a price to pay for power like that."

"He's dying. Power like that destroys you."

"In his case, even faster than it's destroying Sam's lap dog. Robbie is deteriorating as fast as his power is growing."

"That's why he's deaf and slowly going blind." She got it, suddenly, but the revelation was horrible. "Oh my God... He wants your blood, doesn't he?"

"Very good, Little Red. Yes. If he becomes a vampire, he won't die. It will halt the damage being done, even reverse some of it."

"And all of you are opposed to turning him? I find it hard to believe every single one of you is so tenaciously loyal to your code of indifference. How hasn't he found one corrupt vampire to give him what he wants?"

"There are several layers to that answer." He shifted. "One, he hasn't done it yet. Because he's trying to be diplomatic. If he gains it freely, without trickery, he thinks that will make us trust him and want to follow him. Two, as bad off as he is, he needs an old vampire's blood to really fix him. Not one of these new whelps. Old, old vampires are not easily swayed or persuaded. There's also a third, really big, really terrifying reason. How much do you know about vampirism, June?"

"Just what I've learned from the others." She frowned. "What am I missing?"

He leaned toward her. "Not only would becoming a vampire stop Robbie's deterioration, it would keep him from being affected by anyone else's powers. Do you know what kind of monster that would create?"

She gasped, the full weight of it hitting her. "An invincible one."

"Nearly. Unless you left him out in the sun for a couple hours. We do have our weaknesses."

"But you couldn't chain someone like Robbie out in the sun. You couldn't do anything to him."

"And that's the third reason no one will turn him. We don't want to get involved, but we'd like to have a city left."

"Why doesn't he turn himself? Eric Greerson gave himself the virus."

"First of all, don't call it a virus." His tone darkened. "Secondly, he didn't turn out exactly the way he planned, now did he?"

"So the vi—the blood doesn't work correctly when it's used that way?"

"Eric Greerson is far from the first person to shoot himself up with vampire blood in hopes of turning. We have a name for people who do that: zombies. They're not quite human and not quite supernatural, but entirely disgusting and mindless."

"Eric didn't die when he was shot, though, and Aaron was concerned even shooting him in the head didn't actually kill him. So wouldn't Robbie at least get what he wanted and not be dying?"

"Eric's healing wasn't as fast as ours. Bleeding? He shouldn't have bled out at all; the wound should have closed at once. Robbie needs a much bigger boost than that to survive."

"Why does it only work coming from a vampire?"

"Do you think I'm going to tell you that?"

She pressed her lips together and shook her head. "You have to be careful. He's going to come back, and he won't take no for an answer this time. He'll get someone to do it, even if it's not an old vampire, even if it's only half-assed through one of the young ones."

"There won't be any young ones soon. We're going to cleanse our society, as I told you."

She refrained from expressing her disgust and outrage at that. She couldn't say anything that would change his mind, and honestly, she didn't know much about their "society," not enough to have an opinion on how they handled things.

"What does Robbie want?" she asked. "Yes, to get all the paranormal people to storm the Institute, but what's his end goal?"

"What do all madmen want? Control. He wants to rule this city with fear. He wants humanity to cower. He wants paranormal people to become the monsters most normals think they are."

"And none of this fills you with any particular emotion? You don't want to break your neutrality beyond reacting to the inconvenience it might bring you?"

"You mean, do we care about the normals or the paranormal people he'll control?"

"Yes."

"No."

"Why?"

"We don't owe normals or paranormals anything. We don't have any sense of community with either of them. Someday, you'll understand." He leaned in closer and whispered, "When you're one of us."

She barked out a surprised laugh. "You think I want to be a vampire?"

"Don't you? You're already like us. It would suit you."

"Am I? Would it?" She laughed again.

"I know all about you, June Coffin. I learned about you. When I first saw you in the newspapers, I was smitten."

She made an exaggerated gagging sound. "My very own vampire stalker."

"You don't feel any sense of community with paranormal people. You removed yourself from your kindred long ago and made yourself an outsider, to the point you don't even understand them. You didn't know about most paranormal matters until you came to Chicago."

"What I am tore my family apart. I grew up wanting to be as normal as I could. I don't think being a vampire would give me that normalcy. How am I supposed to go back to my boring life if I'm a vampire?"

"Do you think you ever will go back to that life, even as you are now?"

"I hope to."

"You may hope, but you know nothing can ever be the same."

She stared into the darkness. "You're going to get rid of the young ones. Why would you make new vampires?"

"New vampires that are to our liking."

She crinkled her nose. This subject was making her queasy. She didn't like discussing genocide.

"When do you think Robbie will come to you?" she asked. "Soon?"

"I wouldn't doubt it."

"What do we do until he comes?"

"Do as you like. None of you are my prisoners, outside of Micha."

She swiveled toward him. "Let him go. He's of no use to you now. Between the FBI and what Robbie is about to do, no one will care about the technicalities of vampires. It'll get lost in the sea of shit that's about to erupt."

"Maybe. Maybe not."

"Why do you care what anyone thinks of you? Why does it matter?"

"The less people know about us, the less ingrained we are in their society. The more we can keep to ourselves. Don't pass judgments. This is not your world. Yet."

"Well if you continue to hold Micha, I'm staying here." She scooted to the edge of the couch and stood. "I'll wait right here for Robbie."

"Do you love him? Your hybrid human?"

She rolled her eyes at this ever-asked question.

"I don't know. I've never had the opportunity to know him outside of this. Maybe someday I can answer that question more clearly."

"I won't hurt him, for your sake. Like I saved your friends."

"Your kindness is endless." She sagged her shoulders. "But thank you for what you did. How did you do that, by the way? Changing the van to make it look like a news van? Sam told me shapeshifters can't glamour objects, only people."

Occam stood, his silhouette rising in front of her. "Sam is just a man, with one lifetime."

"What?"

"Power grows as you get older. When you're much older than a typical human, it grows quite a bit. You learn to control it in ways you can't learn in one lifetime."

"Guess that's another perk of being a vampire."

"Yes, though I don't suppose it's a selling point for you, since you're not fond of your power."

She kept her mouth shut.

"I have plenty of other advantages to tempt you with."

"How old are you?" she asked.

"I made the switch in eighteen thirty-five. I was thirty-two at the time."

She boggled. "You're almost two-hundred years old?"

"I've got a few more years before I reach that milestone."

Her fascination overwhelmed her trepidation. "Is it like in cheesy vampire movies? Are you tortured by the thought of living forever?"

"Do you think indefinite life is a curse? The thing all humans want the most, to not have to face death?"

"Doesn't sound like it."

He chuckled. "You're smart. Another reason I'm inordinately fond of you."

"Thanks." Something else popped in her head. "I wanted to ask you one more thing—why did you give me Micha's ring?"

"Why do you think I gave it to you?"

She hesitated. She could almost make out his face in the darkness. "I thought... It was just to torment me. But now I think it might be something else."

"What something else?"

"You know I can see ghosts, don't you?" She studied him, what she could see of him. "But how do you know that? It's not something you could have looked up. It's not in my records. Even if you've been spying on me, you wouldn't know that. I've only told a few people."

"You saw one at the clinic."

She tilted her head. "How do you know that?"

"I thought Micha was the one who could see, the way he reacted." He stepped closer to her. "But it was you. You saw Rose Bellevue."

"How do you know that?" The nape of her neck prickled. She subtly drew back from him. "Are you telepathic?"

"It wasn't magic. Much less mysterious. I heard you two talking through the door."

She sagged.

"Also, I can see ghosts too."

She perked. "You can?"

"Yes. I've always been able to, even as a human."

"So you gave me the ring, knowing it would help me communicate better with her? Summon her?"

"I was hoping it would."

"Why?" She shrugged. "Don't tell me you want me to talk to her and get her to say she lied about everything. I don't think you can put a ghost on trial."

"No, you can't. Ghosts are just ghosts. They're nothing. I admit, seeing her pissed me off, but there's nothing I can do about it. No, I gave you the ring because I wanted to see if it would work. And it has. Thank you for letting me know."

"What are you talking about?"

He moved closer. She stood her ground, though the prickling on the back of her neck grew stronger.

"A lot of people can see ghosts," he said. "But not many can communicate with them. Less can control them, even with an object. It takes a special person."

"What kind of special person?"

"Colloquially, a necromancer." He waved a hand. "I think the Institute calls them something else, but I don't care."

She dropped her mouth open. "I don't want to be a necromancer! I hate ghosts."

"Have you seen them your entire life?"

"No. She's the first one I've seen."

"Ah." He rocked back a little. "Interesting. And worrisome."

"Why?" She tried to stifle rising panic. Would she be hanging out with ghosts for the rest of her life?

"You'll find out, one day."

"Occam."

"Everything in time. Don't worry your pretty little head right now." He reached out and touched her shoulder, making her flinch. "I must go. I need to keep my ear to the ground. When I know where and when Robbie will meet with us, shall I tell you? Is that what you wish?"

She was stiff, fighting the urge to throw his hand off her. "Yes, that's what I wish."

"If I can make your stay any more pleasant, don't hesitate to ask." He dropped his hand away.

"You could bring us some food. Real food. I know it's been a while for you, but we can't live on potato chips and popcorn."

"Of course. And I wouldn't want you to be forced to eat anything that might exacerbate your condition."

"Thanks."

She turned toward the stairs. In doing so, she caught another fleeting whiff of cologne. Something struck her—why she noticed it, apart from it not being like Occam to smell pleasant.

"Why does that cologne you're wearing smell..."

Occam was gone, the room silent.

"...familiar?"

Chapter 21

Occam had Chinese delivered for them by Zack.

"Occam sends his regards." Zack dropped the bags in the middle of the bedroom. He smiled a fang-filled smile at June. "You're looking good."

Sam grabbed up the bags. "Thanks. Now kindly fuck off."

"Not going to invite me to dinner?" Zack still gazed at June. "I'm offended."

"Does Occam want you messing with us?" Sam asked. "More importantly, would he be upset if I had to kill you?"

Zack sneered at him. "I'd like to see you try."

"Would you?" Sam stared him down.

After a moment of dangerous silence, Zack sneered again, turned, and left the room. June breathed a sigh of relief. Sam glanced at her. She suddenly forgave him for his hot-headedness earlier.

The bag contained several Styrofoam boxes. One of the boxes had "June" scrawled across the top. She opened it and peered inside. The box contained a bunch of Chinese vegetables: snow peas, watercress, baby corn, and broccoli. She sniffed them to make sure they weren't sautéed in anything she couldn't digest.

She thrust the box at Micha, who sat beside her. "Taste these. Tell me if you taste any peanut oil or butter flavor."

Sam tossed them two wrapped sets of chopsticks.

"I don't know how to use chopsticks," she said. "Is there any plastic silverware in there?"

Sam peeked in the bag. "Nope. Time to learn a new skill."

Micha opened his chopsticks and dug into the vegetables. He took a bite and chewed slowly. He swallowed. "No. I think they're good."

"I'm sure Occam took your food issues into account," Sam said. "He'd prefer you undead, not dead."

She glared at him.

He looked down at his own open box. "Sorry."

"Guys, no more fighting." Cindy sat next to Sam. "Let's just...enjoy our food."

They fell into silence for a few minutes as they ate. June used her fingers. The vegetables were greasy, but they were cooked in vegetable oil.

"Occam says we're not prisoners here?" Sam asked, after a few bites of his stringy brown noodles.

"Just Micha," June said. "He said we could leave anytime we wanted."

"Then we should leave."

She sucked oil off her thumb and narrowed her eyes at him. "And just leave Micha here? Seriously?"

"He's not going to hurt him. You said so yourself."

"We're not leaving him here." She picked up a piece of broccoli.

"We can't stay here. Robbie may come to Occam, but do you think we have the power to fight him? Do you think he and I are just going to thumb wrestle?"

"You want to find out where Muse is, don't you?"

"Yes." He plunked his box down on the bed next to his hip. "But again, we can't face Robbie unprepared. He's not just going to tell me where she is."

"What do you suggest we do? We're on our own. You can't even trust your own people."

"Maybe. But I know who we can trust. Aaron's people. Aaron."

"Yes, we definitely need to get in touch with Aaron." June held up her hands. "But how can we do that, even if we do leave here?"

"There's only one line to Aaron. Our burner phone."

Every week, they swapped out the phone they used to contact Aaron, just in case.

"Where's that phone right now?" Micha asked.

"Muse had it," Sam said. "She kept it when I went to the protest."

"Maybe she's already called him, then," June said. "Maybe she's in hiding with him." Her heart lifted. Maybe Trina was all right, too.

"That's what I'm hoping," Sam said. "But if not, Muse and I had an agreement. If either of us had the phone and we were captured, we'd stash it somewhere. That way Aaron wasn't compromised. If they came for her and she didn't have time to get out, she would have hidden it to make sure Robbie didn't get his hands on it."

"So it could be back at the apartment," June said.

"We have to find out if it's there. That'll give us some answers." He looked at Cindy. "I was so upset earlier, I didn't even think to have you go inside and look for it. I haven't been thinking straight."

"It's understandable," Cindy said.

"So send her back." June set her box aside. She wasn't hungry anymore. "It's less dangerous than us going there."

"It's not dangerous," Sam said. "They wouldn't expect us to come back there. They don't know about the phone. Why would we go back to a place where they could easily catch us?"

"Exactly," June said sardonically. "It's a stupid idea."

"What else do you suggest we do?" Sam sat forward. "We can't fight Robbie on our own. We need Aaron."

"Send Cindy back!" June pointed at her. "She can search the apartment."

"She wouldn't know where to look. I know Muse's mind. I know where she might hide it."

"Then tell Cindy that."

"Why does everyone keep forgetting I'm a shapeshifter?"

June didn't answer, as she was distracted by a familiar bloat-like pain in her stomach. A wave of nausea rolled over her. "What the hell?" she muttered, looking down at the box.

"What's wrong?" Sam asked.

Her head swam and she started salivating, another familiar sensation.

She barely got to the hallway before the vegetables exited her stomach, along with the partially-digested corn chips from earlier. Puke wouldn't exactly ruin the bedroom's décor, but putting everyone off their food by blowing chunks in front of them wasn't exactly polite.

Micha came out and placed a hand on her shoulder as she leaned miserably against the wall, her forehead pressed to the cracked paint.

"You okay?" he asked.

"That"—she wiped at her mouth—"didn't make sense. What the hell?"

"Were the vegetables cooked in something bad after all? Shit, I'm sorry I couldn't taste it…"

She lifted her head and wiped at her nose. "No, this is like the thing at the restaurant. It doesn't make sense."

"I'm gonna go grab you some water." He left her side.

Sam took his place. "I hope you don't need the EpiPen," he said. "We don't exactly have one."

She wiped her forearm across her mouth. "I got it out. I should be okay."

"Allergic to vegetables now? You're running out of things to eat."

"This doesn't make sense. I've never had problems with vegetables. Maybe it was a seasoning or something."

Micha brought her the jug of water. Sam slunk back into the room. June swished a mouthful around and spat it on the floor.

"Maybe it's from stress," Micha said. "Doesn't stress exacerbate stuff like that?"

"I've had stress before, but yeah, not like this." She wrinkled her nose at the puddle on the floor. "I don't suppose I made the vampire house any less appealing."

"You improved it, actually."

She was still a little shaky but no longer nauseated. She lowered her voice. "I'm not letting Sam leave you here."

"Maybe he should go, though. He needs to get that phone. You guys can't face Robbie without backup."

"Why not send Cindy?"

"I think he needs this. I think he needs to feel proactive." He glanced over his shoulder and then looked back at her. "And I don't think he wants to put any more of his people in danger."

"I'll stay here, then." She clenched her fists. "He can go after the phone. I won't leave you here by yourself."

"He might need your help. Nothing is going to happen to me here. If it were, it would have happened by now."

"Micha…"

"Sam needs your help." He squeezed her arm. "He's not thinking straight. He's being rash. He needs someone with a good head on their shoulders to watch his back."

"This is insane." She peeked into the room. "What, I'm supposed to be his bodyguard now?"

"He's not going to change his mind. You can either let him go alone, or you can follow him and try to keep him from doing something stupid."

She huffed. "I couldn't do that earlier. That's why we're here now."

They walked back into the room. Sam and Cindy sat on their bed, Sam eating again—apparently puke didn't faze him—and Cindy frowning, her brow furrowed.

"You okay?" she asked June.

"Yeah." She took a deep breath. "All right Sam, you want to do this, I'm going with you. Same song and dance as always."

Sam glowered at Micha. "You weren't out there long enough to bang her. How did you talk her into it?"

Micha picked up his box. "When you convince someone gently to see reason, it's more effective than pushing them around."

"You learn that being an activist?"

"Yes." Micha resumed eating as well.

"If we do this," June said, "we have to do it fast. We'll have to disguise ourselves and take public transportation again."

"That was the plan," Sam said. "You don't have to go with me, though. You can stay here and babysit your boyfriend."

"I think you'll need more babysitting than he will."

Sam patted his crotch. "Babysit this."

June had enough. She picked up her box of vegetables from the bed and flung it at Sam. He dodged, but not fast enough to keep from getting splattered a little. They hit his arm and hip and splashed across the bed, a few tumbling to the floor.

"Jesus Christ!" Cindy jumped to her feet. "You two!"

Sam flung his box at June in return. She sidestepped swiftly, and it sailed past her. Noodles painted the wall next to the door.

Micha pinched the bridge of his nose. "Oh my God."

"Stop being a child!" June lunged at Sam as he got to his feet.

He caught her by the arms and threw her on the mattress, where Cindy had been sitting. She kicked at him.

Cindy flung herself across June's body. "Stop it! Stop fighting!"

"You're so stupid!" June raged at Sam, pointing over Cindy's shoulder. "You keep throwing yourself into the lion's den, and for what? To prove you're brave? To prove you're some kind of savior? Your people need more help than you can give them right now. But they need you alive! I need you alive!"

"What am I supposed to do?" He bent over Cindy's back. "All I can do is throw myself in the lion's den because we're surrounded by them! We have to get in touch with Aaron, no matter how dangerous it is, and I'm not throwing Cindy to the lions for that. I'm not throwing you!"

June struggled under the weight of Cindy's damned enormous body. "You stupid motherfucker." She pushed at Cindy's shoulder. "If you die, this will all be for nothing. I could have left Chicago months ago!"

Sam frowned, the rage in his eyes simmering down, his face smoothing. June kicked Cindy in the shin.

"Ow!" Cindy yelped. "You better calm down, you little bitch, or I'll twist your nipple rings out."

June sagged beneath her, struggling for breath.

Sam gripped Cindy's shoulder. "Get off her," he said gently.

Cindy hauled her huge ass off June. June sat up, yanking angrily at her shirt, as it had ridden up in the struggle. Sam offered her a hand.

She slapped it away and got to her feet. "We'll meet back here," she said, pushing her hair back. "We're coming back for Micha. What time is it now, Cindy?"

Cindy pulled her phone out of her bag. "Eight sixteen. How long do you think it'll take you to get there and back?"

"If we're near the Nocturnal District, around two hours," Sam said. "But we might have to tear the apartment apart." He paused. "Midnight. We should aim to be back by then."

"And if you don't show up?" Cindy asked.

Micha dug around in his box with the chopsticks, not looking at them. His posture was stiff.

"If we don't show up," Sam said, "find a way to get to Aaron."

Cindy tinkered with her phone. June stalked around the room, what little space there was to stalk around in, smoothing her hair and clothes.

"This is where we are." Cindy showed Sam her phone. "There's a train station three blocks from here. You can catch the brown line."

Sam took the phone and studied the screen.

"I'll see you in a few hours," June said to Micha. "Are you staying here with him, Cindy?"

She nodded.

Micha looked up from his food, his expression blank and guarded. "All right. I'll be here." His frosty tone matched his demeanor.

June couldn't deal with any more drama right now. She walked out to the hallway and turned, looking into the room at Sam.

"Come on," she said. "Let's go stick our heads on the chopping block again. It's our favorite game."

Sam handed Cindy the phone and walked out to the hallway.

"Good luck," Cindy said. "Watch your asses. And stop fighting with each other."

Sam grunted at June. "I think we needed to get that out of the way, don't you?"

June just scowled, hands on her hips.

"Midnight," Sam said. "If anything delays us, I'll call you, Cindy, because hopefully I'll have the phone by then. If we haven't arrived by midnight and you haven't heard from us, assume the worst."

Cindy clutched the phone to her chest. "I always do."

* * * *

At the train station, they purchased tickets from the ticket machine, not an easy task while holding hands, and had to wait about ten minutes. On the train, they sat close together, not making eye contact with the people around them.

Sam was a woman once again, his hair blond this time, and June looked like a hipster dude once more. Sam wore pink leggings and knee-high boots—those had to be Cindy's fashion choices, too.

"I really don't get your disguises," she murmured. "Do you secretly wish you were a woman?"

"You better be grateful I can even do this."

The car emptied after a dozen or so stops, and they were able to talk freely.

"This is the plan," Sam said. "We sneak up on the building. We watch for anyone hanging around. If any—former—Paranormal Alliance members are there, I'll be able to pick them out."

"You know what everyone looks like? What, do you have a photographic memory or something?"

"Trust me when I say I know my people." He paused. His feminine features sagged, his eyes sad. He'd kept them brown. "At least, what they look like."

"Don't get maudlin right now. Focus."

He drew a deep breath. "If it's all clear, we go inside."

"You know how to pick a lock? We don't have the keys to get in." They hadn't taken them to the park, since Muse and Trina would be there to let them back in.

"Yes, I do."

"Do you have any idea where Muse might have stashed the phone?"

"I know how she thinks. We need to check unlikely places."

June rubbed her thigh. "I hope this works." The lights of the city rushed by in the darkness, the train speeding them along to either salvation or doom.

"And I hope Aaron can actually help us," Sam said.

"He can at least stash us in another hole. Life goes on as usual."

They had to switch trains downtown, and June was hoping the transition went smoothly and without incident, that none of Robbie's people were on the lookout for them. Her stomach tightened, like she might puke again, this time from nerves.

"I'm sorry about that, back there," Sam said. "I'm really on edge right now."

"Yeah. I started it, though. Sorry I flung my food at you."

"It's not like you could eat it." He shrugged, a smile jerking the corner of his mouth.

She would not be amused, not right now.

"I don't think Micha likes us being friends," Sam said. "He seemed a little put off."

"We're more than friends." The words tumbled out before she could stop them. "I mean... We're like, soldiers. Fighting together."

Their legs were touching to keep contact; however, Sam took her hand and squeezed it.

"I think he has more feelings for you than you have for him," he said. "I'm sorry I've been riding your ass about it."

"What if he only cares about me because it's comforting? Outside of all this, maybe we don't work at all."

Sam didn't respond.

"And I'd like to know that." She flexed her fingers. "Before I make any choices."

"You sound like a soap opera."

"I'm being practical. I'd like to think at some point down the road, I'll be out of mortal danger. Then I can focus on my love life."

"What if you're never out of mortal danger?"

"Is this really the time to discuss this?"

He rubbed his thumb over the back of her hand. "If you really feel the way you say, if you really don't want to get involved with someone while the weight of the world is hanging on your shoulders, you wouldn't be messing with anyone. But you are."

She let out a sharp laugh. "Messing with someone?"

"I mean in the sexual, emotional, whatever sense."

She narrowed her eyes. "Are you jealous? Really. I've asked you before, but I've never gotten a straight answer. Are you jealous of Micha?"

"Why would I be jealous of Micha?"

"Because either you want the comfort we have in each other during this shitty time, or you want me."

"You're quite full of yourself. If I wanted you, I would have made that plainly obvious." He crossed his legs and bobbed his boot-clad foot.

"You do make it obvious."

He huffed.

"You do all the time." Her throat tightened, emotion creeping in. "And you won't tell me what's going on between you and Muse, like it's some secret. Like it'll ruin your chances with me or something."

"You couldn't begin to comprehend what's going on between me and Muse."

"Try me."

"I don't think this is the place for it."

"But it's the place to talk about me and Micha?" She yanked her hand out of his. "It's complicated between you two, right? Well, it's complicated between me and Micha, too. There's a hell of a lot going on that has to be addressed first, and I don't know what's going on between us because we don't know each other outside this mess. That's how I feel."

"But you already know when this is over, you won't like him. He holds ideals you've actively separated yourself from. He's the kind of guy you don't mingle with."

"And you are?" She snorted. "You're my type?"

"I didn't say anything about me."

"So tell me about Muse. Tell me the short version."

He still bobbed his foot. "I'd rather not talk about it until I know she's safe."

"Are you in love with her? Tell me that much."

"Love is a versatile word. There are different kinds of love."

They were coming up on the stop where they had to change trains. She almost got up and walked to the door, to get away from him, to get this damn thing started, but she would have lost his glamour. No one was in the car, but keeping mindful was important.

"I know there are different kinds of love," she said. "Sometimes love is holding and comforting each other. And sometimes it's throwing food at each other in frustration because you can't figure crap out."

The train slowed. She grabbed his hand and got to her feet.

"And sometimes," she said, "it's doing really dangerous, stupid shit together just so you can be there to make sure the other person is safe."

"Yeah." He gazed up at her. "Sometimes it is."

Chapter 22

From the final train station, they had to walk several blocks to get to the apartment building. They stuck to the shadows, keeping their heads down, avoiding the headlights of passing cars. June's frazzled nerves were a hideous accompaniment to her aching empty stomach and her overall sense of un-wellness and exhaustion.

If they survived this, she was going to spend a couple years in bed.

Upon reaching the building, they hid in the parking lot behind a dumpster. The lot was empty of people, most of the windows in the building dark.

"I'll circle around the lot," Sam whispered, "check out the perimeter."

"Are you nuts?" she whispered back. "We shouldn't split up."

"Yes, we should." He still held her hand. "You stay here. I'm the one that can change how I look, remember? If I run into somebody, I can get away by changing my appearance."

"It's still risky."

"We can't go in there until we know no one is watching the place. If anything happens, you get the hell out of here. We'll meet back at Occam's house."

She let him go because she didn't have a choice. As soon as he released her hand, she blinked back to herself. Sam remained a woman. She sat down on the pavement behind the dumpster and wiped her sweaty palm on her jeans.

"Be careful," she muttered as he took off.

She didn't have anything to keep track of time, but Sam seemed to be gone forever. Then suddenly he returned, startling her by popping around the dumpster. She scrambled to her feet.

"There's no one around," Sam said. "I told you, no one's going to watch the place because they don't expect us to be dumb enough to come back."

"Ha, jokes on them. We are dumb enough."

Sam took her hand, and they crossed the lot to the entrance of the building.

Inside, the small well-lit foyer presented them with two options: stairs or an elevator. The stairs were their only safe choice, though—the elevator had cameras in it and one of their rules since they'd gone into hiding was avoid cameras as much as possible.

She groaned. "Stairs are my new mortal enemy."

By the time they reached the second floor, where their apartment was, her chest ached and her breath was short. Combined with the rest of the unpleasantness in her body, she would probably die before Robbie ever got a chance to kill her.

"We have to get you in shape," Sam said.

"I was shot. I haven't even had a day's worth of physical therapy. I think I'm doing pretty good, given the circumstances. Shut your trap."

They walked to the apartment door. Sam looked up and down the hallway. They were alone. He let go of her, and she blinked back to herself. He also turned back to himself.

He pulled a key from his jeans pocket.

"I thought we didn't take a key with us?" She was still huffing.

He knelt in front of the door. "It's a bump key. You need to learn about lock picking, too."

"I need to get in shape. I need to learn about lock picking. I need to learn to use chopsticks. Sorry I'm not up to your standards."

"Don't worry, I'll make a soldier out of you yet."

After wiggling the key a few times, the lock popped. He stood up and turned the knob.

"We need to be quiet," he whispered. "Just in case."

They slunk into the apartment, Sam going in first. The lights were off. All was silent.

Sam grabbed a broom from beside the kitchen door. "You already have a weapon," he whispered, pointing at her mouth.

"Sure," she whispered back. "Except Robbie's deaf."

"Do you think I can kill Robbie with a broom? This is for anyone else who might be here."

They crept into the living room. Cool night air flowed through the broken window, stirring the curtains.

A struggle had taken place in the room. The couch was out of place, a table toppled over. The remote for the TV lay in the middle of the floor.

"Fuck," Sam whispered.

They checked the entire apartment: bedrooms, bathroom, every closet, nook, and possible hiding place. They were alone. Sam turned the lights on. He tossed the broom on the couch.

"There was a fight here." June surveyed the mess.

In the bedroom June and Trina had shared, things were worse. The bed had been pushed across the room, and oddly, the bedclothes were missing. One of Trina's shoes lay by the open window. June's stomach turned.

"God, what did they do to her?" June asked.

Sam walked to the window. "She probably tried to jump. They most likely killed her and wrapped her body up in the bedclothes to take her out of here."

June covered her eyes, tears burning behind her eyelids. "She was innocent, Sam. She wasn't part of our bullshit. She didn't deserve this!"

"None of us deserved this. Okay, maybe I did, a little. But not the rest of you."

"You should have left her at the clinic."

He pulled her hand away from her eyes. "What was it you told me earlier? Don't get maudlin. Focus. There will be plenty of time to cry once we get back to relative safety."

He left the room. She wiped angrily at her eyes and followed him.

They tore the place apart, searching through and under furniture, in cabinets and drawers, behind things, under things, looking anywhere a phone could conceivably be stashed and in less likely places, like the toilet tank and in the freezer. After a half hour, during which the search grew increasingly frantic, they met in the living room.

"I've looked everywhere I'd expect her to put it." Sam fidgeted. "And in places I wouldn't. Where the hell is it?"

"Maybe she didn't stash it. Maybe she thought it was better to keep it with her."

"No, she would have stuck to our plan."

"Maybe she couldn't stash it. Or they found it."

He gnashed his teeth. "What the hell are we going to do?"

The clock on the wall above the TV showed they were closing in on ten fifteen.

"We have to leave soon," she said. "We can't stay here."

Sam turned in a circle, arms out. "Where is it?"

"I could always ask someone."

He turned back to her. "What are you talking about?"

She pushed a hand into her pocket and drew the ring out. "I can ask Rose. I can get her to appear, anyway. I can't guarantee she'll give us a straight answer."

"With Micha's wedding ring?"

She turned it in her fingers, her skin already prickling with the heebie-jeebies. "I can make her appear at will by using it. She still gives me cryptic messages, but maybe it's worth a shot."

He stepped aside. "Fine, try it."

She took a deep breath and held the ring out in front of her.

For a minute, nothing happened. June stood there tense and anxious. Would Rose choose not to show up the one time June actually wanted her?

Then, she flickered into existence, standing in front of the TV, her dead gaze focused on June.

June took a step back.

"She's here?" Sam said.

"Yes."

"All right, do it."

June licked her lips. "Rose. Can you tell us where Muse hid the phone?"

Of course, Rose couldn't just point and go away. She kept staring at June.

"Come on," June said. "We don't have much time. Do you know where she put the phone?"

"The dead are useless." Sam huffed and started pacing. "About as helpful as a drunk coed at a frat party."

Rose moved forward, and June backed away.

"The one that got away," Rose said in her whispery, emotionless voice. "The safest place is with him."

"Okay," June said. "Anything else? Maybe something a little less nonsensical?"

"What's she saying?" Sam asked.

"Rose, anything else?" June prompted.

Rose drew closer. June struggled not to lower the ring and get rid of her.

"The vampire," Rose said. "He holds all the cards. Listen closely to what he's saying."

"Awesome," June said. She lowered the ring and Rose vanished.

"What did she say?" Sam asked.

"Nothing that made sense. She said 'the one that got away' and 'the safest place is with him.' And then something about Occam."

"What does any of that have to do with the phone?"

She stuffed the ring back in her pocket. "I'm sorry. I didn't guarantee anything. I'm grasping at straws here."

Sam drew a heavy exasperated sigh. He paced in a circle.

June tilted her head. "The one that got away…what if Trina got away? What if Muse gave the phone to Trina?"

Sam held his arms out. "If they didn't catch Trina, why's her shoe in there? Why would she leave a shoe behind? Because it's more fun to run with a limp?"

June walked back to the bedroom. She went over to the window and picked up the shoe—a black, dressy flat.

"Maybe it's a message."

Sam entered the room. "So where did the bedclothes go, then? Is that part of the message?"

"I don't know. Why did Rose say 'the one that got away?'"

"Why do ghosts say anything?"

She turned the shoe over and examined the sole. She pushed her fingers inside the toe, searching for a note. Nothing. Then, an idea struck her.

She held the shoe out in front of her. "Trina? Are you there?"

Sam frowned. "What are you doing?"

"I know it's crazy. But if she's dead, maybe I can summon her like I summon Rose."

"Screw ghosts and their stupid messages. We need to—"

"Shut up!" she snapped. "I'm trying, all right? We got nothing else. You have a better idea?"

Sam kept his mouth shut. June continued brandishing the shoe. If Trina actually appeared, June would probably have a despairing, guilty breakdown.

Trina didn't appear, though, and June lowered the shoe.

"She's either not dead, or she doesn't want to talk to me. Can't say I blame her."

"Now that we got that out of the way, let's look for the phone again. If we can't find it, we'll leave."

They did another search, covering all the spots they'd already looked, just in case. June kept the shoe, convinced it meant something. She jammed it in the back pocket of her jeans.

The phone remained unfound.

"Damn it!" Sam kicked over a table in the living room. "I can't believe this."

"We have to get out of here."

"She had to have left it. She had to!"

"I know ghosts are wishy-washy, but trust me when I say Rose has never told me anything that didn't make sense later. We just have to figure it out."

"We better. Or I'll dig her up and kill her again."

"Classy. We'll find another way to contact Aaron. Maybe Cindy can get in touch with him somehow."

"I have to find out what's happened to Muse." Panic tinged his voice.

"We will."

They headed for the door—however, as they entered the kitchen, it flew open as if kicked from the outside, making June nearly jump out of her skin.

"Shit!" Sam grabbed her arm and dragged her back.

Ethan strolled in the door. June didn't recognize the man who stalked in behind him, but he had a mean grizzled face and held a silver handgun.

"Oh God." June gripped Sam's arm, heart racing.

"What have you two been doing up here?" Ethan asked. "We've been downstairs, waiting for you. It's rude to keep us waiting."

June clung to Sam's arm with both hands, trembling, adrenaline pounding through her veins.

"We're impatient," Ethan said. "An old friend wants to say hi, Sam."

The man with the gun stayed behind Ethan, his gaze sharp and glittering.

"Robbie is no friend of mine," Sam said. "Why did I ever trust you?"

"Why did you?" Ethan focused on June. "Don't try to use your voice on me, by the way. Paul here, he's a telepath. He'll know what you plan to do before you do it, and he'll put a bullet right there." He tapped the center of his forehead.

"How did you know we were here?" Sam asked. "No one was watching the building. I checked!"

Ethan stepped over to the counter and slid his arm behind the microwave. "We weren't in the parking lot." He drew his arm out and held something up—a little black box. "Paul was listening from a few streets away. He gave me a call when you came in."

Sam gritted his teeth.

"Don't beat yourself up about it," Ethan said. "You couldn't have gotten away even if you didn't drag your feet up here. Paul was downstairs waiting for you. If you tried to take off before I arrived, he would have detained you. Everything was covered. You did your best. Gold star."

"How long have you been working with Robbie?" Sam snarled. "In fact, how long has Robbie been working against me?"

"All your questions will soon be answered. You can ask Robert yourself. He'll be glad to tell you. He's eager to share."

"Robert." Sam sneered. "All grown up now, is he? Where's Muse? She better be alive, or you'll pay."

Ethan chuckled. "So cocky. Always thinking you have your hands on the controls when the truth is, there's more buttons and levers than you're smart enough to work. Nice time we had in the park today, wasn't it?"

"Where's Muse?" Sam demanded again, louder.

"Don't worry. She's alive and in one piece. For now. Maybe you'll get to see her, if you behave yourself."

Sam sagged against June's side. She clutched him tighter, her muscles stiff, body poised to run.

"How could you do this?" Sam lowered his voice. "Killing your own, setting us back decades. Destroying everything we've worked for."

"It's been a long day, Sam. I understand this is a bit trying for you, but as usual, you simply don't understand the scope of what we're trying to accomplish. You don't see the big picture."

"Please, enlighten me."

"This is what always should have been. What you should have been aiming for the entire time: superiority. But you couldn't stay on track. You started listening to the activists, letting the normals have too much say in our future. You aligned yourself with the SNC."

"The SNC want what we want. They want the Institute shut down."

"Only because the Institute gives us validity. It makes us part of the normals' society. They really want us back underground, in the dark, and in graves."

Sam shook his head. "That was Aaron's father. He's not his father's son."

Ethan drew closer, and they shrank back.

"Your alliance with them is the reason your brother is dead, Sam. Who else do you want to die?"

Sam didn't reply. He was breathing through his nose, chest working.

"Robert has been highly visible," Ethan said, "where you were not. You weren't smart enough to notice him. He's done his recruiting out in the open, even more so lately, while everyone's been worried about finding you and Aaron. You could say you helped this happen by being a short-sighted fool."

"You won't get far with this," Sam said. "You can't expect this entire city to bend to your will."

"Can't we?" Ethan focused on June again. "You know, it's sad, Siren. Seeing you like this. Being lied to and led astray by this moron."

"I tend not to take the side that kills their own." Her voice shook. "It's a pet peeve of mine."

"You're powerful," Ethan said. "Don't you want to tap the full potential of what's inside you? Don't you want to be with the people who can help you do that?"

"I'm the wrong gal to tempt with power. I wish I didn't have it at all."

Ethan curled his lip. "That's an ignorant thing to say. You've never had the opportunity to explore who you truly are. But now you can."

"Leave her alone." Sam put his arm across her. "You're giving me a headache. Just do what you're here to do."

Ethan laughed. "I'm not here to do anything. Robert will take care of you personally."

"Then shut up. I don't feel like being pumped full of propaganda right now."

"You know all about propaganda, don't you, Sam? I thought you enjoyed the sound of rhetoric."

"I like the sound of *my* voice."

A beep sounded. Ethan drew his phone from inside his jacket and peered at the screen.

"Ah, that was quick." He looked up at them. "Robert has arrived, and he's eager to see you."

June searched for a means of escape. She couldn't get past the angry dude with the gun, without taking another bullet or six. Jumping out a window spelled broken ankles or worse.

"If by some chance you survive this"—Ethan strolled up to Sam—"I do hope you won't think too badly of me. I really do admire you and all the things you tried to stand for. Being a part of the Paranormal Alliance was the highlight of my paranormal existence, however brief a time." The light flashed on his glasses. "And if you don't survive, well—at least you'll go to the great beyond knowing that you touched me, Sam, so very deeply."

Sam touched him again then, with his fist to his jaw.

Chapter 23

Paul had his gun pressed to Sam's temple. June had plastered herself against the wall next to the kitchen doorway, her heart pounding in her ears. Sam, despite his situation, didn't cower or beg forgiveness. He clenched and unclenched his bloody fist at his side.

Ethan clutched his broken glasses in one hand, mopping at his bloody nose with the other. He was red-faced and seething.

"You better not move an inch," Ethan snarled at Sam. "Robert's on his way up right now."

"Don't shoot him," June begged. "Please!"

Paul narrowed his eyes at her. Ethan stepped forward.

"Get over there." Ethan placed a hand in the center of Sam's chest and pushed him toward June.

Sam shuffled backward to where she stood and pressed his back to the wall next to her. She clutched his hand. His palm was slick with sweat, his knuckles slick with Ethan's blood. Paul backed off but kept the gun pointed at Sam.

"You're going to pay for that." Ethan clamped a hand over his nose. "I hope you enjoyed it, because it's the last shot you'll get."

"I loved it." Sam's voice was dark.

June clutched his hand tighter. "Don't make this worse."

Ethan let out a wet, harsh laugh. "Oh, it's about to get as bad as it can get, Siren." His hand muffled his voice.

The door to the hallway, still half-open, pushed inward and swung open wide. A gangly, narrow figure dressed in black breezed across the threshold.

"Hello there, Sam," Robbie said.

His hair was pulled back, making his visage strikingly gaunt, and the scar that striped his face stood out deep red against his pale skin. A milky film covered his eyes, their iridescence shining through the haze. A smile twisted his thin lips.

"This jackass punched me," Ethan complained through his hand.

Robbie's smile widened, stretching freakishly over his teeth. "Still feisty as ever, Sam, I see."

Sam fixed his gaze on Robbie, hard and burning. He looked almost as crazy as Robbie. His hand trembled in her grip.

Robbie shifted his attention to her. "June Coffin. It's good to see you again. You're my hero, you know."

"I am?" she squeaked.

"Yes. You escaped the Institute and got your brother out of there as well. You didn't let them steal your secrets. Good job."

"And my life has been wonderful ever since."

His face smoothed and he stared at her. Her skin crawled under the weight of his milky gaze. She forced herself to think hard and graphically about the time Diego got raging drunk and threw up on the side of her car.

Robbie tilted his head. "Too late. I already know where he is. It's easy to snatch information out of that thing you call a mind."

She pulled in a sharp breath. "He's of no use to you."

"He's of great use to me." He shifted his attention to Sam. "I'm glad to see you again. I wanted to ask you what you thought of the show today."

"You're a monster." Sam's voice crackled with rage. "A sick, twisted, psychotic piece of filth. I'm going to rip you to pieces. Mark my words."

Robbie tutted. The light gleamed on his hair. Everything about him seemed to glisten, in an unnerving preternatural way.

"I only did what you couldn't do, Sam. What you wouldn't do. Don't be jealous because I had the guts to do what the paranormal people in this city have needed for years."

"Except the ones who died," June said.

"The weak die. The strong, the smart—they flourish."

"I never should have trusted either one of you," Sam said. "I should have given that information to the FBI myself."

"Oh, don't worry," Robbie said. "They got the information. Now they just need Micha. They'll close the place down. No more paranormal people will walk in those doors. And once the building is empty of our people, we'll burn it down. Then we'll hunt down every researcher who ever worked there and slaughter them in their beds."

"So that's your plan?" Sam said.

"It's the second part of my three-part rise to power, actually." He held up three long, spindly fingers. "First, I gain the respect of my rightful followers by exerting my influence. I did that today." He lowered one finger. "Two, I gain their trust by giving them a gift I've long promised— the Institute is shut down." He lowered a second finger, leaving his middle finger up.

"And the third part?" Sam said.

June held her breath.

Robbie lowered the third finger and smiled his wide, sinister smile. "I gain their loyalty, by standing before them with your head in my hands. Or on a spike. That would be more festive."

Sam's shoulders stiffened. "I'd make an ugly maypole, trust me. But you, you'd look great on a skewer."

June let her breath out, but she still couldn't get much air in.

"I fail to see how you'd get me on that skewer." Robbie kept smiling. "But if it makes you feel better to do all this posturing in your final moments, then by all means."

"Where's Muse?" Sam asked. "I know you took her."

"Yes, I did." Robbie passed his fingers over his face diagonally, tracing the scar. "That little bitch has to pay for what she's done. She's a fighter, she is. I can't wait to take that out of her."

"I think she improved your face," Sam said. "Still pretty damn ugly, though."

Robbie strolled toward them. June shrank against the wall.

"And is this what you consider beautiful?" Robbie gestured at her. "This frightened, quivering thing, hiding from the truth? So scared of what she is, she doesn't understand her own nature? You claim to stand for paranormal people, but you abide by her self-hatred and the hatred of everything like her."

She opened her mouth but couldn't form words. She might have been belligerent if she weren't terrified.

"There's no use talking to them, Robert." Ethan's nose was still oozing blood, his voice nasally. "They're scum. They're the sort of disease we need to get rid of. They're no better than the normals and the activists."

Robbie lifted a hand to him and Ethan fell silent.

"I want to see Muse," Sam said. "If you've hurt her, I don't care if it's the last thing I do on this earth, I will destroy you."

"She's unharmed," Robbie said. "Do you really think I'd hurt her without you present? I want to enjoy the look on your face while I torture her. But it doesn't have to come to that." He spread his arms. "I thought perhaps if you heard me out, you might change your mind about joining me."

Sam laughed. "You can't be serious."

"It's the only chance you have of living through the night, and a slim one at that."

June glanced at Paul, hovering in the doorway, gun still trained on them. She couldn't get past him no matter how fast she moved.

"There's no way in hell I'd ever join you," Sam said, "or condone the things you've done. You killed innocent people."

"So did you, when you made a treaty with the SNC. You got your brother killed. He was innocent, wasn't he?"

Sam tensed again, his fingers curling around hers.

"Let me tell you a story," Robbie said. "I used to look up to you, Sam. You used to give me hope. I was a lost soul when the Institute first opened. Certainly, I had my books, my vast library of the paranormal. I learned much, but I never felt connected to any of it. Others like me— they seemed scary, so disorganized and angry and shiftless. I found them hard to approach."

Sam grunted. "Yeah, *we're* scary."

"I went willingly to the Institute when it first opened. I thought they were trying to do something good and bring our community together. I thought they were the direction we needed. It only took a few days to discover what was really going on. I managed to escape because I was clever and powerful."

He stepped closer to Sam.

"And then you came along. Your rise to power impressed me, dazzled me even. You hated the Institute, and you hated the SNC. Mr. Jenkins's people didn't care we were being tortured by the Institute. They just wanted us to go back into the shadows. They were killing us: hate crimes, mobs, oppression. And there you were, a shining hero come to save us."

"I never advocated violence against violence," Sam said.

"But you should have. You had such a promising platform, but instead you chose to make a treaty with the SNC, rather than take their blood in return."

"Aaron is not his father," Sam said. "His father made them a hate group. Aaron wants to clean that up and he has. I aligned with him to benefit both of us, to give us numbers against the Institute."

Robbie's eyes glistened. "And your brother died as a result. Not everyone in Aaron's organization wanted a treaty. Not everyone in yours did."

"And that's how you got your followers, isn't it?" Sam shook his head. "The people who didn't agree with us flocked to you."

"The dissenters were small and powerless at first, but I found my place among them. A place in the world, finally. I didn't have the charisma you had, and I certainly didn't have your political clout and money, but in small groups, people listened to me. Ideas were formed. And they spread, changing minds."

"Like cancer," Sam said.

Ethan had been listening silently, his expression proud, chin tilted up, eyes fixed dreamy and adoring on Robbie. He was clearly full to the brim with Robbie's Kool Aid.

"I built my numbers behind your back," Robbie said. "You ignorant, blind fool. You have no idea how deep I've burrowed in. Nearly all your operatives inside the Institute are in my pocket. I let you find out what I wanted you to find out, including about the serum."

"What?" Sam gasped.

June found her voice. "I don't understand that. You and Sam both want to see the Institute fall. Why would you withhold information from him when you want the same thing?" Occam's words whispered in her head: Robbie wanted the Institute to crumble on his terms. Sam needed to hear this. He needed to hear the truth and finally see.

"Information is power," Robbie said. "I didn't have your money or influence, Sam. But I had information. I was willing to stand by your side at one point, you realize. Your charm and my knowledge? We could have ruled the world."

"It was your ploy," June said, "to get him on your side. Present him with this knowledge and he'd make you his right hand man?"

Robbie looked at her. "No, darling. He'd be my right hand man."

"I can't believe this." Sam huffed. "Here I've thought I was blind to the actions of one man, when it was a giant conspiracy to keep me in the dark. How can you call me stupid when this was engineered to make me fail?"

"You could have noticed it," Robbie said. "You could have noticed me, instead of chasing shadows."

"You killed our people!" Sam lurched away from the wall. "You covered your tracks by blaming the SNC, and you sent me chasing those shadows. This wasn't my fault. It was yours."

"If I couldn't keep our kind from going to the Institute, I had to keep the Institute from using them. It was a drastic measure, but it had to be done. I couldn't let them keep stealing from us."

"Knowing what you knew," June said, "you could have taken that information to the FBI a long time ago."

Megan Morgan

"We needed them to actually conduct the experiment. Eric injected himself before he injected Micha, but we certainly couldn't carry him off to the authorities."

"So you're going to shut down the Institute," June said, "and then you're going to give your people Sam's corpse to chew on, and then— what? You take over the city?"

"It doesn't have to come to Sam being torn apart. I can present his head still on his shoulders. I'm giving you the chance, Sam, to join me." His gaze on Sam might have been beseeching and benevolent, if his eyes were anything but alien. "If you join me now, this doesn't have to end badly. I'll spare you. I'll spare Muse. I'll make sure all your friends are exonerated."

Sam leaned forward. He lowered his voice. "I somehow must not have made it clear how much I want to reach down your throat and rip your spine out."

Robbie shook his head. "I figured as much. I don't need you, as you can see, but it would have been nice."

"This is one city," Sam said. "The whole big bad world is out there, beyond the boundaries of Chicago. You can take over this city, but what are you going to do about the rest of the world?"

"Others will join us."

"Your megalomania is truly astounding." Sam backed off.

"My voice will be heard. People will follow me because I have alternatives for them. I can give them freedom and safety."

"For how long?" June asked.

Robbie jerked his head to her, like a blind animal sensing vibrations.

"You're dying," she said. "Every day it's getting worse. You can barely see now." She was still terrified but caring less. They'd die fighting or they'd die chained up. The former held more appeal.

"And the vampires won't help you," she said. "Occam told me. They don't want an invincible monster running loose in this city."

Sam looked at her.

"He wants the vampire virus," she told him. "Eric failed at injecting himself with it—all the bad side effects, none of the good ones. Turns out you have to get it right from the source."

"I will get it," Robbie cut in. "If I have to drain one of them myself."

"It won't work," she said. "There's some magic in a vampire willingly making you one of their own, something Rose couldn't uncover."

Robbie's eyes appeared to glow, as if his evilness powered them.

"Even if I were to die today"—his voice was low and deadly—"others would rise to take my place."

"Would they?" she said.

Robbie grabbed her by the forearm and jerked her forward. His touch was like electricity, hot and prickling. He gripped her painfully tight.

"I'm not the only one in this room who's actively dying," he snarled in her face. "Don't you think your vampire friend has a hidden agenda? They all do."

"Let go of me!" She jerked at his grip.

"You don't understand yourself at all. It's shameful."

"Let her go!" Sam said.

Robbie didn't. "You're powerful too." He grabbed her stomach in a claw-like grip with his other hand. "Just because you don't use it, doesn't mean it's not there, gnawing away at your guts."

She stopped struggling and stared into his eyes, her blood running cold.

"Vampires love powerful people," he said. "They swoon all over a paranormal person with vast abilities. Occam knows how to make bargaining chips."

"What are you talking about?" His hands on her were hurting, his fingertips hard pinpoints digging into her skin.

Robbie laughed. His breath was stale. "She doesn't know she's dying, Sam? You haven't told her?"

The air left her lungs. "What?"

"Your allergies," Sam said. "I suspected it."

Her throat tightened. "No…"

Robbie let go of her and flung her away. She stumbled back against the wall.

"Are you sure you don't want to join me?" Robbie taunted her. "We can die together." He burst into uproarious laughter, high-pitched and evil.

She clutched her stomach, the sensation of his fingers still there.

"As beautiful as this moment is"—Robbie made a sweeping motion at the door—"I'm afraid we must go. There are things to be done, people to take care of. Last chance, Sam." He gazed at him. "Would you like to come to the good side of the fight?"

"Go to hell," Sam ground out.

"After you. After her."

Robbie swept out the door. Paul jerked the gun at them. Sam grabbed up her hand again, clutching it tight. She was numb.

Robbie led them out of the building, Ethan and Paul at their backs.

June was reeling from what she'd just learned and couldn't focus on her current situation or survival. Robbie led them down the stairs, seeming to float down them.

"Where are you taking us?" Sam asked. "You can't just finish us off in private?"

"What fun would that be?" Robbie's voice drifted up the stairwell. "My followers want to enjoy it, too."

He led them outside into the night. The air smelled fishy and briny like the lake, and June's queasy stomach lurched. A small group of people stood under a security light, a short distance from the building's entrance. Robbie approached them, arms raised.

"Stay right here," Ethan ordered.

Sam and June stopped.

"He'll summon you when you become pertinent."

"My children," Robbie crowed.

Five people stood under the light, two men and three women. One woman held up a cell phone as Robbie approached, obviously recording him.

"I have brought you a gift." Robbie spun around dramatically toward Sam and June. "As promised."

All attention focused on them. The woman with the phone pointed it in their direction.

"I promised you I'd bring him to us." Robbie's eyes glowed in the darkness. "He'll be brought before our gathering tomorrow, and I'll put an end to his weak reign."

"I trusted all of you," Sam said. "You betrayed not only me, but your own kind!"

"No, Sam," Robbie said. "It was you who betrayed your own kind. I'm freeing them from your ignorance and oppression."

His followers were nearly swooning. One of the women started weeping.

"Bring him his gift," Robbie said. "I want to show him my hospitality."

The two men broke away from the group and started across the lot, toward a black van.

"You disappoint me, Sam." Robbie strolled toward them. "You had potential."

"Save it," Sam said. "I heard this already. You're just showing off for the camera."

The girl with the phone followed Robbie. Robbie looked at her. "I don't need to threaten him, now do I? He's helpless. He always has been."

The girl giggled, holding the phone up to him.

The men slid the side door of the van open. June stood stiff, barely able to breathe.

"He won't be so snappy when we leave here," Robbie said. "I'll give him a little something to weigh on his heart."

The men dragged someone out of the van, someone small and short and dressed in white.

"Muse!" Sam lurched forward.

Ethan threw an arm across his chest.

"I told you," Robbie said, "she's unharmed. For now."

The men carried Muse between them. She didn't struggle, hanging limply from their arms.

June looked around, desperate, searching wildly for an escape, or for something—anything—to fight Robbie with. She looked around and caught Paul's gaze. He stared at her, his eyes glittering. She froze, her breath catching.

Those eyes. Gray, pale.

Paul tilted his chin down, arching an eyebrow. The gesture struck her. She'd seen it several times in the past week: that cocky know-it-all look.

"Don't hurt her!" Sam lurched forward again.

"Watch it," Ethan barked at him, pushing him back.

"Now, Sam," Robbie said. "I need to spill someone's blood for the camera. I can't—"

Robbie stopped short and snapped his head around. June caught her breath. She couldn't chase what she'd just realized out of her head. It was too late. Robbie had heard her thoughts.

"Robbie, Robbie, Robbie," Paul drawled behind her. "Oh, I'm sorry. It's Robert now, isn't it?"

Chapter 24

Ethan looked around at Paul, confusion in his eyes. Paul swiftly stepped forward and socked Ethan in the gut. Ethan doubled over and collapsed to the ground with an agonizing groan. Sam and June stumbled back.

Paul disappeared in a blink, replaced by Occam.

"You've been a very bad little monster, Robbie." Occam waggled a finger at him.

"Jesus Christ," June breathed out.

Robbie stood stock-still, staring at Occam with his wide white eyes.

"You pissed off the one legion of people your powers are useless against," Occam said. "Shame on you." He then called out, "Oh, kids! Say hi to Robbie."

Two figures streaked from the darkness at the edge of the lot, so fast June thought she was seeing things at first. Zack and Belle leaped on the two men holding Muse. The men let go of her and she stumbled, almost falling. Zack and Belle dropped the men to the ground without much struggle. What the vampires did to them was unclear, since June was too far away, but only one of the men had time to cry out before they were both still and slumped on the pavement.

The woman with the phone shrieked and backed away, still recording.

Occam pushed past Sam and June and strode toward her. "Honey, vampires don't like their picture taken."

She screamed as Occam grabbed the phone from her. She took off running across the lot, into that terrifying darkness where more vampires surely waited.

Before the other two women could run as well, Zack and Belle jumped on them too. Belle fell into the bushes with one woman, and Zack threw the other one to the ground and attacked her neck. More screams shattered the night, before they were quickly and brutally cut off.

June's heart was pounding out of her chest.

Sam rushed over to Muse. He grabbed her around the shoulders and pulled her against his side.

Zack and Belle leaped away from their victims, and the three vampires circled Robbie in a wide, slow, ominous loop.

"I'm not alone," Robbie said. "More of my people are here."

"Not anymore," Occam said. "More of my people are here. We got rid of your people, just like we got rid of Paul." He held up the cell phone. "Tell the viewers how that makes you feel."

The phone flew from Occam's hand and smashed on the pavement. Occam laughed.

"I will kill you all," Robbie snarled.

"What, by throwing stuff around?" Occam chuckled. "None of us have anything you can hurt us with. My gun wasn't real."

June un-rooted herself from her stunned position and hurried over to Sam and Muse. "Is she okay?"

Muse peeked out from beneath Sam's arm, her face twitching. She didn't have any visible injuries, at least. "I'm okay," she whispered.

"I can still rip their guts out." Robbie pointed at the three of them. "Quite literally."

"Go ahead," Occam said. "But I should warn you, if anything happens to them, my followers are out there in the darkness, ready to jump on you like rats on a corpse. And Robbie, around vampires, you're just a man."

Zack clicked his teeth at Robbie. "And we're hungry."

"Why are you doing this?" Robbie demanded. "You're neutral! Now suddenly you jump in the fight? This war doesn't concern you."

"You're right," Occam said. "Kill each other. Slaughter each other down to the last and let the blood flow through the streets. We don't care. We'll pick over your bones when you're done."

"Then why? Do you want me dead, so our groups will clash and kill each other in some glorious battle, so you can have the city?"

"Yes, of course we want that," Occam said. "But that's not my motivation tonight."

"Then tell me what's going on." Robbie turned in a circle. "Why are you crawling out of your hole and putting me in a corner? Just because you can?"

"It's because you're fucking with my investment, Robert," Occam said. "And self-interest is my only interest."

June's head was spinning from confusion. Occam looked over at her, smiled, and waggled his fingers at her in a little wave.

"Her?" Robbie grew incredulous. "The reluctant Siren?"

"The very powerful reluctant Siren."

June gaped.

"Who's dying," Robbie said.

"Yes, exactly, who's dying. You know how that goes, don't you?"

"Shut up!" June stepped forward. "Stop saying I'm dying. I'm not."

"The cleansing is coming," Occam said. "Do you think we would repopulate our ranks with weak vampires? We'll own this city one day, but it will be because we built a careful empire to inherit it, brick by strong brick."

"I'm not becoming a vampire!" June said. "I'm sick of you acting like you've made a decision for me. Whatever this is, whatever you're trying to prove, you can stop it right now."

"The only reason any of you are alive right now," Occam said to her, "is because I've made this decision for you."

Robbie flung his hands up. "Fine. I won't touch your prize. Take her and go. She's of no interest to me, anyway. She's exactly the kind of cowering scum I don't want in my ranks."

June gritted her teeth, a mixture of furious and horrified.

"Now," Robbie said. "Are you going to get out of my way, Occam? You've already said this war is of no interest to you."

"I'm protecting the rest of them because it's what June wants," Occam said. "I'm making her happy. A happy Siren is a good Siren. For me."

Robbie gnashed his teeth. "Fine. Take all of them except Sam. I want him."

"No," June said. "He's not taking Sam."

Occam shrugged. "My darling has spoken."

"You're overstepping your bounds, Occam!" Robbie clenched his fists. "If you try to stand in my way, I will take you out. You'll be among those I get rid of."

"Is that so, Robert?" Occam remained unruffled. "Do you think you have the power to take out the vampires? All of us? We've already disposed of the minions you brought here with you. Bring some more. We like easy pickings."

Sam stumbled forward, Muse clinging to him. "Enough of this. No one else has to die. If you want to do something to me, Robbie, do it. We'll do this one-on-one. This doesn't have to be a war."

"It was a war long before it came to you and me," Robbie said.

Occam sighed dramatically. "This is the most fruitless pissing contest I've ever seen. Fanatics never prosper. They have a glorious blaze-up, and then they fall into their own ashes. Sam need not worry about taking you out, Robbie, you've already taken yourself out. You've wounded a city and made it furious. The normals will hunt you and your people down. They'll string you up."

"You lie." Robbie brandished his fists at him. "My beliefs will spread. We'll grow, and survive, and flourish!"

"Pretty sure every cult leader on the planet has had the same idea. Right up until a bunch of men in body armor carrying rifles put a cap on their hopes and dreams."

"You have no idea what I'm capable of."

"Yes, I do, because I saw it today. You blew your wad too soon. Don't you know the key to any successful takeover is patience, not jumping as soon as you feel froggy?"

Robbie's eyes bulged, and his jaw clenched. He was breathing hard and fast through his teeth.

He unleashed his fury. The bushes next to the building ripped out of the ground and flew across the lot, spraying clumps of dirt. June barely stepped aside in time to avoid being hit. The windows above them shattered, and glass rained down. She and Sam stumbled back from the building. Sam covered Muse's head with his arm.

"You're a child," Occam yelled over the noise. "No one is impressed. And you're drawing all kinds of attention to us. Good job."

The destruction ceased. Stray pieces of glass tinkled onto the pavement. Shouts sounded from the apartments above.

Robbie spun toward the girl Zack had attacked and left lying in the parking lot. He lifted his arm.

Something flew from her to Robbie's outstretched hand—a small black object. He whipped around and pointed the gun at Occam's face.

"You didn't disarm my people," Robbie said.

Occam stared down the barrel of the gun, unflinching. June held her breath. Zack and Belle backed off.

"You better hope you do that right," Occam said. "I've been shot before. It pisses me right the hell off."

A shriek sounded above. A woman was leaning out a window. She quickly drew her head back in.

"The police will come soon." Occam remained calm. "So you'd better make a decision. Do you think you can do this right?"

June silently willed Robbie to drop the gun.

"As an addendum"—Occam took a step forward—"if you pull that trigger, you'll have a whole mess of vampires feasting on you."

Don't do it, June thought fiercely. As much as she hated Robbie, she'd seen enough blood and gore.

Robbie's hand faltered.

"Come on. Make your move," Occam said. "You can take out a whole crowd of people, but not one vampire?"

Robbie's expression sagged. The sudden passiveness was more terrifying than his outrage.

"You're right," he said. "The time for hesitation is over."

He turned away from Occam and pointed the gun at Sam.

Time stuttered into slow motion, like when June had been shot in the parking garage. Robbie pulled the trigger. June stood frozen, helpless as everything unfolded in front of her. Sam didn't move, either. He didn't have time.

But Muse did.

She leaped in front of Sam. Time sped up again as the impact of the bullet hitting her threw her back against him, hard enough Sam nearly toppled over. He caught her under the arms, and they both collapsed to the ground.

June's ears rang from the blast. Objects started flying again: bushes, glass, rocks—a furious hurricane of debris. The cars in the parking lot awoke like disturbed slumbering beasts. Car alarms rang out, glass shattered, tires blew out. Robbie streaked away in the chaos.

She didn't think to tell Occam to stop him. She dropped to her knees next to Muse and Sam.

Bright red coated the front of Muse's tunic. She clutched her throat, more blood spilling over her fingers.

"No!" Sam screamed, cutting through the static in June's ears. "Do something!" His voice was helpless and horrified. He clutched Muse against his chest.

No help could get there fast enough, though. Blood ran from the corner of Muse's mouth. Her face had gone as white as her clothes. Her eyes were wide and lucid and filled with terror. She opened her mouth as if trying to speak, but more blood spilled out.

June whipped around. Occam, Belle, and Zack stood nearby, watching passively.

"Do something!" June demanded, and would have used her power if she could have. "Help her."

"What would you have me do?" Occam asked. "There's only one thing I could, and Sam would never allow it."

She turned back to Sam. Muse looked up at him, shaking, gripping weakly at his shirt. Sam's face was twisted and wet with tears. He gazed bitterly at June, eyes shining.

June gripped Muse's shaking hand on Sam's chest. Her skin was cold. June closed her eyes.

"Don't feel the pain," she said, over the noise around them. Warmth coated her throat and spilled across his lips. "You're not suffering."

Muse's hand went limp. June opened her eyes. Muse sagged against Sam, her face placid and eyes distant.

"I'm sorry," June choked out. Tears spilled over and streaked down her face.

Sam cried out, a half-scream, half-sob, an excruciating sound of pain. He sounded like a little boy. He hunched over Muse and gathered her against him, his tangled hair falling across her shoulder.

Lights flashed over them. A car had pulled into the lot.

"We have to go." Occam gripped June's shoulder. "Unless you want to talk to the police."

The car pulled up next to them and drew to a stop—Occam's car, the black one. They couldn't end this horrible night in jail.

"Sam"—June gripped his arm—"we have to get out of here."

Belle and Zack hurried to the car.

Occam held a hand out to her. "We're all leaving. No one will be here to protect you."

"We're coming." June struggled to her feet, pulling at Sam. "Sam, we have to go!"

Sam got up, still holding Muse, keeping her gathered to his chest. Her arm dropped away from her body and dangled, limp and lifeless, blood running from her fingertips.

Chapter 25

June sat on the porch of Occam's ramshackle prison house. The neighborhood was so still it seemed abandoned—no lights in any of the houses around them, no one out on the street. Vaguely, in the distance, the city hummed in its constant cacophony, but the noise seemed from another world.

She ached for a cigarette. Wounded lung be damned. Luckily, she didn't have one, because she would have sucked it down and paid for it all night.

A floorboard creaked behind her. Her brief respite was over. She'd been out on the porch for at least twenty minutes.

Occam stepped beside her and stood at the edge of the porch. "What a bloody end to a bloody day," he said.

She drew a deep breath. "Is he okay?"

"He's where you left him. As okay as he can be." No real concern filled Occam's voice.

The world teetered around her as she waited for something to happen, for a final shove to send things spiraling into the abyss. The tension hung so heavy it bowed her shoulders.

Occam squatted beside her. He gripped her arm. She snapped out of her stupor, frowning.

She had a fresh cut from Robbie's temper tantrum, where a piece of glass nicked her forearm. The wound was scabbing over, but when Occam rubbed his finger across it, the cut opened up fresh. She winced. Occam brought his finger to his mouth and sucked the blood off, like licking cake icing.

"Stop." She jerked her arm away. "Don't touch me."

He popped the finger out of his mouth. "I'm not snacking on you." He ran his tongue over his lips, gazing across the yard. "I'm trying to figure out something."

"What?" She held her hand over the wound.

"You can tell a lot about a person from the taste of his blood—well, if you've been a vampire long enough, you can." He rose. "Your power is incredibly strong. It's grown vast and quick over the past couple months, like a cancer multiplying. That's why the necromancy started. As your power grows, other abilities may open up to you."

"And that's why I'm dying." She forced the words out. "That's what the food allergies are."

"Yes. I knew it at once. I'm not fond of you just because you're powerful. I feel a kinship with you. I've been there."

She looked up at him.

"Back in my day, my human days, we didn't call them allergies. We didn't have such things. But it was horrible and painful nonetheless. I've forgotten a lot of things over the years, become detached from many things from my past, but that... That I remember."

"The same thing happened to you?"

"Yes. I was lucky the vampires found me when they did." He kicked at the porch floorboards, sending a tiny stone tumbling down the steps. "It had come to the point I couldn't consume anything, even water. Starvation and dehydration are a grisly way to die. Not to mention the pain from my guts deteriorating. There's no pain like being eaten from the inside out. I will never forget."

She closed her eyes, cold horror gripping her and settling deep in her chest. "That's what will happen to me?" she whispered.

"That's what will happen to you."

She opened her eyes. Anger replaced fear.

"It's not fair," she choked out. "After everything I've been through, as hard as I've fought to survive... It won't matter. I'll die anyway."

"We all die anyway. Well—not all of us. And you don't have to."

She blinked tears from her eyes. "Maybe there's something they can do now. Some medical intervention they didn't have back then."

"Nothing will stop it. That's the curse of what we are. It uses us up until we are no more. Maybe—the abominations that we are—it's how nature expels us from the ecosystem. But there's a way to fight nature, hand-to-hand. You can be victorious."

"This is your bargaining chip. You get me for your vampire princess, because my alternative is suffering and death."

He chuckled. "You won't be a princess. No more than I am a king."

"What if I choose death?"

"Death is scary." He rocked back on his heels. "You have time to decide, perhaps longer than you expect. But it will be an increasingly painful time. I'm a patient man. I will wait. I have nothing but time."

She couldn't speak.

"We will build our army, one strong soldier at a time. And one day, we will conquer. You're not overly special, but you are rare and strong. We value your future service."

"I don't know how to be a soldier. I don't even know what the hell you're fighting for."

"You will. Time heals all wounds and shows you the way. Better than you could imagine, in one lifetime."

The hum of a car engine coming down the street interrupted the quiet. Headlights splashed across the broken pavement. The vehicle slowed and stopped in front of the house, a red pickup truck with a cap.

"Ah, the party guests have arrived," Occam said.

"Who is it?" She rose slowly and cautiously to her feet.

"Don't worry, no one who wants to hurt you."

Her trepidation turned to shock, and then relief, when two people got out of the truck and walked across the yard toward them.

"Aaron! Trina!" June rushed out to meet them.

"June!" Trina called.

June clutched the other woman in a tight, trembling hug. Trina hugged her back.

"You're alive." June gazed at her in amazement as she drew back.

"So are you," Trina said. "I'm glad. I really am."

Aaron stood beside them, silent and grim.

"It looked like there was a struggle in the apartment," June said. "I found your shoe."

Trina wiggled her toes in the pair of flip-flops she wore. "Aaron was nice enough to provide me with some new shoes. It sucked running barefoot."

"Muse—gave you the phone, didn't she? We went there looking for it."

Trina nodded. "She knew they were coming, but not soon enough for us to get out. She told me who to call, what to say." She gestured at Aaron. "I hid out and he picked me up."

"How did you get out of the apartment, though?" June asked.

"Saw it in a movie." She smiled sheepishly. "Sheets around the bedpost, climbed out the window. It wasn't graceful. They came undone and I fell most of the way. Thankfully, the bushes were forgiving. But damn, am I sore."

Aaron gazed at the house, his expression stony, but consternation shining in his eyes. "Is she inside?"

June nodded.

Aaron walked stoically toward the house. Occam still stood on the porch.

"Welcome to my humble home, Mr. Jenkins." Occam bowed dramatically. "I'm sorry the butler isn't here to escort you. It's his night off."

Trina touched June's arm. "What happened? He was talking to someone on the phone, but I didn't know where any of you were or if you were even still alive."

June swallowed. "Muse is... Robbie killed her."

Trina clamped a hand over her mouth. "Oh, God... She saved my life. If she hadn't done what she did...oh, God."

"She saved more than one life tonight. But if it's any consolation, I think that's exactly how she wanted to go."

Occam beckoned to them. "Come along girls, it's not safe out here. Might get attacked by vampires."

They followed Occam inside. A few candles were lit and one lamp now had a bulb and was turned on, revealing how shabby and broken-down the place was: peeling paint, holes in the walls and ceilings, water damage everywhere, stained floors. The furniture was rotting and tattered, probably full of enough creatures to start a zoo. Everything creaked and smelled, and the whole structure seemed like it might collapse at any minute.

A sun porch sat off the living room, most of the glass walls broken or missing. Light shone out from the living room, pushing back the shadows.

Sam sat slumped on a patio couch. One hand lay limp in his lap, the other propping up his head, his elbow on the bare metal arm of the couch. His expression was blank.

Aaron stood inside the room next to the doorway, staring at the same thing Sam did.

A small white figure lay on a second bigger couch across from Sam. Her utter stillness was profound. The light showed the black drying blood on her white clothes. Her head was turned to the side, toward Sam, a smear of blood stretching from her mouth, up her cheek, and into her hair. One hand rested on her stomach, fingers curled.

Trina, standing next to June, gasped softly. She touched her lips, her eyes sparkling in the dim light.

The night was still, not even the wind blowing, yet it felt so impossibly heavy, hanging over them like a hammer about to fall.

Aaron drew a deep breath. "I always knew this day would come." His voice seemed muffled by the quiet. "Since Mary Ellen was three, I knew this was how it would end."

June blinked a few times.

"That's when her mother and I realized she was reading our minds. When we understood what she was. That was the beginning of the end. For her. For my wife. For everything."

Who he spoke this eulogy to was unclear—maybe all of them, maybe no one.

"My wife hated my father," he said. "But somehow she loved me, at least for a time. When we realized we had to keep Mary Ellen away from him, from us, to save her life, my wife had a hard time abiding it. She didn't love me after that. We sent Mary Ellen off to boarding school at the age of six, and we didn't see her much after. She spent most of her life 'away.'" He nodded to Sam. "Until the day I sent her away again, into the only protection I could really provide for her."

Sam didn't move or react.

"In her childhood, my wife never saw the practicality of it, though. She wanted her daughter, and she comforted herself the only way she knew how—with the bottle, with pills, with any chemical that would make her forget. She found a final comfort when Mary Ellen was ten. I didn't bring her home for the funeral, because my father would be there."

June tried to draw a breath in. The air seemed as thick and stifling as water.

"I don't know if my wife's death was intentional or accidental, but it doesn't matter. I hope she's at peace. I hope they both are now. Gone from this terrible world that only wanted to destroy them."

He'd sacrificed as much as any of them, even more. June hadn't considered his plight in all this. She hadn't understood it until now.

Aaron spoke to Sam. "I'll make sure she's taken care of, that she's put respectfully to rest in a good place."

Sam lifted his head a little. His gaze was distant.

"It's the least I can do for her," Aaron said. "I have some people waiting to take care of her. I'm sorry we can't have a proper funeral, but if you want to have some sort of ceremony in her honor later, I will support it."

The pain was palpable—a bleak thing filling the room, the house, the world.

"Are you taking her now?" Sam's voice came out thick.

"We unfortunately must hurry things along."

"Can I have a few more minutes with her?" Sam asked. "I'll bring her out myself."

"Of course." Aaron turned to June. "I must go speak with Occam."

June stepped aside so he could get past her and out the door. She couldn't leave, not with Sam sitting there like that, so lost and broken.

"I'm very sorry for your loss, Sam," Aaron said over his shoulder.

June frowned as he stepped around her. "What about your loss?"

His eyes were shining, but otherwise, his face was stoic. "I barely knew her, dear." He walked out of the room.

She swallowed around the salty sludge in her throat and struggled to breathe, her vision blurring.

Trina touched June's arm, smiled a watery smile, and then followed Aaron.

Tears streaked down June's face, and she didn't wipe them away. She walked over to Sam, steeling her resolve. She reached out and touched his hair. He looked up at her with glittering eyes.

"He was aiming for my heart," Sam said. "That's why he got her in the throat. The bullet is lodged in her neck. If it had gone clean through, I wouldn't be sitting here. That doesn't make me feel any better."

"I'm sorry," June whispered, tears continuing to fall. "There's something I can do for you, if you want it, if it's not inappropriate."

He slid a hand over her wrist. Blood crusted his fingers. His grip was weak. "You've done enough."

She dug into her pocket and pulled out a glass tube. "I'll give you my blood." Her hand trembled as she held the tube out to him. "I hate this thing, but I'll give it to you. I know what it was meant for now. And I'm powerful enough, apparently."

Rose's voice whispered in her head, from the hallway in the clinic: *It wasn't meant for you.* Could Rose see the future? Or had Occam already devised to give it to June at that point?

Sam kept his hand on her wrist, his grip weakening more, until he let go and dropped his hand back into his lap.

"If you want it, it's yours," she said. "I just—I don't want to watch."

Wrinkles creased his forehead, a frown on his lips.

"You gave up your chance," she said. "You gave it to me. I'm giving it back to you. Find out who the fourth murderer was."

To wake Muse, to hear her speak, might be too much for him right now, or maybe it would be a gift, to hear her one last time.

He took the tube. "How did you get this?"

"Occam, of course. He loves to give me presents." She glanced at Muse's body. "Is it all right if I don't stay? I don't want to watch, and I think maybe this is something you should have for yourself."

Sam's eyes glittered brighter. She couldn't stand to see him cry again.

"Three drops, right?" She held out her arm, the one with the cut Occam had reopened. "That's not much to give."

"It's a lot. After everything else you've given."

"Why stop now?"

She dug her fingernails into the cut, gritting her teeth. A trickle of blood started, oozing over her ink.

"If you want this," she said, "it's the least I can do. The only thing I can do. But if you don't, I completely understand."

The cut burned. The blood wended its way down her forearm.

Sam gripped her arm.

He opened the tube with his other hand, pushing up the cork with his thumb. He turned her arm gently so the blood streaked toward her wrist. As the blood dripped off her skin, he caught it in the tube.

He let go of her arm and she withdrew it, covering the cut with her hand.

He held the tube up. She widened her eyes as the fluid inside glowed for a moment, not brightly, but bright enough to notice in the darkness. A pale blue flash.

"The scientists will never figure out this magic," Sam said. "Magic is magic, and it's ours, for better or worse."

"Occam was right." Her fascination turned to anguish. "I am that powerful."

Sam touched her hand. "Go clean that up. Don't let it get infected."

She fled the room.

She went into a bathroom on the lower floor, unsurprisingly dirty and disgusting. The tile floor was broken and covered in a thick layer of filth, the toilet and tub stained black. A ripped shower curtain dangled from a rusted rod above the tub, and her mind went back to the night in the tub with Sam. A crooked mirror hung over the sink, beneath a bare bulb, and she stared into her own haunted luminescent eyes as she scrubbed her arm beneath the sputtering tap.

Her hair was limp, barely still in a ponytail. Her roots, a bright contrast to the rest of the dyed black strands, were dark blond, the color of Jason's hair, the color of a person she hadn't been since she was young. She looked much older, gray and sagging and gaunt, her glowing eyes rimmed with red, her lips dry and cracked.

How would she look when the thing eating her insides finally took over? She'd turn into a skeleton, a walking corpse. Would she even be able to walk?

She scrubbed harder, clawing at the wound, hating her very blood. She pressed her forehead to the mirror and cried so she wouldn't hear anything beyond the walls of the bathroom, so she wouldn't hear Muse's dead voice.

An interminable time later, in a daze, she walked through the silent sagging house and outside.

Everyone was outside: Occam, Trina, and Micha stood on the concrete walkway that stretched from the porch to the sidewalk. She'd forgotten Micha was in the house. Aaron stood next to the truck at the curb. She walked slowly down the porch steps.

"There's Little Red," Occam said. "Will Sam be joining us soon? The hour is late. Especially for some of us."

She floated through a fog, her brain not connecting to the thoughts it was trying to generate. Micha gazed at her, his face sagging and his eyes tired.

"I don't..." She stopped in front of them. "I don't know."

"Ah"—Occam turned toward the house—"finally. Time to get this show on the road."

June turned.

Sam stood on the porch. The streetlight turned him into a ghost, washed-out and pale. He held Muse. Her arm dangled from her side, the sleeve of her tunic dark with blood, her hand coated in a black glove of it. Nobody spoke as he descended the stairs, slow and ponderous.

He walked through their midst. Muse's head was tucked against his chest, her face hidden. They followed him out to the truck like a funeral procession. Aaron opened the gate on the truck cab.

Sam walked to the back of the truck and gently placed her inside. He leaned in and over her, close to her face.

Micha touched her arm and she looked up at him.

"Good-bye," he said softly.

She frowned. "What?"

Occam cleared his throat. "Your friends are going on a little trip. But don't despair. I think everything will turn out just fine, if they do what they're supposed to."

"What are you talking about?" June asked.

Occam held up a folder. "We found this when we were ransacking Robbie's vehicles at the apartment building. We're good at looting. It's how we get all our nice things."

Trina took the folder from him. "Thank you."

"What's going on?" June asked.

Sam walked over to them, dazed and unsteady. He had a smear of blood on his chin.

"We're turning ourselves in," Micha said.

"What?" June gaped at him. "To whom?"

"The FBI," Aaron said. "I'll probably spend some time in a cell, but hopefully not long." He pointed at the folder in Trina's hands. "That's the documentation on the serum."

"And Micha is the proof," Trina said.

"Robbie said he already gave the information to the FBI," Sam said. "But we're not taking any chances. The way he does everything on 'his terms?' I'm sure he only gave them a little, or he's dangling it over them. Or he lied. Better to cover our bases."

She looked desperately at Sam, breath catching. "Are you going too?"

He shook his head.

"And don't forget what else is in there," Occam said to Micha. "The important part."

Micha tilted his head back. "Of course. The proof of my wife lying about vampires."

Occam shrugged at June. "Turns out she fabricated all her research. Our scientists uncovered the truth. Lying tramp."

Micha rolled his eyes.

"There's a safe place for you and Sam to go," Aaron told June. "Occam has assured me he will deliver you there safely, on pain of losing the benevolent payments from my lawyers his friends receive every month."

Occam bowed to him.

"Cindy will continue to be your liaison," Aaron said. "Hopefully, you won't have to stay in hiding long."

"Robbie's still out there," Sam said. "I don't intend to hide anywhere long."

June turned to Occam. "You're really letting Micha go? This bullshit is over?"

"This bullshit is far from over," Occam said. "But he's free to go fight the Institute. What I want will be taken care of." He clapped Micha on the shoulder, making him flinch. "I know he'll do right by me. I make good threats."

Micha pulled away from him.

Aaron walked to the truck. Trina followed.

"You're letting me go too?" June asked. "Aren't you afraid I'll skip town?"

"You're not going anywhere." Occam smirked. "You won't leave this city anytime soon. We'll see each other again. Maybe much quicker than you'd like."

Aaron and Trina got in the truck, Aaron behind the wheel. Trina left the passenger side door open.

"You don't have to do this." June gripped Micha's wrist. "We can find another way."

"If there were another way, we would have found it." He squeezed her hand. "Be careful, and stay in hiding for now, so you don't get hit by the fallout. If everything goes as planned, we'll see each other again soon."

"I don't have a lot of faith in our plans working out."

"Yeah, neither do I."

"Micha." She squeezed his wrist. "Don't let them hurt you."

He smiled a slight sad smile. "I don't know what my fate is, but I'm glad we got to share some of this road together. I'm sorry you ended up in this mess, but you're strong and you'll make it out. I promise."

He leaned down to her. She lifted her mouth for a kiss, but he missed her lips and kissed her cheek instead. She stared at him as he drew back.

"Take care of him," Micha whispered. He glanced at Sam. "He's smart, but he's not as tough as he acts."

Micha walked to the truck. She was stunned, her heart aching. After he closed the door, he gave her another sad, winsome smile and waved.

Sam stepped up beside her. "God speed," he whispered.

She reached out and took his hand as the truck pulled away from the curb. Aaron honked once.

Occam cleared his throat behind them.

"Don't just stand there. Let's get you to your hideout before the shit hits the fan."

Chapter 26

Another clean white penthouse high above a downtown street, surrounded by massive stone and glass towers—removed once again from the world by height and anonymity. A well-stocked kitchen and every need fulfilled, showers and beds and clothes. A prison that wasn't a prison.

Cindy stopped by, and she cried. Sam didn't want to talk to her, so June had the necessary conversation. June hugged her before she left and promised to pass her condolences on to Sam, who was sequestered in the bedroom he'd chosen.

After Cindy left, June sat in the kitchen at the island counter, nibbling on a carrot and drinking water. Dawn approached, paling the dark sky beyond the huge walls of windows. She was tired to the bone but sleep wouldn't come easy.

She approached the closed door of Sam's room. She knocked once, received no answer, and let herself in.

Take care of him.

The lights were off. He wasn't on the bed, or on the couch in the room, or in any of the chairs. The door to the bathroom was open and the light off.

The door to the balcony was open as well, and for one awful, heart-stopping moment, she feared the worst. However, he sat in a chair out there. She stepped outside.

The air was warm and humid, ruffling her freshly washed hair and new clean clothes. The buildings around them reflected the dull pre-dawn light.

"I just wanted to check on you before I went to bed," she said.

Sam had one bare foot propped on the short glass table in front of him. He still wore his jeans, red splatters across the denim. He was shirtless. He'd cleaned the blood from his skin.

"Maybe you should try to get some rest too," she said. "I know it won't be easy, but you must be exhausted."

He didn't move. She couldn't leave him sitting out there, even if she had to stay up and watch over him.

He stirred and rubbed his temple. "How could so many terrible things happen in one twenty-four hour period?" He didn't sound like himself, stripped of everything vital and raging and brilliant, whittled down to bone and emotion and vulnerability.

"Seems to be the way of things." She gazed over the city. "It only takes a second for everything to fall apart."

He didn't reply.

"Cindy was here," she said. "She gives her condolences. She said anything we need, just contact her."

He dropped his leg and got to his feet.

"Sam?"

He approached her, his gaze fixed intently on her face. He stopped in front of her, towering over her.

"Get some rest." She gently gripped his arm above the elbow. "When you wake up, we'll try to…figure this out. Maybe you should eat something first, though. I know it's hard, but—"

He leaned forward, closing the small gap between them, and slid his hand onto her waist, into the curve of her side where it met her hip. His touch was light and yet overwhelmingly possessive.

"Sam," she said softly, warningly. "You should rest."

He tilted his head down, his hair sweeping around his face. She stretched up to meet him, despite her misgivings, too tired to fight what was probably the wrong thing to be giving in to at this moment.

The kiss was different than any kiss they'd shared before—not stolen or forced, but deep, willing, and consuming. A gasp gusted out of her and into him.

He moved his hand around to her lower back, up under the tank top she now wore, and up the curve of her spine. She arched toward him and gripped the thick muscle of his hip peeking over the top of his jeans. He pulled her against him, tight against the solid heat of his body.

They broke the kiss and she sucked in a breath. Her lips tingled.

"Sam, is this really what you want right now?"

He answered with an even more powerful kiss and wrapped his arms around her, lifting her off her feet.

Guilt surged through her, chased by desire. She didn't deserve such a good, vibrant, alive feeling, when they were still so close to tragedy and grief. She didn't deserve him, like some spoil for a battle she hadn't fought.

This didn't stop her from undoing his jeans when he placed her back on her feet. She didn't tell him to stop when he tugged at her nipples through the thin fabric of her top, sharpening her desire. She didn't keep her tongue from meeting his as he devoured her mouth again. Through the guilt, she burned for his hands on her. She wanted this to happen.

He gripped the bottom of her top and pulled it up over her head. The warm air caressed her bare skin, adding to all the lovely sensations she didn't deserve to feel. He dropped the top on the balcony floor, and she grabbed him by the belt loops.

They stumbled inside, into the cool darkness of the bedroom. Guilt rose sharply one last time, trying to talk some sense into her, but she pushed it aside and continued dragging him toward the big perfectly made bed. They had to mess it up, destroy it, like they were destroyed, like everything in the world was messed up.

The bedspread was soft and silky against her back as they tumbled onto it. She had on lounge pants, and he dragged them down over her hips. He moved so quick and confidently, making her more eager, more willing to ignore everything else for him.

He pushed his jeans off. He wore dark-colored boxer briefs, and she gripped him through the soft, sweat-damp cotton. The hard, thick heat that filled her palm snapped the tension inside of her, a powerful longing born of something kindling for a long time. That thrill of wanting so bad, so deep, for so long in secret.

She hooked a finger beneath the elastic of his briefs and tugged them down.

Unless Sam was overcome with remorse and stopped this, she would not fight any longer. If he did stop, she would probably wither from sexual frustration, but she would understand.

Thankfully, he didn't stop, and she emitted a soft relieved moan when he pushed his fingers into her. She was soaked. Ready. He smoothed his thumb over the ring, and his touch was perfect, not too rough, not too gentle.

They'd wasted too much time in the past few months to stall now with more agonizing, pointless hesitation. She pressed her knees against his sides, and with every inch of her body, begged him to end the senseless circle they'd been dancing around each other.

The thought of protection flashed through her head, and she wondered if there were any condoms around, but they were already so hopeless and shameful it didn't matter anymore.

He slid into her, filling her at last, the sensation so intense it was nearly painful. She gasped, arching beneath him, gripping a handful of his hair. He breathed raggedly against her neck.

She dug her knees into his sides. "Sam."

He thrust into her. Slow, and then faster. Harder. He braced his arm above her head and gripped her thigh with his other hand, pushing her leg up. Getting in deeper.

They didn't talk, just gasped and moaned and begged each other silently with touches and kisses and the rolling of hips for more. Talking was pointless. What they wanted was obvious, finally laid bare for each other.

She usually couldn't get off without a little extra stimulation, but this time, to her breathtaking surprise, his cock inside her was enough. He had the right angle, coupled with the much longed-for weight of his body above hers, his desperate gasps in her ear, the scent of him, and just him. The reality merging with fantasy was enough.

She cried out helplessly against his shoulder as she clenched around him, the orgasm so deep and hard her vision went gray. She dug her nails into his back, pressing them into his taut, sweaty skin. He tangled his fingers in her hair and licked over her jaw.

He worked her harder, his muscles tense, his shoulders flexing beneath her gripping hands.

"Sam," she panted out, scrambling for some sense of practicality. "Now would be a really bad time for us to become parents."

"I know," he grunted against her ear.

A moment later, he abruptly pulled out of her. She shivered at the sudden burst of sound from him—deep, delicious, satisfied groans, very much like him, like the Sam she knew and wanted for months. He shivered above her, and she stroked her hands across the quivering muscles of his chest. Wet heat slicked her stomach.

He slumped, his hips lifted delicately above hers.

He rolled off, leaving his scent hanging above her—sweaty, raw, masculine, a faint trace of that musky cologne he always wore, even when they were in hiding. To impress her, maybe? She was impressed.

She got up and went to the bathroom, her legs weak and body buzzing. She brought him back a towel.

Megan Morgan

They lay in the blue light of early morning, naked, still not speaking. Her guilt expanded to touch other things, other people she had betrayed by doing this. The kiss Micha had placed on her cheek blazed in her memory.

Apparently, she had a thing for screwing guys who had recently lost the woman in their life.

Sam lay on his back. She was on her stomach, her face turned toward him. He reached out and stroked her shoulder. The moment seemed charged and yet unspeakably sacred and humble.

"Sam..." she whispered.

"Get some rest."

"You should too." She reached over and stroked his hair back from his face.

"Help me," he murmured. "Help me rest."

She didn't need to ask what he meant.

"Forget what's happened, until you wake up." Heat rose from her chest to her throat. "Be at peace until your body is rested." She chose her words carefully, so she didn't have a repeat of Micha.

His eyelids drooped, and his hand sagged against her shoulder. She rolled onto her side and took his hand and held it between hers.

He faded out, and he wasn't like himself at all again as he sagged into the bed—too vulnerable, too human. The slickness between her legs reminded her he was still Sam, the man she'd fought alongside, the man who was perfect for her.

The sun rose, golden and bright, driving back the long, terrible night. As the dazzling rays warmed the room and chased out the demons, she finally closed her eyes and joined him in sleep.

* * * *

The room was still filled with sunlight when June opened her eyes, and for a second, she didn't remember how dark the world really was. Sam sleeping next to her brought her back to reality. He was sprawled on his stomach, the sheets gathered around his waist, the light tracing the curve of his spine.

She'd dreamed about waking up to this. She did not dream about waking up to it under these circumstances, however.

Her old friend guilt sat on her chest like a nightmare hag, driving her to crazy thoughts.

What she'd done to Micha earlier that year, making him forget, screwing up his mind, was not something she could ever put someone else through. Still, part of her considered getting up, dressing, and making it seem like she had never been in the bed—and then speaking to Sam immediately when he awoke and making him forget what they'd done. He didn't need to feel guilty on top of everything else.

She couldn't do that. She rolled toward him and rested her hand on his shoulder. His skin was warm.

He stirred, shifting against the pillow, and opened his eyes.

She held her breath. The command she'd given him to forget and sleep seemed to fall away as he lifted his head. One moment his eyes were wide and placid, and then they darkened and his eyelids drooped.

"Hi," she said softly. "I wanted to make sure I didn't completely erase your memory last night."

"No." He rubbed his face. "I remember, trust me." He looked around the room. "What time is it?"

"A little after two."

He grunted and dropped his face in the pillow. "It's late."

"Not like we have anywhere to be."

"No, I guess not."

They lay in silence for a few minutes. The room was cool, even with the balcony door still open. The dull roar of the city drifted in.

"Thank you for helping me rest." He turned his face to her. "My body needed it."

She was thirsty. Hungry. She was used to being hungry, which would be helpful in the future, apparently.

"Sam…" She had to get the words out. "We were both emotional last night and we needed comfort. I don't want to hurt you or make this any more difficult for you."

"You didn't make it difficult. Don't apologize."

"I thought she was an amazing person. I liked her. I respected her. I still do. Even now, I don't want to step on her toes. I seem to have a flair for this." She winced. "I swear I don't have a fetish for other people's loss."

He touched her arm. "You're not stepping on any toes. I told you, don't apologize."

Despite his voice being calm, it was also firm. She dropped the subject.

"Occam played his card," she said. The sunlight stretched across the ceiling, and she was amazed at how the world went on, the sun shined, the sky was still blue. "He's been playing me right into his arms."

"Yet you're still lying here in this bed, with me, in broad daylight."

"He went through the same thing I'm going through, the food allergies. It gets worse, according to him. It's what nearly killed him. He said it was terrible. It ate him away, and there was so much pain." Her voice caught. "He'd nearly wasted away by the time the vampires took him."

"It was a different time. I know Occam is old. He's bragged about it."

"That doesn't mean there's a cure now. They couldn't cure Muse, could they?"

Sam didn't respond.

"It's my fate to die horribly, in pain. To have my guts eaten away." She shook her head. "It's not fair, not after all this."

"You believe what he says?"

"He's never lied to me. He's many things, but he's not a liar. He doesn't need to be."

"And so Occam has offered you vampirism as an alternative, I take it?"

"He says I'll be a good soldier." She blinked against tears. "I'll be all the things I never wanted to be, all the things I never had to be until I came to this awful city."

Sam lifted his head. He scooted closer, pushing his hair back behind his ear. He gazed down at her. "Do you want to be a vampire?"

She struggled with the answer, because it was more complicated than a simple "yes" or "no." "I don't want to die." Her voice was strained. "That's all I know."

He stroked his fingers down her cheek. "Then we'll find another way. Occam is taking too much delight in this. We won't let him have his way."

"He says I may have a while. I don't know about that. I've had this my entire life, but it's progressing faster now."

Sam lowered his head and rested it on her shoulder, his fingers curled against her cheek.

"Sam. About last night—"

"Shh…" He placed a finger against her lips. "It's all right to just leave some things the way they are. We don't have to talk about everything."

He sounded too much like Micha.

She convinced him he should get up and take a shower, that it would do him good. She'd make breakfast while he cleaned up. They needed some sustenance other than fast food and snacks.

"There are clothes here," she said. "They're in one of the other bedrooms. I'll bring you some stuff."

Sam was in his underwear, and she appreciated his sculpted body, despite all the other things in her brain fighting for attention. She had put her tank top and pants back on.

He glanced at his bloody shirt in a heap on the floor, next to the balcony door.

"I can get rid of it," she said softly. "If you want me to. And your jeans."

He nodded. "I think you should. I would be inclined to keep them, for no good reason. She'd tell me not to be so dramatic."

She studied him—still so wounded and too real for her to be comfortable with, yet majestically beautiful, standing nearly naked in the sunlight. And hers? Maybe? Finally.

"Thank you," he said. "For what you did for her, in those last moments."

She picked up his shirt. "Go shower. I'll make a breakfast better than anything we've had in a long time."

Sam walked to the bathroom door.

She steeled herself. She had to know.

"Sam?"

He stopped.

"I just need to ask. Was she—your lover? Your girlfriend? I just want to know for my own peace of mind." She held up a hand. "I'm not apologizing. But I've been here before, and I kinda want to know how big of a bitch I am."

She held her breath, waiting for his response.

"We loved each other," he said flatly. "It was just that. Love, of some sort. I don't know what else to say. We loved each other, but we couldn't be in love."

He turned back to the bathroom. The answer didn't make her feel any better.

"I will tell you one thing, though." He turned back. "Every time Micha touched you, I wanted to strangle him with my bare hands."

She bit her lip.

He gripped at the air. "Just grab him and—" He gritted his teeth.

She looked down, fighting a smile. She lost.

"Anyway." He lowered his arms. "Yeah, I was jealous of him."

She looked back up at him, smiling. "Go get your sexy ass in the shower. I'll make waffles. I saw a waffle iron out there. Hopefully Aaron left some gluten-free waffle mix for me."

"Not blueberry."

"Not blueberry. I know you hate blueberries." She knew a lot about him, actually.

He slipped into the bathroom and closed the door.

Chapter 27

Cindy didn't visit for three days. In that time, they didn't hear a thing about Aaron and Micha turning themselves in, neither on TV nor online. The city was consumed with Robbie's massacre.

Cindy finally showed up with her usual bustling air and several bags of groceries. June practically pounced on her.

"What the hell is going on?" June demanded, wearing an oversized T-shirt and a pair of boy shorts. "We haven't heard a thing. Where have you been?"

Cindy dropped the bags on the island counter in the kitchen. "Aaron told me there was enough food and toiletries here for you to be comfortable for at least a week, so I didn't think there was any rush. Also, I didn't want to come until I actually had news."

"You didn't think we could use the company? Some contact with the outside world?"

"Why would you want contact with the outside world? I wish I could hide in here with you." She glanced toward the kitchen doorway and lowered her voice. "How is he? Aaron put her to rest. That's part of what I need to tell you. Is he all right?"

"He doesn't talk much about it."

"Sounds like him."

June started unloading the bags. "I don't want to push him. If he wants to talk about it, he will."

"I don't even know what to say to him. I miss her too."

"I wouldn't say anything if I were you. So what's the news?"

"Get Sam in here. I don't want to have to repeat myself."

Sam walked into the kitchen. "I already heard you whispering about me. It's quiet in here, you know."

June slapped on a poker face. Sam wore a pair of black lounge pants, which fit except that they were struggling to cling to his hipbones. He was surprisingly shirtless—though June had seen him shirtless a shameful number of times in the past few days. He had his hair pulled back. He looked like he'd just come from the gym. The sexy gym.

Cindy blatantly stared at him.

He began rooting through the bags. "Did you get Nilla Wafers? You better have."

"Yes, of course I did, Sam." Cindy shifted. "Haven't I, every time I bring groceries?"

Sam pulled the yellow box out with a flourish. "You forgot, that one time."

"Yes, and I've apologized at least fifty times." Cindy kept her gaze fixed on Sam as he wandered over to the sink and leaned against the counter. "So, uh…"

Cindy grew fidgety. Perhaps it was their lack of clothing, or the absolute reeking sin of what they'd gotten up to on the couch roughly an hour ago. June had made a list of things they needed the next time Cindy showed up—including condoms. June hoped she wouldn't ask.

"Aaron buried her?" Sam asked, without emotion, as he tore into his wafer box. "He has her interred safely somewhere?"

"Yes," Cindy said. "He wanted to do that before he turned himself in."

"That's why it's taken him three days?" Sam opened a cupboard above the sink and pulled down a bottle of whiskey. "I'm assuming he just now did it, and that's why you're here."

"Yes." Cindy snatched the bottle from him as he held it out.

June rustled around in the groceries, not watching as Cindy chugged the whiskey, uncomfortable and more than a little unsettled by the reason she needed it. And maybe a little jealous.

Cindy finally seemed to breathe easy. She wiped her mouth. "He also had to get some things in order before they turned themselves in."

"He's a fool," Sam said. "The serum information and Micha? Yes, they'll be interested in that. But they think Aaron killed Eric Greerson. They won't let him off the hook. We never discussed doing this."

"That's why he had to get things in order," Cindy said.

"What do you mean?"

"He has something else. That's why it took him three days. He had to talk to someone first."

"Nice of him to keep me in the loop." Sam popped a wafer in his mouth.

"You've been a bit preoccupied." Cindy took another swig of whiskey, winced, and licked her lips. "Someone gave him evidence that will clear both of you."

Sam stopped chewing. "Wuh?" he said around the mouthful.

"Someone he knows hacked into the Institute databases. Aaron has the real footage of what happened that night." She nodded at June. "And the night you escaped."

June widened her eyes.

"There's a lot of other information in those databases," Cindy said. "Stuff the FBI will also be very interested in."

Sam finished chewing and swallowed. "Who the hell could get into the Institute databases? You would have to have some pretty high clearance for that."

"He didn't say a name." Cindy set the bottle down. "But he told me to tell you something. He said you'd understand."

"What's that?"

"He said the old guard isn't dead. They're just in hiding."

Sam stared at her, his brow furrowed. Then his face smoothed. His eyes popped wide, mouth falling open.

He dropped the wafer box, and it landed with a whack on the tile floor. "Holy shit!"

"Do you know what he's talking about?" June asked.

Sam strode toward the island counter, gripping his head. "Michael Paulson."

June frowned. "The first head of the Institute?" She was getting better with names.

"Aaron must have gotten in touch with him," Sam said. "He's not dead." He slammed both hands on the counter. "That sneaky bastard."

"Michael Paulson isn't dead?" Cindy's voice rose.

"It's perfect." Sam lifted his hands. "Of course Michael Paulson would be able to access their databases. He'd know where they hide their secrets. That's why Aaron suddenly wanted to go to the FBI. His cards are in order."

"Wait." June frowned. "How could Michael Paulson still get in there? Wouldn't they have changed the passwords and stuff?"

"Not if they thought he was dead. And even if they did change things, I'm sure he knew other ways in. It has to be him. The 'old guard?' Of course."

"How did Aaron know he was alive?" Cindy asked. "Or where he was? Michael Paulson never exactly got along with the SNC. The SNC and the Institute were bitter rivals back in the day."

"That's how." Sam snapped his fingers. "Aaron's father would have had intelligence on Michael Paulson, kept close tabs on him. He would have known where he was."

Cindy snorted. "You think Alan Jenkins knew Michael Paulson was still alive? And he let him live?"

"Alan died not too long after Michael Paulson vanished." Sam winked at June. "You enjoying this history lesson?"

"If it keeps you out of prison, sure."

Sam shook his fist triumphantly. "Aaron is going to the FBI with the intelligence I gave him and Micha and the footage showing we killed Eric in self defense. They'll clear us and put the Institute under a very strong microscope."

"God," Cindy said. "This could all be over soon."

June gripped the edge of the counter, afraid she might collapse in a sobbing puddle. The wave of emotion was painful, a mixture of soul-shaking relief and profound fear to hope.

"It could all be over," June repeated. "Oh my God."

"Not all of it," Sam said. "I have to find Robbie."

"Don't put the cart before the horse." Cindy shook her finger. "Even if everything works out, even if the FBI does everything you hope they will, it could take a while."

She was right, of course. June still envisioned having her life back before the end of the year, all this suffering a distant nightmare by next summer, something she told her therapist about and drank to forget. Remember that one time Chicago tried to kill us?

Sam pushed back from the counter. "All we can do now is wait."

Cindy snatched up the bottle. "And drink to the light at the end of the tunnel." She took a deep drink and held the bottle out to Sam.

June was so happy to have even a spark of hope she didn't balk at the exchange of backwash and took a drink when the bottle was passed to her. The burn cleared her head.

"I have something else." Cindy dug into her massive purse. "For you, June."

She pulled out a small box. A red ribbon graced it, knotted up in an elaborate bow.

"You didn't have to bring me a present." June took the box. "I forgive you now for leaving us in the dark the past three days."

"It's not from me." Cindy grimaced. "Occam came into my bar last night, the creepy bastard. Like I need vampires visiting me at work."

June frowned. "I didn't know vampires liked the bar scene. I thought they preferred to practice their vices in their slovenly hovels?"

"He told me to give that to you." Cindy pointed at the box. "He said if I opened it, he'd know and he'd send someone to pop my eyeballs out with a soup spoon."

"Such a charmer." June fingered the bow. "And really good at wrapping gifts, apparently."

Sam walked over next to June. "There can't be anything good in there." Her stomach tightened. Another Oracle?

Cindy took a step back. "Should we get a bomb dog to sniff it first?"

June tugged at the ribbon. "He wouldn't hurt me. It's probably just something obnoxious." Maybe it was a bag of cocaine. Or a picture of him naked. Or a dead bird, like a cat trying to impress its owner.

She undid the ribbon and opened the box. Cindy and Sam inched closer.

On top was a folded piece of paper. June took it out. Beneath was a piece of thin gray velvet, hiding whatever was inside. She read the note first.

I can wait forever, but I don't want to. The note was signed "O."

She lifted the slip of velvet.

Her insides went cold. All the hope she'd had a minute ago was sucked away, along with her breath. Two small innocuous items were inside the box—innocuous, except for what they signified.

A long strand of hair dyed bright artificial red, and a watch.

The box nearly tumbled out of her hand, but Sam caught her by the wrist and peered inside.

"He has Diego and my brother." She could barely get the words out because she couldn't get any air in. "They never got out of Chicago."

Cindy gasped. Sam's eyes turned stormy.

"He said he had more than one string to pull me with," June said. "If I don't care about myself, he knows I'll care about them."

Everything made sense now: Occam's ominous warnings, the cologne she'd smelled on him. She recognized that cologne because she'd smelled it in her shop before. If it was on Occam, that meant a struggle had taken place. Diego was a fighter. *He holds all the cards*, Rose had said. *Listen closely to what he's saying.*

"What the hell?" Cindy gaped at June. "Why would he do this?"

"Because he wants June to be a vampire," Sam said. "But we're not going to let him have his way."

June crumpled against him, tears slipping from her eyes. Not tears for herself, or even Diego, but for Jason. He was a prisoner again, and the ransom this time was her. Once more, she had to save him or die trying.

"Looks like we added another name to the list of bastards we need to destroy." Sam wrapped an arm around her.

"Damn it," she choked out.

* * * *

June sat on the balcony, the afternoon sunlight beating down on her. She sat with her elbows on her knees, holding the watch in front of her.

The glass face of the watch reflected the light. The silver band gleamed. The watch didn't even tell the right time. Jason hadn't used it for the time, just to cover up the scar.

Had he given it up freely, the way Micha had given his ring, to let her know he was all right? Whether or not, she would shove a stake through Occam's heart. Maybe staking a vampire was just the movies, but she could damage his heart enough to kill him.

If he even had a heart.

The box sat on the glass table in front of her. Diego most likely hadn't given his hair up freely. He would be trouble for the vampires. He never had the good sense to back off and give up, which was how he'd found her. She was terrified for him.

Sam stepped out onto the balcony. He'd put a T-shirt on. He walked over and sat down in the chair next to her.

"We'll get your brother and friend back." He gripped her knee. "I promise. And we'll make Occam pay. Maybe we can stick him and Robbie in a shallow grave together."

She continued gazing at the watch.

"I know you're worried." He leaned toward her. "I understand this is hard for you, especially since your brother has been a prisoner before."

"He won't hurt or kill them. He won't harm them unless I say no."

"You don't have to become a vampire. We'll find a way to save you, and them."

She rubbed her thumb over the watch face. "Why's he gotta be so obsessed with me? This is insane."

"Vampires have a tendency to fixate." He let go of her knee and sat back. "They need strong recruits. They're getting more serious about this 'cleansing' thing."

"He told me that. I don't normally approve of genocide, but in this case…" She cupped the watch in her palms. "Do you really think this could be over soon? That they'll clear your name?"

"If Aaron really has the ace in the hole I think he does, then yes. We'll be free. Any of my followers still left will rally to me. But I'll be walking on ashes." He fell silent.

"At least not having to hide will make hunting down Robbie and Occam a hell of a lot easier."

She dropped the watch back in the box with Diego's hair. She told herself again Occam wouldn't hurt them, so the nervousness in her gut would go away.

She took a deep breath, stood, and stepped over in front of Sam's chair, facing him, hands on her hips. He gazed up at her, the light making his eyes dark and shiny.

"We're gonna have to do this again," she said. "Take on the world. Muse would want you to kick ass and take names. Just like I know my brother wants me to do the same."

She cringed. Someday, she would say something and it would sound cool and inspiring instead of like something she heard in an action movie.

Sam sat forward, gripped her wrist, and pulled her toward him. She was considerably smaller than him, so she had no real choice but to fall gracelessly into his lap. That was okay. Once again, she was tangled up with a man, unsure if it was real or temporary comfort, and once again, she didn't care as much as she should have.

"At least I get the girl this time around," he said.

She arched an eyebrow. "Maybe if you had given my questions a straight answer before, you would have had the girl by now."

"And ruin the thrill of the chase?"

"I've been chased a lot lately, and none of it was thrilling. We got a lot to talk about." She patted his chest. "But not right now. We have plans to make. Because we're coming out of hiding soon. I can feel it."

"So can I." He squeezed her thigh.

"Stop." She poked his chest. "It's time to be serious. Tell me what we do next, smartest man in the city."

"We wait. Aaron is sitting in a cell right now and can't pull his usual strings. I have no idea where my trusted operatives are or where Robbie and Occam are. We can do nothing but sit here and hope the tide turns our way."

She sighed. "We'll go stir crazy. What are we going to do with ourselves?"

He smirked and slid his hand around onto her ass.

"I have a few ideas."

Meet the Author

Megan Morgan is an urban fantasy, paranormal romance, and erotica author from Cleveland, Ohio. Otherwise, she is a bartender by day and purveyor of things that go bump at night. For more info please visit meganmorganauthor.com.

Twitter @morgan_romance
www.facebook.com/megan.morgan.author

http://www.kensingtonbooks.com/author.aspx/31645

Keep reading for a peek at the first book in
Megan Morgan Siren Song series

The Wicked City

Whatever June Coffin says, goes—literally. And it's not just because she's a chain smoking rebel. As a Siren, June has the ability to force people to obey any command she voices. But in a world where those with supernatural powers quickly become lab rats for science, she'd rather look out for herself than fight on the front lines…until her similarly gifted twin brother, Jason, is captured by Chicago's Institute of Supernatural Research.

To save Jason, June has no choice but to enter a hidden world of conspiracy, murder—and strange bedfellows—including a widowed paranormal advocate whose memory June accidentally erased, and a fiery paranormal separatist leader. Soon the lines between attraction and strategic alliance become blurred. But in a city exploding with paranormal crossfire, and her brother's life at stake, June will have to face her inner demons and finally take a stand.

A Lyrical e-book on sale now.

http://www.kensingtonbooks.com/book.aspx/31127

Chapter 1

The first time June Coffin saw Micha Bellevue, he was giving a lecture at the Chicago Institute for Supernatural Research. June and her brother Jason weren't yet prisoners of the unholy place and June had sneaked into a conference room. Though the subject of the lecture—something insipid about paranormal rights in the workplace—didn't interest her, the lecturer certainly did. Micha was tall and rugged yet boyishly handsome, all her weaknesses. *Meesha*, not *Mi-ca*, much easier to yell in bed. He had sandy brown hair with gold highlights, cut shaggy with a swoopy fringe. He also had sky blue eyes and a crooked smile.

June, in contrast, was five-four, lean, and petite. Her father once called her "diminutive," and she'd hated the word ever since. She had a flowing mane of jet-black hair, though at the moment it lacked volume or luster and she'd been keeping it in a ponytail. Her eyes were vivid green, nearly iridescent, but their color was real, unlike her hair. She was also over-fond of tattoos and piercings.

She was Micha's exact opposite, which was fine, because she believed people needed to explore sexual pursuits outside their peer groups.

In the fifteen minutes she spoke to Micha after the lecture at the Institute, the lovely man revealed himself to be full of ostentatious ideas and painfully corny jokes. A bit later, June stood in an atrium, smoking a cigarette while he led a string of eager young supernatural neophytes across the courtyard below. She narrowed her eyes against the smoke curling around her face. *I'm so gonna hit that.* She hadn't, not yet, for huge moral reasons.

Namely, because Micha had a wife.

Except, his wife currently lay trussed up in her casket, awaiting her funeral service in the morning, and June had kind of helped put her in it.

But right now they also had this issue with the gun.

Hanging out with dead people on a Sunday night didn't rank high on June's to-do list, despite her last name. But as she stood in a darkened funeral parlor staring at the tall, buxom, red-haired woman with said gun, she realized how much her priorities had changed.

"What the hell is that?" June's question was rhetorical, but she still wanted an answer.

"It's a Glock." The redhead—whose name was Cindy—said this coolly, as if she were describing a pair of shoes. Cindy had dressed all in black for the occasion, like a cat burglar.

The three of them—June, Micha, and Ms. Congeniality herself— weren't in the funeral home to steal anything. Even after the events of the preceding week, June wasn't cracked enough to snatch a body.

"Why do you have it?" June asked. "We don't *need* a gun."

The whimpering aged gentleman on his knees next to Cindy probably welcomed this news but clearly was no less frightened, as Cindy had the muzzle pressed against his temple. The man wore a handsome silk robe with wide lapels, the kind rich guys sported in movies. Were all funeral directors so dashing in their choice of nightclothes?

"I brought it just in case," Cindy said.

"Why would we need to shoot someone in a funeral home?" June raised her voice, no longer worried about being quiet. The director had probably heard them clamoring through the window at the rear of the house. June possessed some nifty skills: she was an excellent self-taught artist, she could shoot whiskey with the boys like she was one of them, and she could make wicked smoke rings. However, grace and athletics eluded her.

"I don't think he's armed," June said. "I doubt you need to defend a funeral home."

"You never know," Micha said behind her. "Necrophiliacs probably like to break into funeral homes."

June closed her eyes; she counted to five, and then ten, but when she opened her eyes again, she wasn't any calmer.

"I won't hurt you," the man on the floor said in a small, pitiful voice. "Just take what you want and go."

June stepped forward and waved a hand at Cindy, shooing away the gun. June had never touched a gun in her life. She had never needed to.

Cindy lowered the gun and stepped back. "I was just trying to help." She spoke with the petulance of an admonished child. A child who didn't get to play with her deadly weapon.

June knelt. The paunchy balding man was shaking, his eyes wide.

"It's all right." A heavy energy, curled in June's stomach like a sleeping cat, rose to her sternum and surged upward again to warmly coat her throat. "Just sit there and relax and think about your favorite things until we're gone."

The man's body sagged. His face slackened. He pivoted to the side and sat down on his bottom with a shuddering thump, his gaze gone distant and dreamy. A smile tugged at the corners of his mouth.

June stood.

"There. Isn't that awesome? Supernatural powers and stuff?" She didn't enjoy throwing around her "hypnotic voice phenomenon," as the scientists liked to call it, but invasive persuasion seemed far less cruel than criminal menacing.

Cindy pushed the gun forcefully into a holster on her hip. June winced, afraid it might go off, but thankfully—or perhaps regrettably—it didn't. June had failed to notice Cindy was wearing a holster, probably because she'd been too busy figuring out how to break into a funeral home.

"Come on," June said. "Let's get this done."

She stepped past the oblivious man on the floor. Micha followed.

The casket, tucked into a bank of flowers and wreaths, rested atop a short dais like a morbid confectionery in a baking contest. June slid her hand along the side of the casket to find a latch. She did *not* want to do this. Despite the mind-obliterating madness she'd survived recently, corpses still jangled her nerves.

"Gah." She lifted the lid a few inches.

She turned into a baby around corpses, despite knowing they weren't going to sit up and strangle her. Earlier, when she'd voiced speculative, mostly joking concern about the dead getting their revenge, Cindy pointed out scientific research had proven zombies non-existent.

"Turn a light on." June took a bracing breath and opened the lid farther. She expected a bad smell, but a faintly chemical, perfume-y odor wafted out.

"Here." Cindy slid up beside her.

A pale bluish light illuminated the space around them and fell on the still, poised figure inside the casket. Cindy held her cell phone aloft, screen lit. June paused.

"What?" Cindy's eyes shone in the faint light.

"I think if you try, you could be a little more disrespectful. Maybe you'd like to shoot her a couple times? Turn on a light!"

"You're the one breaking into her casket." Cindy tapped the screen to renew the light. "We can't turn on a light. Someone might see. Hurry up. This is freaking me out."

"It's freaking you out?" June opened the lid fully. She snatched the phone from Cindy and held it closer to the body to get the grim task over with.

Micha's wife, the esteemed Mrs. Rose Bellevue, had been a lovely woman. Had. Been. She had high delicate cheekbones, plump lips, and dusky skin—the times June had seen her alive, anyway. Her dark hair was fixed in a neat knot atop her head, loose curls spilling onto the white pillow beneath her. A tiny smile touched her lips. Her long-fingered hands rested delicately on her stomach, manicured nails gleaming. She wore a white dress with a boxy neckline and lace sleeves. She looked like an angel instead of a zombie, thank God.

June waited for Micha's response, sort of hoping, sort of not. "Well?"

Micha leaned closer and peered at her face. The light on the phone dimmed. June jabbed the screen, and a moment later a faint jingle came out of the phone.

"Give me that." Cindy yanked the phone from her and looked at the screen. "You just dialed my boyfriend. Good work."

June was aghast. "I can't believe anyone would date you."

"*One* of them."

Cindy disconnected the call and shone the light back on Rose's face. June ground her teeth and pulled a breath through her nose.

After a tense, silent moment, Micha stood upright. "No. I don't recognize her." He shrugged. "Pretty, though. I must have game."

June smoothed a hand over her hair. The strands were greasy and limp and she winced. She hadn't had a shower in more days than she wanted to contemplate.

"All right," June said. "It was worth a try. Let's split, before we get caught. We'll go through the front door this time."

Cindy lowered her phone and patted her hip. "If we have to fight our way out, I'm ready."

"Yes, if the legions of undead try to block our escape."

June carefully closed the lid of the casket, turned, and walked down the aisle, past rows of couches and folding chairs. The funeral would be huge. She had to get the hell out of the place, away from the woman's dead body and her own guilt. She needed to get the hell out of Chicago, but she couldn't. Not yet.

Not until she got her brother back.

Cindy had an apartment in West Lakeview. She told June that's where they were, but June didn't care if they were on the moon. She felt like she *was* on the moon, in some bizarre alternate reality, even if all signs pointed to being on earth. Cindy also had a tortoiseshell cat named Serendipity—Dipity for short—that liked to sit on June.

June lay in bed in Cindy's guest room, a small white box with little decoration or furniture—a twin bed, a sagging sofa, and a hulking, ugly wooden dresser. Dipity sat on June's stomach, kneading her belly as she prepared her for—who knew? Dinner, probably. One paw, then the other. Over and over. Knead, knead. Knead, knead. A cigarette dangled from the corner of June's mouth, one eye open as she peered through the smoke, past the bowl she was utilizing as an ashtray on her chest.

"Will you lay the hell down?" June snarled.

Dipity did, folding herself into a loaf and gazing at June with wide, accusing yellow eyes. Dipity moved up and down as June breathed.

Soft slapping footsteps sounded in the hallway. Cindy peeked around the doorframe. "Did you say something?"

Dipity looked up at Cindy.

"I was talking to your damn cat," June said.

Cindy stepped into the room. June found her pretty in an overbearing sense: Amazonian and bodacious, leggy and curvy in a way most guys liked. All the things June wasn't.

"She likes you." Cindy wore white pajama pants and a pink T-shirt stretched tight across her ample bosom. "It must be your charming personality. Or you smell like Micha."

June glanced over at the sofa. Micha had his back to them, covers bunched around his waist, his white T-shirt twisted and hair a tousled, mottled mess of brown and gold. Despite Cindy's friendship with Micha, she pointed out repeatedly that she was not a "paranormal activist" like him. June didn't blame Cindy for wanting to be clear. June had actively avoided paranormal activists until she committed the grave mistake of coming to Chicago.

"He's been sleeping a lot." Cindy indicated Micha. "Is that one of the side effects?"

June ground her cigarette out in the bowl and sat the bowl next to her hip. "Hell if I know. I've never accidentally messed up someone's mind so bad I couldn't reverse it."

Cindy left the room. She returned shortly with a newspaper.

"Look at this." She walked to the bed and thrust the paper at June.

She gave June the Paranormal section of the *Chicago Tribune*. June had been reading it every day for some mention of Jason. She'd also been reading news online, on Cindy's laptop. The Chicago Institute for Supernatural Research, the first and biggest facility to be given government approval for paranormal research, kept the city alive with supernatural intrigue and gave bloggers something to endlessly blather about. The Institute's presence didn't mean folks in Chicago were hugging their neighborhood telepath, however. The freaks still got persecuted, like in Sacramento where June lived.

The headline on the first page said: HAVE THE SIREN TWINS LEFT CHICAGO? INSTITUTE NOT FORTHCOMING.

June's heart jumped and then sank again after she read the article. The reporter speculated she and Jason had fled, "shaken profoundly by the horrific and untimely death of the Institute's top vampire researcher, Rose Bellevue, her vicious murder still a hot topic of rampant speculation." The article went on to say paranormal citizens were pointing fingers at a normalist group called the Secular Normalists of Chicago or SNC, "a dastardly force polluting this city with misinformation and blatant ignorance."

June could end the speculation, if she dared come out of hiding.

The article also said police were still investigating the possible kidnapping of Micha Bellevue, Rose's husband and one of the paranormal community's most lauded advocates: "last year's recipient of the J.B. Rhine Award for Advocacy, friend of many paranormal people. His generous admirers hope fervently for his safety and the punishment of those involved in this horrendous crime."

June had seen plenty of bloggers speculating Micha had something to do with Rose's death and was on the run, and one particularly amusing guy was convinced Micha had been abducted by the CIA. June could be sneaky, but she wasn't on level with the government.

"I can't believe how lurid this shit is." June tossed the paper on top of Dipity. She emitted an angry mewl and got up. "Reads like a tabloid."

"Ethan Roberts." Cindy lifted the paper off her cat. "He's been the lead paranormal reporter for the *Tribune* for years. He might be colorful, but he knows what he's talking about." She tucked the paper under her arm. "My friend will be here soon. So haul your ass out of bed and get dressed."

Dipity jumped off June and padded slowly around the bed.

"I tried to warn him." Cindy looked over at Micha. "All those years he thought the Institute could do no wrong. He sure took it up the ass without lube this time."

June didn't comment.

"It sucks, though." Cindy dropped her voice a little. "He didn't deserve to lose Rose."

"Look at it this way. Now he can be an advocate for the right people. Knowledge is power. Fight the Man. Rah rah."

June sat up. Dipity moved behind her and rubbed across her back in a sleek caress. Cats forgave easily.

Cindy turned toward the door.

"Hey," June said.

Cindy stopped.

"What's the SNC? I keep seeing them pop up in these articles."

Cindy scrunched up her face. "They're a paranormal...protest group. Can't say 'hate group' since the treaty. The Secular Normalists of Chicago. They wanted to set themselves apart from the Bible-thumpers and fundies, but they still like to beat us up."

"I didn't realize they needed an organized group to do that. Where I come from, that's called a gang."

"It was founded by this guy named Alan Jenkins. He died like five years ago and his son Aaron took over. Aaron says he wants to clean up his father's dirt." She pursed her lips. "I don't believe him."

"Quite a city you got here."

Dipity hopped off the bed and landed on the floor with a thump.

"I don't know how you sleep at night," June said.

"With one eye open." Cindy turned and left the room. Dipity streaked after her.

Micha, undoubtedly having been awake for the entire conversation, stirred and rolled partially onto his back and twisted his head around. He gazed at her with bleary, unfocused eyes. She fought the urge to walk over to the sofa and lovingly smooth his hair back; then grab a fistful.

"I like your ink," Micha said groggily. "I have some. On my back."

June blinked and stretched her exposed arms. She had countless hours and thousands of dollars worth of tattoos up and down her arms, across her chest, some on her back, one down her left side. A lot she'd done herself. She also had multiple piercings: six in one ear, four in the other—minus the gauges—one in her tongue too, not to mention a few other places. A "rebel," her mother called her. She caused soccer moms to cross the street on a regular basis, even when doing nothing more malevolent than smoking a Parliament while holding a latte and texting.

"Thanks," she said. "You'll have to show me sometime."

Micha rolled fully onto his back and stretched, arms over his head, long legs stiffening beneath the blanket. He didn't fit on the sofa, but he'd insisted on taking it, like a gentleman.

"God, what time is it?" he asked.

"A little after nine." She needed to say something but took a moment to choose her words carefully. "I feel bad about you missing your wife's funeral today. But until I figure out how to fix what I've done to your head, I can't send you back into the wild. Let them keep thinking you've been kidnapped by the CIA or whatever. I have a feeling if you surfaced right now you'd fall into the Institute's net anyway."

Micha put his hands over his face. The light caught on his gold wedding band.

"I'm so confused," he murmured through his fingers. "Not only about this woman who's supposed to be my wife, but about the Institute." He took his hands away. "I supported them. I thought they were doing the right thing. I believed they were helping the maligned and oppressed."

June couldn't believe he'd used the words "maligned and oppressed" in seriousness.

"I've done so many seminars there," Micha said. "I've lauded them as a safe haven and a place for paranormal people to understand themselves and help others understand them. When I think of all the people I've sent there…"

The sunlight blazing on the white walls magnified the color of his eyes, making them some inane interior decorating color like *cerulean*. They were desperate though, dimmed with worry and care, darkened and dulled by sadness.

"Well"—she wasn't good at placating—"a lot of people thought Hitler was doing the right thing until they found out the truth. Didn't make them criminals."

Instead of seeming relieved, Micha blanched, his eyes going wide. She popped her tongue into her cheek and looked around for her smokes. Smooth. *Real* smooth.